Tobbi's Amazing Adventures in Cloudland

by
Ilya Simakovsky

Library of Congress Card Number: 2008920341

ISBN 13: 978-1-59713-048-6

First Printing, 2008

Cover by Mark Seliger.

About the Photographer: Mark Seliger is currently one of the top photographers in the world. He is an editorial photographer who was born and raised in Amarillo, Texas. Mark currently lives and works in New York City, and is under contract to **Conde Nast Publications,** where he has shot numerous covers for *GQ* and *Vanity Fair.*

Published by
Goose River Press
3400 Friendship Road
Waldoboro ME 04572
gooseriverpress@roadrunner.com
www.gooseriverpress.com

CONTENTS

CONTENTS

PART ONE

THE BOOK OF ASCENT

Colossal foamy lips parted and a huge white cloud shot out. In February's icy air the cloud twisted and whirled furiously after the rumbling, mind numbing basso blasted through it a second later, "We must have him! He hears. He must come to us. Get it ready fast and send it; time is so short. If this doesn't work we are doomed, all of us...all of them...everything below...."

A WORD TO THE READER

Do you dream? Do you wake up feeling that during the night you went somewhere and did extraordinary things? Some believe that the world is but a map, plain and clear, with every detail already outlined and all roads constructed. To them, destiny is but a chain of stops on these well-traveled roads to be reached and visited for a while. To others, however, the universe is an enormous mystery replete with strange creatures and mystical lands, places to discover, and roads yet to build.

You kids are like that, able to use your imagination to see what only a few others can, to go where no one has ever gone. Like the boy whose story you're about to read, you may stumble onto fantastic adventures in places where others can find only familiarity and boredom. So, use your gift. See, hear, feel, search, experience, believe in the incredible, and most of all, believe in yourselves!

And, oh yeah, don't bother to explain the amazing things you discover to those who refuse to listen, just get more books and read. Heck, write your own life stories: life is a book with clear pages while you're a kid.

When I heard Tobbi's story I nearly choked with laughter but he insisted that it was all true and that I shouldn't change a thing. So, here it is just like I heard it....

CHAPTER 1

Meet the Ladybug

Tobbi, the greatest basketball player of all times, even greater than Mike—the Air—Jordan, whirled swiftly. The frustrated guard swiped at the ball, which was no longer there. Side to side Tobbi darted, leaving two more opponents behind, until the basket loomed like a prize ready to be snatched. He sprung and floated above the earth, like the dudes in "Matrix," helplessly watched by other players. Slam...dunk! The winning points and glory were his, except again, somewhere at the edge of his perception, a deep mysterious voice moaned, "Tobbi...Tobbi..."

"Tobbi Sontag! Come down here right this minute or you're grounded for the weekend." As a mother of a dreamer, Lydia often had to repeat herself. Now she was mad, yet again, because she still could hear the pounding of the basketball upstairs.

"Tobbi!" she screamed. The pounding stopped and shortly she heard the elevator squeaking on the way down.

"Tobbi!" she said the second he rolled into the kitchen....

"Is my beautiful mother angry? Is she going to punish her son, who is so very sorry?"

Tobbi whipped his hand from behind the back and pushed a red rose, which he swiped from a vase upstairs, into Lydia's face. Lydia brushed the rose out of the way, opened her mouth, and just stood there; she couldn't even stay angry with him, since he'd begun using a wheelchair four months ago. She watched him driving the darn thing to the table. His dense, dark-brown hair defied hairbrush and, as usual, bounced on his forehead in a bundle. Beneath the thick arched eyebrows, a pair of dreamy, blue eyes sparkled

1

with intelligence and mischief. With an upturned and heavily freckled nose, large mouth and a mad thick lower lip he looked even more a rascal.

"Well, Mom! Are we eating or you still want to take a swing at me?"

He looked over his shoulder with a sly smile. Lydia turned quickly and marched to the stove making lots of noise with the pots and pans. Tobbi sighed and tore into his food like a hungry wolf. Lydia's annoying instructions soon followed. It went easier if he imagined them as part of the meal: *Grapefruit*, he thought; *yes, today she sounded like a grapefruit.*

"Be extra careful getting onto the bus, and don't you hurry! Everybody will wait. And fold your chair completely or someone may trip over it. Tobbi, are you listening to me?"

"Yes, Mom."

"Don't talk with your mouth full."

"Gees, didn't you just ask..."

"Don't you dare ignore your teachers! I don't want to hear another complaint about it! Your father and I were so embarrassed at the last conference; every teacher complained that your head's in the clouds all the time."

"Yes, Mom. But I'm not failing any classes and..."

"Not failing isn't enough. You can do better! The odds will be against you when you go to college and later on. You must learn to do better for yourself!"

"I'm only eleven years old, Ma! What college? Kid first—college later, you know."

"Don't mock me, Tobbi. You must fight against this...this disease of yours and..."

"Mom! What's the matter with you? It's Friday, the weekend's coming. Chill, okay?"

"Okay, okay you rascal, off to school with you," Lydia said, brushed the untamed flock of hair off Tobbi's forehead, kissing him hard. Tobbi nodded, put the bookbag onto his lap and rolled to the door. He blew her a kiss from the doorstep and was gone. Lydia smiled, Tobbi always found little ways to show his love. She didn't even mind that often it was his way of getting out of trouble. His weird illness was such a hard thing to accept; she dreaded seeing Dr. Golding later today.

Tobbi's lungs tingled pleasantly, filled to capacity with the fresh, cool morning air. Shrieking he rolled down the ramp Father had built for him. Sometimes being in the wheelchair was okay for in some places where people walked, he raced.

Immediately his imagination flared up. There he is in a low-cut race car screeching into the tight turn, at 180...no 220 miles an hour. The wind blasts his face, the engine shrieks—victory! There, just beyond the trees—the finish line. The crowd roars—a few more seconds....

The horn of the school bus ripped him out of his car seat. Oh no, it was his schoolmates that had been yelling all along. The driver, Big Bill, waited at the doors, "Daydreaming again, Tobbi?" he asked. "One day your mind will fly so far away that you'll have a rough time finding it. You'd better start concentrating on what you are doing." Tobbi nodded, pushed with his forearms and moved his body onto the steps of the bus. Bill moved alongside and caught Tobbi shoulders.

"Bill," Tobbi said, "let me do it."

"It's okay, Tobbi. It's getting late. See, I didn't take into account your racing schedule. So, up you go."

Tobbi let him; after all, it was pretty hard. 46 pairs of eyes stared at him when he appeared in the alley between the seats. The girls' eyes he could tell instantly: they were full of compassion. Since he started in a wheelchair, the attention from girls became most annoying: *let me carry your books, Tobbi. Let me get the door for you, Tobbi. You dropped your pencil Tobbi. Whah! What a nuisance, all of them! Except Nelli, she seemed kinda cute...and cool too,* Tobbi thought, *good at pitching, running and even playing ball.* Overall, though, girls were trouble; all the nicknames and gags he had to endure

3

from guys....

Boys' eyes were different. Devoid of reason, they sizzled with a wild energy ready to be unleashed at any opportunity. No such thing—with Bill driving. He just swept the bus with mean, dark eyes and all noise ceased. Tobbi recently discovered that Bill wasn't as mean as he pretended, but kept this to himself preferring peace over riot like when Mary drove.

"Hey, Ladybug!" Tommy's voice attacked from the rear. "Your wheels were stuck, or what? Circling around like a crazy golf cart." Tommy, known as the "Barb," imagined himself a class bully. Yet, he only managed to irritate by sticking onto you like a barb.

"Shut up, Barb, it's better to have stuck wheels then a stuck mind going in circles, like yours!" the bus chuckled.

"You're dead, Ladybug! Don't go to lunch today or you'll be sorry."

"Yeah, sure Barb! Just don't forget to take your finger out of your nose. Can't have a broken finger before finals, not that it would make any difference in your grades."

Now everybody was laughing except Tommy, who was still yelling.

Bill turned and growled. The kids froze. *Like freaking Freddy Krueger,* Tobbi thought, eyeing Bill with curiosity.

"Don't worry about the Barb. He's full of it," mumbled Kenny, the Pouch, in between the swallows. Sprawled over two seats, right behind Tobbi, the Pouch was big, round, and fat, like one of those Chinese porcelain figurines. He never stopped chewing, even when he talked. Tobbi spied on him during sleepovers to see if he did it in his sleep; the jury was still out on that. Kenny was Tobbi's best friend and he was smart.

"Yeah, Pouch, I know. But who wants his lunch spoiled?"

"Nobody, but nobody spoils my lunch," Kenny growled, "and you're sitting with me, so don't sweat it."

CHAPTER 2

The Awakening

The day continued as most days in school, somewhere between boring and very boring. According to Tobbi's parents school was supposed to be this great joy; they insisted that to learn new things was exciting, to study the world was marvelous. Yet, today, he struggled mightily to understand how knowing about cell division or why molecules in things jump around like somebody bit them on the butt is going to help him become a famous pilot or a race-car driver. Adults just didn't dig it—kids should study only the interesting stuff. Take botany for example; Mr. Pierre was talking excitedly in his confusing French accent about the way plants had, you know what...the S word. So, he, Tobbi, should also go goo-goo over the way bees transfer pollen and help Mama and Papa plants make little baby beans, peas, and carrots. He'd been bored to tears at his Aunt Jane's wedding but should be interested in the plants' way of doing it! Huh!? Now, the way bees do it, is cool. If only humans could fly like that... let's see....

He, Professor Tobbi Sontag, the most talented inventor on earth, surveyed his finished project: a pair of slender, power-assisted human flying wings. He strapped on the harness, connected the electric leads, and stumbled onto the high ledge. Far below, a vast grass covered plain stretched to the horizon. There it merged with the enormous, sloping, blue roof of a sky. With his fingers numb and shaky, Tobbi flipped his arms and jumped; up, uP, UP he flew into this marvelous sky.

"Tobbi...Come Tobbi...," a deep moan came suddenly, mysterious, dark, and threatening as a call of death; then— a tiny laughter. Laughter? There he was back, in the class-

5

room. Everyone was laughing and Mr. Pierre was staring at him over his thick-rimmed glasses. Not good.

"Come, Tobbi," Mr. Pierre was saying, "we must have an answer. After all it appeared as if you had raised a hand, or was it two hands?" Tobbi swallowed hard, he hadn't a clue.

"Would you mind repeating it, Mr. Pierre?"

"Mon dieu!" Mr. Pierre growled in French, his thin face crumbling like a wrinkled leather glove.

"Let us evaluate your request, Mr. Sontag. It appears that you asked me to repeat myself, a most worthy request, considering the wide-spread belief that repetition does, in fact, enhance learning. However! Hmmm, hhm..." Mr. Pierre cleared his throat and glared at the hushed classroom.

"However," he restated, "one must assume that what needs to be repeated was heard in the first instance. Therefore, Mr. Sontag, I must clarify your request and ask in return, what would you like me to repeat, the last question, this whole lesson or the entire semester, hmmm?"

The kids were loving it. Mr. Pierre never shouted, never cursed, but the subject of his displeasure was reduced to an ant, always a tiny step away from being squashed. So, Mr. Pierre was never ignored and his classes were rarely missed. Tobbi was one of the few who dared to bait the "Bulldog" (Mr. Pierre's affectionate nickname), by not paying attention.

The ant named Tobbi sensed the weight coming on.

"The question," he mumbled.

"What was that?" Mr. Pierre asked.

"Please repeat the question," said Tobbi tightening his fists till the knuckles turned white.

"Ah! The man made up his mind! Commendable. Well then, would you please explain to us all, how did you come to believe that not knowing about science will benefit you; as you demonstrate repeatedly by not listening to me, Tobbi?"

When the Bulldog bites, it never lets go, that's a fact. His frantic search for something to say was broken off by the bell; and what a beautiful thing it was!

Mr. Pierre labored through a tortured breath and said, "The test is on Tuesday and will cover chapters five and six. I do expect you all to study. Have a great weekend. Mr. Sontag, please allow me the pleasure of your company for a few minutes longer."

Everyone was bouncing, but Tobbi. First, he had to face a trashing by Mr. Pierre, and then the Barb in the cafeteria—not an ecstatic moment.

Pouch wobbled by and winked at him. "Mr. Pierre," he said, compassion practically dripping off his glistening, munching lips, "don't chisel at Tobbi hard. You know he's cool. He's just having a bad time, wheelchair and all. Okay?"

"I so appreciate your consultation, Kenny, it's immensely valuable to me. Now, unless you aim to take over, allow me to exercise my meager abilities as this young man's teacher, and teach. Goodbye."

"I tried, dude!" Pouch said, and then he, too, abandoned ship.

Tobbi remained alone with the most feared teacher in school. As he approached, Mr. Pierre's desk seemed to grow huge along with Tobbi's fear; expecting cruel and unusual punishment, he encountered, instead, a face filled with millions of tiny wrinkles. The wrinkles were caused by...a smile, of all things. This just couldn't be. It could only mean one thing: The Bulldog has bared his fangs and the tongue-lashing would be brutal; the chill went down to the bone.

"Weird, huh?" said Mr. Pierre.

"What?" Tobbi felt like a foul ball flying out of control.

"I bet you thought that smiling wasn't my thing."

"But...but...wha...how...I..."

"You know, Tobbi, I was like you once."

"What...what do you mean?"

"A dreamer, you know how it is. You hear or see something exciting and kaboom! You're away with it, riding, jumping, flying; like a real thing, right?"

"Right," Tobbi agreed, astounded that this dry and vic-

7

ious teacher may actually understand. He squinted at Mr. Pierre suspiciously.

"For me it was always driving," continued Mr. Pierre. "My childhood in a small French village was very—how should we say—boring. Besides school, there was a chicken farm and a movie theater. So, I filled my head with all these adventures. Since there are no rules in a dream, you can do or be anything, isn't it so?"

"Yes," agreed Tobbi, driving his wheelchair closer. *Could Mr. Pierre really understand?*

"It started when Messie...I mean Mr. Arbur, brought his new sport Citroen into the Village. Citroen—a French car, you know. My life went on hold until I could drive this little red monster. However, we moved away soon. I was miserable until the day I imagined it! Oo-la-la! Driving this beautiful car in my dreams was the most exciting thing! Yeah!" Mr. Pierre closed his eyes and inhaled; his face brightened, gaining that excited, joyful look a man gets when he tastes the fresh morning sea breeze or when his dad smells Grandma's world famous beef stew.

"I became a full-time day-dreamer." Mr. Pierre continued, "It annoyed my parents. All my teachers complained and... well, you know how that is, don't you Tobbi?"

Tobbi nodded enthusiastically.

"What gets you going, Tobbi? Is it flying? I mean, just now, in class...?"

Tobbi hesitated and then opened up, like never before. Unbelievable, but he was telling his innermost fantasies to someone who only minutes before scared him half to death. He told Mr. Pierre about his dreams of becoming a basketball star and his racing around in his Formula 1 wheelchair. The flying fantasies, however, were his addiction. Mr. Pierre learned about Tobbi's recurrent dream in which he slowly transformed his bike into a car, and car into a plane. Eventually his invention could also submerge as a submarine. The whole world chased him and his amazing machine like Captain Nemo in *Ten Thousand Leagues Under The Sea*. He continued to improve his car-submarine-plane. Finally, it could fly into space, too. When chased by F16's, he would dive under water. Escaping from submarines, he'd flee into space. Night after night this dream recurred, continuing where he'd left it the night before. His parents were amused by his eagerness to go to bed. Tobbi saw that Mr. Pierre understood and stumbled over words in his excitement to share his dreams. Today's fantasy came next; he explained how free he felt flying...and remembered the Voice.

"What is it Tobbi?"

"It gets weird sometimes, Mr. Pierre."

"Oh, yeah? How?"

"I don't know, it's just nuts."

"So far, Tobbi, all I see is a lot of great imagination. Don't worry. Shoot."

"Well, Okay. But don't tell anyone, promise?"

"Of course. Now, what is it?"

"I've been hearing this voice calling me."

"You mean you dream about it."

"No...yes...I don't know. For a while now, whenever I dream of flying, this really gruesome voice calls me...like it wants me to fly to...wherever. I get scared and shake it off. But now—"

"But now?" prompted Mr. Pierre.

"Now I hear it more often."

Mr. Pierre raised his bushy eyebrows and said, "You have quite an imagination, Tobbi. This last thing, however, worries me a bit. Maybe you should mention it to your parents or your doctor."

"See, I told you! You think I'm crazy!"

"No, I don't. I'm just concerned about you. Well, okay. Let's leave it for now. I've been watching you lately and I see things that you can and must do something about."

"Like what?" Tobbi bristled.

"Let me first tell you what'd happened to me."

Mr. Pierre smiled again and made Tobbi feel safer. "My fantasies got out of control," started Mr. Pierre, "instead of confronting a problem, I'd dream myself out of it. I fell behind in school. Kids made fun of me constantly. I didn't care; I could always handle myself...in a dream. My busy parents were content as long as I wasn't stealing, cheating or fighting, and if it weren't for Mr. Bordoux I'd be lost."

Tobbi smiled and met Mr. Pierre's infamous, above-the-glasses stare without fear. There was compassion, interest, and intelligence in his brown eyes that previously stayed hidden under the gray, frowning eyebrows. Mr. Pierre smiled back and continued. "Oh, yes! Mr. Bordoux. He's the reason I became a teacher, you know. A small fellow he was, forever stuck in his fifties, it seems. His face was long and narrow with a sharp protruding nose and slightly bulging eyes that were green and clear like a calm sea. Always so warm they were..." he paused.

"Well, hmm, yes; because of the thin hair splashed over the forehead and large yellow teeth, kids nicknamed him Rat. Boy, were they off the mark! Yes, he was pretty much ignored by everyone between classes; always quiet, he never reprimanded or disciplined students. But in his classroom you could hear a whisper of time. He didn't teach history, he lived it! He transported you across centuries and miles. It was as if we, the students, argued the fate of Rome on the Senate floor or fought as gladiators for our lives. In ancient Egypt, we were Pharaohs commanding thousands in the building of the Great Pyramid. This was his gift. Nobody missed his classes; it was like going to the movies, always exciting and fresh. After teaching for 30 years myself, I still don't know how he made everything seem so fresh. He had another gift also. Kids in trouble sought his advice and he found those needing it, even if they themselves didn't know it."

"Like you?" Tobbi said quietly.

"Yes, I was one of many. Interesting, by the time a class graduated no one called him a Rat anymore. When former graduates visited, he was always their first stop. Isn't it strange how it works sometimes?"

"So what did he do?" Tobbi asked.

"Patience my dear flier, I'm getting to it. One day, just like today, he asked me to stay after class. I nearly ignored him but stayed. It had changed my life."

He sighed and looked at Tobbi.

"So...?" Tobbi said, eagerly.

"So nothing. The end of story."

"But! What...why did you...? I don't understand!" Tobbi slapped his forehead.

"It's all right, you will. Now the way you and I can fantasize is special. People like us grow up to be inventors and researchers, writers and adventurers..."

"...and teachers?" added Tobbi with a sly smile.

"Some. Good ones," agreed Mr. Pierre. "But there's danger. Some people fall victims to their dreams unable to control them."

"How's that?" Tobbi held his breath.

"See, when fantasies take control, you forfeit your understanding of reality and what is real becomes a fantasy and what is fantasy becomes—"

"Real!" finished Tobbi beaming.

"Exacteur! Life loses direction and meaning this way. Dreams aren't meant for escape. They should expand one's mind, not shrink one's life! You must learn to control you dreams, understand?" Mr. Pierre put his hairy, claw-like hand on Tobbi's shoulder and looked deep into his eyes. He must've found his answer, for he leaned back and broke out with cheerful wrinkles.

Tobbi perked up, "That's what he told you, right?"

"Who?"

"Mr. Bordoux."

"Ahh! You truly understand now, don't you Tobbi?"

"I think so. What now?"

"I noticed that you let other people do your work for you."

11

"But—" Tobbi objected.

"Your duties are your responsibility. This wheelchair's your reality. You must deal with it. This way, you can claim victory in the end. You can win, Tobbi, but YOU must fight for it!"

"That's what my mother says."

"Smart woman—your mother. Listen to her."

Tobbi nodded. He wanted to go and think now. Mr. Pierre understood. "Just one more thing," he said. "How are you doing with this condition of yours?"

"It's not getting worse anymore. I'm going to my doctor today. I'll see what she says."

"Tobbi, don't let anybody discourage you. You will beat it. Believe me, we dreamers have our ways. okay? Oh, and another thing. This conversation and my secret identity are for your eyes only. Top secret! I have a dreadful reputation to protect, you know," he allowed a tiny smile. "I can rely on you, can't I?"

"Yes, sir!" answered Tobbi brightly and cringed when he saw Mr. Pierre transform. As if possessed by a mummy his face shriveled into a prune; his eyes slithered back into dark sockets; his shoulders sagged and the old Mr. Pierre now glared at Tobbi scaring him to death.

"Mr. Sontag," he said dryly "those absences of the mind we experience in the classroom frequently, they're going to stop, aren't they? I will make it much tougher for you if this silly behavior continues, UNDERSTOOD?"

Despite the fearsome stare, Tobbi smiled his understanding back.

"Hmmm...You're dismissed then. I expect a better effort from now on in all your subjects."

Mr. Pierre turned away and Tobbi started for the door. Halfway through he backed out. "Mr. Pierre!" he said, "thank you!"

"Right," he answered, "go on. You'll miss your lunch. A hungry stomach makes for a dim mind, goodbye."

CHAPTER 3

The Confrontation

Tobbi rolled along the corridor ignoring greetings and usual stares. Mr. Pierre was awesome and yet, he couldn't even tell Pouch about it, a promise is a promise. It was funny how Mr. Pierre's words echoed his mother's. Bummer, it was nice to have people do things for you but he needed to rethink that if they were right.

The noise got louder as he neared the corner. The feeding frenzy had begun. Tobbi's stomach growled and his mouth watered. Then it hit him—the Barb! Oh, what the heck! He rode in.

The brightly lit cafeteria was in turmoil. Kids, even while sitting, squirmed, flapped their arms and talked, talked, talked. Since every kid attempted to speak over the others, the noise was incredible. Why did it look so weird all off a sudden, as if he was inside a cartoon surrounded by a wacky characters? This sea of unrest was traversed hopelessly by teachers. Like Arctic ice-breakers they climbed the waves of turbulence and crashed them, leaving quiet spots in their wake for a whole two...seconds. Then the mayhem returned. Tobbi saw one calm spot and chuckled. At the head of the table intended for six people sat the one and only Kenny, the Pouch, King of all Kitchens and Master of the Chow. He was, of course, chewing. Kenny ruled his small kingdom with menacing growls that rumbled in his giant stomach as in a subwoofer. Trespassers were warned once. Next, food was removed from the cavernous mouth and chewing stopped—a mortal threat. Kenny's dark, slightly slanted eyes focused on the poor disoriented soul. At this point to save his life a kid had to run or he would find himself airborne. For a fat guy, Kenny could really move.

Soon Tobbi found himself a recipient of the growl. He lingered on, so Pouch focused, "Tobbi!" he yelped, and his thick, glistening lips parted in a surprisingly engaging smile. "You're alive." Pouch lifted his stomach off the table and wobbled over. He picked Tobbi's hands up, turned him around, and boosted him up like a toy.

"Hey, chill out, dude. What are you doing?" Tobbi asked, laughing.

"Just checking if any parts are missing."

"C'mon, Pouch. It wasn't that bad."

"Yeah sure! And *Star Wars* is just a flick! Famous last words. First you don't feel a leg or an arm missing then poooof...you're dead." Kenny's head lolled to the side and his tongue came out: he made a very convincing zombie. Tobbi roared; Pouch could be as silly as he was mean.

"Take my word for it—Mr. Pierre is not at all what he seems. And keep the lid on it, okay?"

"Hey! What's that? Puppy love for a Bulldog."

"Kenny don't call him that, ever again," said Tobbi, "I mean it."

Pouch stared at him hard. Tobbi wasn't backing down. "Okay, I don't know what's come over you, but it's a deal."

"Thanks, Pouch," Tobbi said, "you're the greatest and don't you forget it."

"Unforgettable, that's what I am," Pouch sang, showing his softer side, horrendously off tune.

"So, Ladybug, you came!" the voice screeched from behind Pouch's broad back. Pouch hopped around and crouched with arms reaching forward, growling like a bear. The Barb stepped back. "Pouch, I have no beef with you, man," he said.

Pouch hopped forward and snarled, "It's Mister Pouch to you, retard!" The Barb lost volume like freshly poured coke in a cup but still tried to walk around Pouch, who hunched down and turned to attack.

"It's okay, I'll handle it." Tobbi said.

"There's nothing to handle here. He's interrupting my meal. Beat it Barb or—"

"Cut it out, Pouch. I said I'll handle it," Tobbi said firmly, and a miracle: Pouch backed away. Strangely, the Barb retreated also, eyeing Tobbi suspiciously.

"So what are you goanna do, huh?" he asked, glancing at his small group of supporters. Jimmy, Barb's best friend, Barb's only friend, shrugged his shoulders, as if saying—it's your mess. The Barb began to panic. Tobbi rolled forward and dropped a bombshell: "Tommy, I'm sorry I said your brain was stuck. I don't think you're stupid," He said, and reached with his hand. The Barb raised his fists and jumped back, and then his jaw dropped as did many others.

"Tommy? Who's Tommy?" Pouch demanded. Tobbi wasn't finished yet. "You know, you'd be okay if you didn't try to be a tough guy. Chill out and we could be friends. Okay Tom?"

The kids froze in shock. No less then two teachers came over. Mrs. Jeremy, the English teacher, inquired, "What's going on here?"

Her words animated everyone as if by remote control. Pouch fell into a chair. Others were shaking their heads. Tobbi, on the other hand, remained unmoving. The Barb dropped his fists, not letting his eyes off Tobbi's hand. Then, suddenly, he turned and ran from the cafeteria. Mrs. Jeremy asked again, "What's happened here? Tobbi! What did you do?"

"Oh, nothing" answered Tobbi cheerfully. "I just told him how much I liked him." Mrs. Jeremy was suspicious but couldn't do anything. She resumed her rounds.

Pouch reached over, felt Tobbi's forehead, and asked, "T-man, are you sick? Or maybe you're taken over by an alien or something. That's it! Why, that explains everything: Bul...Mr. Pierre, I mean, is the alien who infected you. Just tell me this is so, because the alternative's worse—madness, total madness."

15

Ilya Simakovsky

Just then Nelli came over and in her high, clear voice that, of course, could be heard everywhere, declared: "Tobbi! I just want to tell you what you did was beautiful. I think you guys are all cruel the way you treat the Ba...I mean Tommy. I think Tobbi did good. It's cool and I like...like..." She got lost. "Well, that's what I think." She turned, shiny dress whooshing, her ponytail bouncing proudly on her way out. Now, everyone wanted to know what'd happened. A flurry of stares came to rest upon Tobbi. He, meanwhile, was stuffing his face with one of Pouch's hamburgers.

Pouch for once, wasn't chewing on anything at all! "Weird," he said. "I just want to make sure that the dude, stealing my food here, is the same old buddy of mine."

"Yep. It's still me," Tobbi said, choking and spitting pieces of Pouch's hamburger all over. "I've jhuscht leahhrned a few shhinksh. Mmm this is mad good!"

"What? Stop mumbling! And stop spitting! Hey, yo, that's mine!" Pouch cried out, seeing another hamburger leaving his plate.

"Dude! You need to lose weight." Tobbi clutched the burger and bit in.

"What!? That's too much! You, thief, gimme back my burger!" Pouch lunged and grabbed the remains of the burger out of Tobbi's mouth. Tobbi snatched fries off his friend's plate. Pouch blocked with his elbow and fries went flying. He turned ready to strike, his face red as a beet.

"So, going to hit a cripple, are you?" Tobbi said, smoothly. Kenny sat down, hugged his plate and turned his back on his friend, muttering.

"What's that?" asked Tobbi.

"Are you deaf too? It's too weird. I don't know if I wanna be around you. Maybe I'll catch it too; and yeah! You thief! Get...your...own...FOOD!"

"Hey, chill, man. I'm sorry. You know I like you just the way you are. About the weight though, you know I'm right; even though I like hanging around...and around, and around

16

you; sort of like the earth around the sun; takes a year to go around." Tobbi started laughing again.

Pouch looked back and despite himself smiled. "Okay, I'll forgive you," he declared. "About the chow though, go get your own. I'll start losing weight tomorrow. Right now I'm still hungry."

Suddenly Tobbi paled. He bent his head as if listening to a faint sound.

"Gees, not one of your fantasies again,"

"Did you hear that?" Tobbi whispered.

"Hear what?"

"That voice."

"What voice? There's no voice. You're hallucinating, I didn't hear noth'n'. You must be hungry!"

"The voice called me. I swear. I'm not crazy!"

Pouch frowned. "Sure thing. You just imagined it. Just eat. It'll do it. Here, take my burgers, take my fries, take anything...eat!"

Tobbi ignored him. For the first time he heard the voice clearly while awake. With shaking hands he pushed his chair towards the exit. Pouch shook his big head and went back to his cold food without much enthusiasm.

CHAPTER 4

Premonition

Lydia looked at the clock for the fifteenth time. She spent the day doing meaningless things and now was cleaning the kitchen again. Becky walked in.

"Mom, didn't I see you doing this before?"

"Yeah," answered Lydia and cried. Becky, her 16-year-old daughter, hugged her tightly.

"What's the matter Mom? Please don't cry. It's Tobbi, isn't it? It'll be all right, you'll see."

Lydia wiped her tears and kissed Becky on the forehead, "Thank you, darling. I know. I'm just worried about Dr. Golding's visit. I'll be okay."

Becky, a tall, slim girl with a graceful neck, full head of blond feathery hair, and bright freckled face hugged her mother again and then nuzzled her. When Becky was little Mother would tickle her nose back and forth with the tip of her own nose whenever Becky was upset, and invariably she'd feel better. Now Becky returned the favor. Lydia couldn't help but smile.

"Now, what do I see here?" inquired Richard Sontag. "Sontag's female hugging club, is it?"

Mr. Sontag had a giant voice. It boomed like distant thunder, echoing between walls. The women chuckled, seeing their husband and father skipping the stairs on the way down. He looked deceptively small and thin. It was comical the way his narrow, graceful wrists and ankles were framed by powerful, ballooning muscles. A former track and field athlete, he was capable of unbelievable bursts of energy. On family outings he was always in front scouting. Lydia frequently complained that they were like Tom and Jerry because like in the cartoon, she could never catch up with

18

him.

His mind worked just as fast. Engineer by trade and inventor by nature, Richard was building and destroying things faster than a baby in a sand box.

His children adored him, when little, they found him an unending source of games. They could do just about anything to him; Tobbi once bit him on the nose just to see if Daddy could cry. Tobbi cried; Daddy didn't. He became a source for interesting stories, ideas, and adventures when they got older. It was no wonder that ladies smiled when they heard Richard. After all, he could cheer up a mummy.

Richard asked, "So, can anyone join or is it an exclusive outfit?"

"Sir, the privilege is usually reserved for people with higher voices, but in certain rare instances we can make exceptions, can't we Becky?" answered Lydia.

"Yes, indeed, Mother! But they must earn it."

"Of course, of course, my wise daughter. Question is: how?"

"I'll show you how," roared Richard and became an avalanche. Before the ladies could properly prepare, the avalanche swept them off the floor, blew them across the kitchen and living room like fallen leaves in a gale and deposited them on the couch.

"No way!" exclaimed Becky, angrily combing her messed up hair. Lydia laughed.

"Well, let's try around the yard once or twice then."

The answer was a frantic "NO!" Followed by an unconditional surrender.

Richard hugged and kissed his daughter, then his wife. He noticed a stubborn tear drop in Lydia's eye and sat up straight. "Honey!" he said, "listen to me, Tobbi's condition is temporary. He'll get well. So, no matter what Dr. Golding says today, remember this, he'll be fine. He'll win and we shall help him. Everyone agrees?"

When there wasn't an answer he raised his awesome

voice, "Well?"

"Yes, yes, okay," Lydia and Becky cried out, covering their ears.

"That's better," he said.

CHAPTER 5

The Family Stuff

"What's going on? I thought I heard an explosion," Tobbi slammed the door behind him and sat in the foyer roaming his eyes around.

"Oh, it wasn't dear. Your father's talking, that's all" purred Lydia. Tobbi stared at the whole family entangled on a sofa. He grimaced; his upturned nose squashed into a pancake. Lydia giggled. Becky giggled too. Richard followed and finally Tobbi. They laughed until they had trouble breathing.

"What's this about?" Tobbi asked when he was able.

"Oh, Daddy just threw his.., actually our weight around," Becky answered.

"Huh!? Never mind. I'm not interested in your craziness; I've got enough of my own." Tobbi took the elevator upstairs. Lydia frowned and followed. She knocked on his door.

"Yeah?"

"It's me, honey. Can I come in?" asked Lydia well aware of NO PARKING sign strategically placed beneath the skull and cross-bones.

"Just a second, let me put my pants on."

"Need help?"

"NO!" he yelped, then quieter, "okay, come in now."

Lydia looked around the room with a critical eye and found that she still enjoyed her son's style. Many posters and photographs covered the walls. Around the bed on the opposite wall basketball stars performed in scores of photos. To the left and across from the window racing cars of various shapes and colors were now spotlighted by the afternoon sun. The rest of the room was devoted to birds and airplanes, helicopters and spaceships, superheros and robots, acrobats and bats pictured or photographed in flight. Lydia walked in

21

further, ducking various models of flying machines suspended from the ceiling. It seems that any moment the house would be lifted and carried away by them all. Then she noticed a new and totally out-of-character addition to her son's interests and lifted her left eyebrow.

"I think she's cute that's all," Tobbi said quickly.

"I'll say!" said Lydia eyeing the photograph of a scarcely dressed woman in the niche behind Tobbi's bed. "Is it that time already?" she asked.

"It's just a picture, Mom!"

"Oh, really? First a picture, then live ones begin to pop up here and there. What's the name of the one you like? Nelli is it?"

"It's not like that, really, Mom! Come on...." Tobbi mumbled, looking away.

"All right, all right, but I'll get father to talk to you. You know, one of those birds and bees talks."

"Who? Dad!? The closest he'll come to the subject would be a law of physics, like heat exchange or something."

"You don't say," said Lydia her voice suddenly thick with luster. "Obviously you don't know your father very well, son. There are times..."

"Oh yeah? Tell me?" Tobbi insisted. Lydia shook her finger at him and said, "Never mind you; better tell me why you are upset; something I need to know?"

"No, Mom. I just learned a couple of hard lessons in school, that's all."

"Good or bad?"

"A little of both."

"Do you want to talk about it?"

"No..." Tobbi paused, not sure about what to tell her, "It's just that I..."

"Go on." Lydia inched closer.

"It's nothing, really, Mother. Don't worry, I'm okay."

"Cross your heart and hope to die?" asked Lydia. Tobbi nodded finding no sense in worrying her just yet.

"Okay, sonny, I'll let you off the hook, but promise me that you'd talk to me if needs be."
"I promise, okay? Let's not be late. I don't want to see Dr. Golding as it is."
"Right you are, Tobbi. Let's hurry. You're being very adult about this. I'm proud of you."
"Mom, make up your mind, okay? One minute you treat me like a kid, another—like an adult."
"So what, if I'm a little confused? I'm your mother; I'm allowed. Go!"

CHAPTER 6

The Warning

Mr. and Mrs. Sontag had been in the waiting room for a while. Lydia could not take her eyes away from the door. As if an entrance to an unknown and dangerous universe it kept her under a spell. Lydia squeezed her husband's arm nervously: the door opened. Richard patted her hand gently.

"Please come in, the doctor is waiting for you," said a tall nurse. Lydia looked at her and hesitated until her husband pulled her up.

Dr. Deana Golding was a tall, stringy woman in her late forties. She wore little make-up on her tired face and her hair was always slightly messed up. Nevertheless, she was one of the top specialists in Neurology.

"Please sit down," she said and continued her writing. Lydia's anxiety skyrocketed, even Richard fidgeted. Just then Dr. Golding looked up and smiled. The room seemed to gain color.

"Is he doing better?" Lydia asked hopefully. "Not quite," the answer came, like a blow. But Dr. Golding continued quickly, "Still there's good news. It appears that his condition has stabilized. It may be that we are turning toward remission."

"That's wonderful." Lydia was hopeful again.

"His blood values, other test results have not worsened since last month, unlike before, so we have hope."

"Oh, thank you so much, Doctor."

"Well, it's too early to celebrate. As I told you before, things could change again. Therefore, we must do everything we can to help your son. It's extremely important to have a healthy lifestyle and healthy attitude. Tobbi must be ready psychologically to defeat his disease. He takes his medications on time, right?"

"Of course."

"What about exercise and vitamins?" Lydia nodded. "Good!" said Dr. Golding, "now, last month I recommended Dr. Lubkin, the chiropractor to you. How's it going?"

Robert answered, "You know, Doc, his back pain has gone away like magic, and you know what? He says he feels better after each treatment. Dr. Lubkin's fixing my old neck too. Thanks."

"Oh, you're welcome. I've referred others to him, including my pain-in-you-know-what husband. He had chronic headaches. Now he's much happier because he's only giving them to me." Everyone laughed as the tension eased.

"Now," Dr. Golding said gravely, "there is one aspect of this condition I have not yet discussed with you, since it's somewhat rare." Lydia's frowned as Dr. Golding continued, "You know that for reasons yet unknown some patients spontaneously recover almost completely."

"Almost completely...?" inquired Mr. Sontag.

"Well, some weakness usually remains in the large muscles, not a big handicap. A few patients, however, have a different reaction. In some people disease may flare up more aggressively, and they go through a crisis."

"What sort of crisis?" asked Lydia, blinking moisture out of her eyes.

"Well, the sudden activation of the condition is met with the all out effort of the body to resist it."

"So, what happens?" Lydia pressed nervously.

"If—," Dr. Golding coughed, "a patient wins then he or she recovers without any weakness. Most do nowadays, but some don't."

Lydia's looked at her husband blinking rapidly.

Richard patted her on the hand and said, "Listen, Doc! With all due respect, I know that Tobbi will be well. I know! Don't ask me how, but I know. So let's see how we can make it easier for him, okay?"

Ilya Simakovsky

The doctor looked long and hard at Richard. "Very well," she said, "let's hope you're right. It appears he's heading toward remission, anyway. Just continue the good things you're doing: plenty of rest and exercise, good food—no junk, and most important, a good mental attitude, like yours Richard; give him some of yours."

Dr. Golding got up. "I'll see everybody in a month. Hopefully there'll be more good news. Goodbye."

Tobbi was already in the waiting room. He perked up when his parents walked out. Lydia hugged him, while Richard punched him easily on the shoulder saying, "How was it soldier?"

"Not so bad, Dad. I'm sort of getting used to it. Needles suck, that's all."

"That's my boy! No Sontag will ever be scared of a few needles."

"Yeah, sure! Why don't you take it instead of me?"

"No needle ever touches me. I was talking about the other Sontags."

Richard recoiled, making a sign of a cross with his right and left index fingers.

"Yeah, yeah," growled Tobbi, but he smiled.

Lydia looked into Tobbi's eyes and said, "Doctor thinks that you're on the mend, how about that?" Tobbi grinned. "She also said that we still got lots of fighting to do and that you've got to be strong and positive mentally. You think you can hack it, Tobbi Sontag?"

"Yes, ma'am! With you on my back I have no choice, I think."

"You better believe it, sucker!"

"Mom!"

"Lydia!"

"What? What did I say?" Lydia asked flapping her long eye lashes like a Barbi doll.

Richard chuckled and reminded everyone about Dr. Lubkin's appointment. Tobbi hurried to the door. He looked

26

forward to a chiropractic treatment; it was called an adjustment, like he was some kind of a robot. Oh, yeah! A robot! He suffered a major malfunction. On this alien planet it meant death. He's heading to his engineer for repairs. Giant insects, with poison dripping of their long black stings, attacked from above. His tank tracks were slipping, yet his laser cannon zapped the vicious beasts right and left.

Lydia flapped her arms and pointed at Tobbi who wheeled his chair side to side, mouthing off gun shots. She caught up with him, braced her mouth and bellowed, "Earth to Tobbi; repeat—earth calling Tobbi, come in please."

Tobbi snapped out just in time to avoid driving off the pavement, turning to their car instead. In ten minutes they were there. Terry, Dr. Lubkin's receptionist, saw Tobbi and immediately punched the intercom, grinning all the way: "Dr. Lubkin—office alert! The terror on wheels is here. Come and get him."

Tobbi snickered. He remembered how on his first visit he crashed nearly everyone's toes with his wheelchair. Even now Terry hid her feet under her chair, chuckling quietly. He loved being adjusted. Here he rested from needles and probes and it made him feel good. Dr. Brad Lubkin walked in. He was a lean, muscular guy, with shoulder length hair and thin ironic mouth. Tobbi couldn't help but grin when he saw Dr. Lubkin's broad smiling face. They shared a common passion—cars. Even now he tossed the latest issue of *Car and Driver Magazine* into Tobbi's lap.

"Hi, Tobbi. Great issue. Wait till you see the specs on the new Ferrari, and check out the new GM concept cars—mean little things. I'd kill to get my hands on one of those!"

"I can't help you, Brad, just spare me pleeeease!"

"Huh?" Dr. Lubkin was lost for a second, "Oh, you're a smart aleck. Okay, I'll let you live, maybe. Get on that table!" he commanded.

Tobbi parked his chair next to a knee-high, narrow bench covered in maroon leather; it was divided into three sections for the neck, torso, and pelvis (what a spastic name for a butt!).

Dr. Lubkin moved Tobbi onto the table where he stretched on his stomach relaxing. Like two dancing snakes Dr. Lubkin's fingers slithered up and down Tobbi's back. He must've found something because Tobbi felt a quick, gentle thrust. Snap-crackle-pop went his back and it didn't hurt one bit. More of the same happened in different parts of his body. Dr. Lubkin then stretched his legs and poked at his muscles. He called it acupressure and it hurt a little. Then it was over. Tobbi felt like he grew a mile when he sat up, more importantly, there wasn't an ache in his body.

"So, how do you feel?"

"Great! Thanks."

"Let's see, this is your ninth treatment. How's your back pain?"

"What back pain?"

"As I said before—a smart aleck. But, I'm glad you're feeling better. I'm going to see you less frequently now, so you stay cool and keep those car ambitions honed, okay?"

Feeling lighter and stronger, Tobbi raced down the hall right into Terry, who yelped and scrambled furiously for the safety of her cubicle.

"That's it" she whimpered, "from now on I'm on vacation whenever you're in the office. And next time you WILL get a traffic ticket: my brother's a cop and I swear I'll get you one. The speed limit here's 55 miles per year, got it, speedbreath?" She stood with her hands on her hips, barely controlling a smile.

"I'm sorry, Terry. I won't do it again. I promise."

"Fat chance! You and my boss, Mario Andretti here, are hopeless speed freaks all of you. So, you'd better speed on out of here before somebody gets hurt. You catch my drift, Tobbi? And, oh yea! Have a nice day."

Tobbi waited for his father outside. He dreamed of a hot red French car which he drove like an absolute maniac.

CHAPTER 7

The Mysterious Visit

Several things happened in the next two weeks. The Barb had mutated. He stopped bugging people and turned into a quiet, intelligent boy, with a strange sense of humor and Tobbi even started to like the kid. Tobbi became more popular too, so much so he had to assure the jealous Pouch that he was still Tobbi's best friend and nothing could come between them, except, of course, there was Nellie.

All of a sudden, she decided to adopt Tobbi for her own and since she was a very popular girl the other boys tried to break into their budding relationship. Her devotion or whim seemed quite firm, she even tolerated Pouch's unavoidable presence since Tobbi made it clear if Pouch goes so would he. The three were seen everywhere together. Nellie was surprised to discover a very engaging, smart, and humorous side of Pouch. Not spoiled by a long shot with female attention, Pouch positively bloomed in the company of a pretty girl. In other words, they were having fun.

Today, though, Tobbi felt weird: like his grip on reality was becoming loose again, and the Voice came back, stronger than ever. He almost went to Mr. Pierre, but decided to wait. It was Thursday. The day after tomorrow Dad promised to take him fishing and he didn't want to jinx it. Yet, by the end of the day Tobbi became scared: he felt haunted. When he came home he was nearly in tears.

Lydia was cooking when Tobbi came in. "Hi, honey," she said—no answer. *Well, maybe he didn't hear,* she thought; he'd come and greet her in a minute. When, instead, Tobbi went straight upstairs, she frowned. "Tobbi!" she called—no answer again. That wasn't like him at all. Lydia lowered the flame under a pot, wiped her hands on her apron, and went upstairs.

She knocked on Tobbi's door, once, twice, three times—still no answer. "Tobbi, open the door this minute!" she ordered, "what's the matter? Are you all right? Tobbi!"

"I'm okay, mom, just tired. I'll just rest a little, okay?"

"Tobbi, honey, let me in. You don't sound well." The lock clicked. Lydia followed Tobbi who rode towards the window. Lydia ran ahead and kneeled by his chair. "What's the matter, honey? Please tell me."

Suddenly Tobbi turned to her and slapped the wheelchair angrily. "It's this damn thing! Why can't I be like everyone else? Why did I have to get sick?" he yelled, sobbing.

Lydia hugged him; he struggled briefly then relaxed. She said softly, "We all wish our lives were easy and sweet like a tasty bowl of ice cream, but they rarely are. We're constantly tripped by bad things and put in front of barriers. It's the way we handle them that determines what kind of people we are. And, honey, you're strong. You're so strong, you don't even know..." She kissed him on the forehead forcefully. "Besides, you're not alone. We're all by your side every step of the way. Nothing can defeat the Sontags united, you know that, don't you?"

"Okay, Mom. I'm sorry. I just...had a tough day."

"How so?" she fixed him with her particular radar-like stare; the one Tobbi couldn't dodge.

"Okay! I feel strange today; like something's about to happen; something big. I just don't know what. It sucks."

"Do you feel like talking to Dr. Golding?"

"No. I..." Tobbi hesitated but decided not to tell her about the Voice. "It's okay, don't worry. I can handle it," he said confidently.

"Are you sure?"

"Yes. I'm sure. Let me change and I'll be downstairs in a minute."

Lydia nodded, got up and went downstairs. In the kitchen, she walked to the stove, stared at it with her hands on her hips, turned around sharply, and walked to the phone. She dialed quickly and waited, rapping her fingertips on the counter. "Richard?" she yelled because the noise in the background was loud.

"Yes, honey. What's up? I'm right in a middle of trials and—"

"I'm worried about Tobbi, Rich."

"Just a second," she heard him scream off the phone, "Jerry...Hey, Jerry, would you shut it down for a bit. I know it's up to speed. Shut it down! It's important. Thanks. That's better, I can hear you now. What about Tobbi?"

"He came from school disturbed and angry, and...worried. It's not good."

"So? It's happened before."

"Richard! Not like this, I'm telling you. He's scared; I can feel it. He says he feels like something's going to happen. Remember about another way it could go?"

But, Lydia, did you see any changes?"

"No, but who knows how it starts. Do you?"

"Okay, okay. It's just that these trials are very important and—"

"As important as your son, Rich?" Lydia said very quietly.

There was a pause on the other end. "I'll be home soon, honey. Don't worry, we'll handle it, and Tobbi will be all right. See you soon." He hung up. With a deep sigh of relief, Lydia went back to finish cooking.

Meanwhile, Tobbi sat at his window and stared at the sky. Always a point of interest and inspiration, it now stirred a dreadful anxiety in him. The clouds seemed swollen, pregnant with menace, and drifting close enough to touch. Suddenly, he noticed a big, strange cloud shaped like a human head. It seemed to pause, letting the other clouds drift by. How weird, he even could see its mouth. Tobbi shook his head and rubbed his eyes. He definitely saw two thick lips now and above them a huge bulb of a nose. Through its big nostrils he could see the bright blue of the sky. Tobbi gulped too much air and hiccupped; above the nose, two enormous, slightly slanted eyes became visible. He yelped when the white puffy lids lit up with gold; the afternoon sun seemed to aim its rays there like some kind of monstrous projector lamp.

"Mom," Tobbi whispered, shivering, then louder "Mom! Come here...."

Downstairs, Lydia stopped moving her pots around; was Tobbi yelling? Nope. She heard nothing. She shrugged her shoulders and went back to work. Meanwhile, Tobbi was about to call again but his voice froze in his throat. The giant eyes were opening. The gold drained out of the lids as they slowly lifted, revealing enormous, blue orbs. They seemed to look right at him. They WERE looking at him! Tobbi opened and closed his mouth but nothing came out. The big mouth in the sky moved instead.

"Tobbi," a familiar basso called. Tobbi's heart was beating so fast; if it had wings it would rip through his chest and fly away. He wanted to run away too and he wanted his mother here, now. These conflicting impulses paralyzed him, he couldn't even think. Yet, his initial fear was being squashed by fascination and a growing belief that the head in the sky meant him no harm. Then, it spoke again: "Tobbi come. We need you."

"Who?! Who needs me? What are you?" asked Tobbi, greatly disturbed that he was talking to a cloud.

"Come, Tobbi, we need you." The voice faded, the great eyes closed, and the cloud floated away.

Instantly angry, Tobbi shouted, "What do you want from me? Leave me alone. How do you expect me to get up there? Fly!? I can't even walk, you stupid cotton wad. L-e-a-v-e... me...alone!"

"Help!" the voice insisted very faintly, and Tobbi heard no more.

Lydia dropped everything and ran upstairs. She busted

through the door like a tank, yelling too, "Tobbi. Are you okay? Why are you screaming..." Tobbi was sitting at the window, his chest heaving, and staring into the sky. Lydia moved closer.

"Tobbi, darling, what's the matter? Tell Momma, come on," she stroked his hair gently glancing out the window, trying to see what had upset him so.

"What does that look like to you?" he asked at last.

"What? What are you pointing to?" Lydia peered hard into the sky.

"That big cloud over there to the left, see?"

"Oh, that one; yes, yes, I see it. It looks like...hmmm let me see...it looks like a head, I'd say. How funny. So...?"

"It...it...looked at me." He just couldn't say that it talked to him.

"Come on, baby! No matter how imaginative you are, it's still just a cloud, hardly worth being so worked up. Besides, how could it look at you?! Need eyes for that."

"There were."

"Stop it Tobbi!" Lydia put some steel in her voice. "Don't let some fantasy ruin your evening. Your father will be home soon. Don't let him see you like this. Okay?"

Tobbi perked up. "Dad's coming home early tonight? He hasn't done that this whole month. Are you sure? Doesn't he have some kind of field trial today?"

"Yes, but I asked him to come home earlier."

"You might as well ask that cloud to come back. It'll be more likely."

"Tobbi! Your father's work is very important to him, but when he heard that something's upsetting you he didn't think twice. He'll be here soon. Your father loves you. We all love you, don't you know this?"

"More than his work?"

"More than anything, Tobbi."

"Okay, cool," said Tobbi cheerfully. Dad didn't allow gloominess, with a joke, advice or plain silliness he could make a corpse feel better. Tobbi rolled away from the window and went to the bathroom. Lydia asked if he was coming to eat. "Yep," he yelped through the door, and she went down to get ready.

After the meal Tobbi went to do his homework. There was a lot to do in mathematics, which he liked, but when he opened the textbook everything blurred. The sense of detachment returned. He was so tired of it: a gray fog seemed to fill the room separating him from the things he loved, even his family. Anticipation, excitement, and dread combined into one overwhelming feeling—certainty—something was about to happen. *But what? What?* he asked himself. The open textbook provided no answers.

"Tobbi!" the voice came again. Tobbi yielded this time.

"Tobbi come. We need you."

"What do you want from me? Where are you?"

"Up here...above...look...."

Tobbi went back to the window, and sure enough, the cloud head was there. It stared at him, now with the violet-blue eyes of the evening sky. Tobbi said, "Am I going crazy? I don't understand! How can I help anybody up there? It is I who need help. I've got to tell someone. I wish Dad was here already, he'd understand."

"No, Tobbi. Tell no one...come up...fly up...."

"Fly?" the magic word had been spoken.

"How? 747, space shuttle!"

"Just wish...Tobbi...believe...believe...believe...believe..." The voice and the cloud faded away. At the edge of the great unknown Tobbi sat, watching the sunset, thinking of the incredible thing that was happening to him.

CHAPTER 8

Daddy's Home—Richard's Story

"Tobbi," the basso called. Tobbi, still deep in thought, recoiled in fear; the Voice came from behind his door now.

"May I come in?"

"Of course, Dad, please..." Tobbi said greatly relieved. The door opened and his dad, a wonderful little giant walked in. His son's headlong rush nearly knocked Richard off his feet. "Ahha! You wanna play rough, do you?" he bellowed and picked Tobbi up, chair and all. "I'll toss you like a snowball for tackling me down without warning—you sneak!" But something was wrong: Tobbi grasped him like a desperate, drowning man. Very gently, Richard lowered Tobbi down. Tobbi wasn't letting go so Richard hugged Tobbi back, and they sat like this for a couple of minutes in silence. Finally, Richard pulled back and searched his son's face. It was full of uneasiness, eyes bathed in tears.

"What's the matter, son?" he asked. "Talk to me. Your mother's worried and so am I." Tobbi just shook his head. "Why not, I can't help you unless you talk to me."

"Dad, I just don't know what to tell you. I just...don't feel right."

"Is something's hurting you? You feel weak or..."

"It's not that, Dad!" Tobbi snapped. "I feel strange, like I don't belong here anymore, I'm scared, Dad!"

"Tobbi..."

The door flung open. Becky waltzed in. Seeing the two men sitting close, she said, "Oh—oh, I think I walked in on something. Is this one of those male bonding things we women know nothing about?"

"Don't you know how to knock anymore, Bubbles?"

Becky hated that nickname; she shook her hair indig-

Ilya Simakovsky

nantly and retorted, "My knocking is reserved for important people and..."

"Becky, this isn't the right time," Richard said.

"Daddy, he started it!"

"Becky, you didn't knock."

"He doesn't have to call me names. Let him lock the door, I never knock."

"Becky, that's enough. Please, let us talk."

"Okay. You can take this bonding thing and shove it," and spinning on her heels, she waved them off with her freshly manicured fingers.

"Women!? Who can understand them? Not me. Can you?" Richard took a flustered breath and turned back to Tobbi who shook his head in denial. However, a little fight with one's sister was all one needed to get his spirit up. Tobbi felt calmer now.

"So, tell me what do you think is going to happen, Tobbi?"

"That's just it, Dad, I don't know." He desperately wanted to tell his father about the Voice, but the cloud-head's warning stopped him.

"Tobbi, none of us knows what's going to happen tomorrow or the next minute. That's the great thing about life; it's always fresh, always full of surprises. For me it is. Then, of course, there are people for whom it's just the opposite; always a dread, always a worry. Which would you rather be?"

"I understand, Dad, but you don't ride in a chair. You're as healthy as a bear, you can't understand."

"I can't, can I...?" he paused. "I've never told you this; remember the big scar I have on my leg?" Tobbi nodded. "When I was freshman in college, I competed in track and field which you know—right? What you don't know is that I had my eyes set on the Olympics—I was that good. One day I was running down the tough woody trail near the campus. Suddenly, another runner passed me. It was our senior track star. He always challenged me; didn't like me either. So, we started racing. The trail was treacherous and twisted wildly

36

but I was beating him." Tobbi saw his father's eyes lit up and got excited too, forgetting his worries.

"Yes, I lead George by a dozen yards when I made a tight turn around a big, old oak tree. I hit a bump and felt my knee buckle. The next thing I knew, I was tumbling down the slope, breaking all kinds of things not the least of them my leg. The bone was sticking out; blood pumping. It looked awful. George surprised me. As tired as he was, he picked me up and ran with me all the way back to school, straining his back and collapsing in the end. I guess he blamed himself for what'd happened to me. We're still friends, by the way."

"You're talking about the big George, who flies in from Chicago sometimes?"

"Yep, that George; became a sports doctor, you know; healed many more people then he'd injured. Besides, it wasn't his fault."

"So what happened next?"

"I had a compound open fracture of both bones in my lower left leg. Doctors laughed when I asked them to fix me quick. I had Olympic trials to get to in six months. The big cheese orthopedic doctor came to talk me into changing my sport interests. He told me that if George hadn't gotten me back so quickly, I would've lost my leg: to continue running was out of the question. I listened and did what I had to do to get out of the hospital. They told me—two weeks; I was out in one. The hardest part came when I started physical therapy. It hurt so bad I nearly passed out several times. I was the first to come and the last to leave the rehabilitation clinic. The doctors told me that I might injure myself permanently. I didn't listen. Even your granddad tried to hold me back, but I was possessed. I stopped only to eat and sleep. Slowly everybody came to support me as I began to improve. The pain of it haunted me for years." Richard flexed his knees as if checking for pain and continued, "To make a short story long, I started running again and eventually got to the trials. Didn't make the team, though; missed it by one spot, rats....

37

So you see," Richard grasped Tobbi's face and pulled him close, "If you really believe you can beat this thing, then nothing should stop you...nothing. Whatever you must go through, no fear—understand?" Tobbi nodded and shook his shoulders as if shedding off snow. "Dad," he said.

"You don't need to say anything, boy. I understand. Look, it's eight already. Let's have some chow and do a man's thing."

"What's that, Dad?"

"Why, son, car racing's on."

"All right. Let's go!" Tobbi rode downstairs on his father's strong back.

Two hours later it was time for bed. However, Tobbi kept delaying: he asked dad questions about various cars they'd seen. He asked Lydia to sit with him and bullied his sister into playing checkers. It was very unlike him. "Tobbi," Lydia said finally, "quit stalling. You won't be able to lift your head off the pillow in the morning. Up you go! Taxi!" She held her thumb up like a hitchhiker. "Beep, beep," went Richard and offered his back again. Tobbi smiled and said, "Dad, you sound like a locomotive not a car."

"Fine," agreed Richard and tooted accordingly. Tobbi laughed and hurried to get on his back before things started falling off the shelves. Becky covered her ears while Lydia, laughing, pushed them both towards the stairs. The women could hear the make-believe train all the way to Tobbi's bedroom.

Richard and Tobbi collapsed on his bed laughing. In a while, Richard got up and helped Tobbi undress. Tobbi let him: he was too tired and feeling feverish. He asked for the window to be opened after which Richard tucked him in, real tight. Tobbi hugged him fiercely and wouldn't let go. Finally, Richard peeled away gently.

"Dad, I'm scared again. What if..."

"There is no if," Richard interrupted firmly. "Son! Are you afraid to fight for yourself?"

"No...Yes, I don't know, Dad. That's just it! I don't know what I'm afraid of and..."

"Precisely!" Richard cried out. "You're afraid of the unknown. Welcome to the human race! All people are the same in this respect. But you know, after living for awhile you may come to a certain understanding: until you know what the trouble is, don't worry about it. Once you know, do your best to fix it. If you can't fix it, then and only then, you worry; understand?"

"I don't know..." Tobbi hesitated. "I guess I understand, but..."

"No, Tobbi. No ifs or buts. Don't be afraid of the future. Many good things will happen and many bad things will happen, but your life is a long story filled with wonders and excitement, struggle and victory, love and sorrow, laughter and tears. Look forward, Tobbi, and let your dreams guide you."

"You sure?" asked Tobbi quietly.

"You bet!"

"You're so...awesome, Dad."

"If I am, my son, then you are as well." They fell silent, and then Richard asked, "Remember our little bedtime rhyme?" Tobbi nodded.

"Chimney soot and dirty boot
Big black wolf and monster's hoot
Thunder's boom and lightning's strike
Witch's brew and howling night
Snake's loud hiss and wasp's long sting
All those scary and nasty things
They are not so frightening
If I know that in bad dreams
Mom and Dad are on my team."

They finished the rhyme together. "Better now?" Richard asked.

"Yap."

"Goodnight then. Sleep tight. See you tomorrow." And he left.

Tobbi lay still, listening to the night conquering his house. Later, when it got quiet, his thoughts became clear. No longer afraid, he was ready to handle whatever came his way. Slowly, ever so slowly, the night conquered him as well. Darkness descended.

CHAPTER 9

The Flight Begins

The darkness filled up with a gray smoke. Was he or wasn't he asleep? Tobbi couldn't tell. The weird smoke whirled and whirled around, as if pushed by clashing winds. Colorful beams of light punctured through the smoke and hacked it into many shapeless clouds. These soaked in the light and began glowing with pink, yellow and other pastel hues. Tobbi shivered: his entire vision filled up with this mosaic canvas which began to elevate pulling Tobbi with it. His body held him down like a harness.

"Tobbi," the Voice rumbled, loud and clear this time. "It's time. Fly, Tobbi. Don't be afraid. Come to us. We need you."

Tobbi wasn't afraid, but he wasn't going either. The fog lifted higher, and from all sides the darkness was pushing in, seeking him. That worried him more.

"Tobbi, you must come!" The Voice resonated with urgency now, "Fly, Tobbi, fly to us. You can fly..." It was fainting quickly.

"I can fly?" whispered Tobbi, and suddenly knew that he could if he wanted to. He felt darkness pulsate around him; it wanted him—it wanted to win. Groaning, he strained to pull up. The darkness smothered him, the bright fog—all but gone. He pulled again with every ounce of power and will. Something ripped and he was free; free like never before; he floated up, without even trying, and flipped in the air. In his bed he saw a body. It took a second to recognize it; how could this be, me there and me here? He agonized, trembling. Maybe I shouldn't do this? Is this a dream? But he felt so liberated, he couldn't give it up, not now, maybe later; he couldn't care less how it came about. It was supremely wonderful and frightfully exciting.

He hovered, undecided. "Tobbi, I'm waiting," the Voice said, "the choice was made. Fly to us, Tobbi. Fly and see...before it's too late...." Tobbi glanced around the room and without further hesitation flew, slowly and clumsily at first, but faster with every second, out of the open window, higher than his house, above the gnarled old oak, over Butler Hill and he was freeee eee-ha! He could fly! Tobbi screamed with joy, twisting and darting to and fro in the early light of morning, savoring the feeling of complete liberation from gravity, from his wheelchair, from his school, from his house...his house? He looked back, but couldn't see his house; the ground had receded and everything became so tiny. He thought of his family but needed to find out what this was about more.

"I'll be back, I promise," he yelled and flew on in search of the owner of the Voice.

CHAPTER 10

The Head in the Clouds

This was mad good! Better then any video game he's ever played. Just by thinking it, he could speed up or slow down and fly in any direction. Some dumb bird was flying below; he swooped down like a hawk and discovered that it was difficult: the strange force was still pushing on him. Up was far easier, "Eee..ha," he yelped, and flipped over causing his hand to drift past his eyes. Suddenly out of control and screaming he flailed his legs and arms, and splashed right into a big cloud, like a kernel of a cereal into milk. A web-like resistance of the cloud stopped him quickly. Tobbi brought the left hand to his face. He felt it moving. He knew where it was, yet he couldn't see it, even worse, he couldn't see any part of himself—good time to panic. Squawking like a petrified chick, he clawed through the murky whiteness as if through jelly. It sure didn't feel like a bunch of floating water droplets that a cloud was supposed to be. Suddenly he was through. The sun flared brilliantly at him, igniting the surrounding snow-like plain with a golden glow. It looked exactly like the videos he'd seen of Alaska with its endless snowy wilderness. Slowly, cautiously he looked down and squinted hard: his arm, his body was fluffy, white like cotton. *What am I?* he thought. It was beyond any reasonable explanation or any scientific principle. He needed help. He needed to find the source of the Voice and some kind of explanation or he would go completely and irreversibly nuts. Unless he was already nuts: after all, he looked like a cloud; he floated like one, but he thought like a human. Which was fantasy and which was real Tobbi no longer knew. He just wanted to go on until something helped him decide.

So he flew, enjoying the incredible sensations; upside

down, right side up, hands under the head—all amazingly good; he did somersaults and loop-de-loops until he got bored. Then he just flew on southeast; he didn't know why, it just felt right. The day became night and the night—day as he continued, driven by some intuition, a sense of direction akin to a bird on its long winter migration. The earth rotated below like some lazy, enormous humpback whale. It was decorated by the brown blotches of cities, blue ribbons of rivers, and green hairy tufts of the forests. Then for the longest time there was nothing but ocean. Tobbi realized that he could spend the rest of his life circling the earth with nothing but vertigo to show for it.

Long after he crossed over the land again a group of mountains seemed to materialize out of a distant haze, far to his left. Jolted by a sudden stab of excitement Tobbi turned toward it. Out of nowhere a thought came: this is it! Abandoning all caution, he flew his fastest. Distances were quite deceiving here; it took a while, but finally, there it was: a huge mountain circle broken only by an equally enormous jagged canyon, the main entrance to the inner space. He approached close enough to see through the split. There was another mountain inside. Wide and conical, it stood in the center with its top completely covered by an enormous white cloud. Another huge cloud, this one thick and flat, encircled the middle mountain like a collar. The whole thing reminded Tobbi of an ancient, silly costume he had seen in a history book: a head sitting on top of a disc-like collar as if on a plate...a head! THE HEAD! Tobbi shivered; the white cloud on top of the mountain looked just like the back of someone's head. Tobbi flew in through the split feeling like a thief entering the king's lair. The brown-gray walls leaned inwards, falling on him as a Venus fly trap on a fly. He now faced the lone mountain. The dense disc-like cloud completely obscured the view below. *Look here, wall-to-wall carpeting,* Tobbi thought as he slowed down and landed on it. Steam was everywhere. It rose to the bright sky in flimsy white columns, making the cloud ring dense and thick. His eyes were glued to the head-shaped cloud. Now he felt really frightened. The head, if that's what it was, was just too huge. Tobbi froze. The cloud-head seemed to be turning, or was it his head spinning? He looked for something to hold onto. Fat chance! He spread his legs and crouched, ready for anything. Indeed, the Head came around. Tobbi's eyes hurt from the strain. "You!" was all he managed to say.

CHAPTER 11

Meet the Cloud Folk

The cloud on the mountaintop turned out to be, a head all right. But it was its face that drove Tobbi literally up the stone wall. The afternoon sun poured liquid gold over the high wall above him. Tobbi happened to be in the shade, shaking in fear. The Head, on the other hand, basked in the brilliant light that filled most of the vast inner circle. Confused by fear, anger, and fascination Tobbi stared into the giant eyes on the fantastic face that was exactly like the one that visited him at home not so long ago. These eyes were black and full of red sparks. The Head spoke. Actually, speaking was too meek a term for the blast of thunder-like echoes it released.

"Amazing likeness, wouldn't you say?"

"Amazing likeness, my butt!" Tobbi answered, still trying to push his way out through the solid rock, "You're just a bad, bad, baaaad dream that's all."

"You got spunk, little one. I like that," the Head rumbled back.

"I got sour cream for the legs and cottage cheese for the body! That's what I got. Spunk doesn't begin to cover it!"

"You didn't enjoy your new flying abilities, then?"

"Yes...No..," Tobbi mumbled, slid back down the wall, and crouched. He grabbed his head in his hands and said, "Look at me! I've gone completely mad! I'm talking to a cloud!!! Even worse—I believe it! I know I'll just pinch myself and wake up; you and this whole place will go away!" Tobbi did just that—pinched himself on the rear. Nothing vanished; instead, his fingers penetrated his butt painlessly. Curious, he brought his hand to his face and wailed in terror: clutched in his fingers was a piece of his you-know-what in the form of a white fluffy stuff. He twisted back and screamed, "I just tore my... ahaaaa...I just ripped my butt." Just as suddenly, he froze, slapped the torn piece back, patted it flat, and was none the worse for wear.

"Ah...ha...ha...ha...oh...ho...ho," laughed the Head shaking and twisting on top of its mountain just like...just like....

"What are you laughing at, you—jumbo Jack-in-the-box!"

"Getting a little thin there, bud," roared the Head. "Who's Jack-in-the-box, some relation of yours, perhaps?"

"Okay! Enough of this! You better start explaining or I'm out of here. I don't care if this is a dream or not; I just need to know."

"All right, all right, I guess you deserve an explanation. You'd better get some sustenance first, or you'll go the way all the good clouds go—into the thin air ah...ha...ha...huh...." The Head failed miserably as a comedian, but Tobbi sure was tired of being rattled around by its earth-shaking attempts at it.

"Now look," he started, but was hopelessly overpowered by the Head.

"No, Tobbi, you look! You think you look okay?"

Tobbi felt okay. Well, a little weak, but okay. He looked down and freaked out for the umpteenth time. His body was flimsy and gray now, more like a fog then a cloud. "What's happening to me?" he howled.

"Oh, just hungry, I guess," the Head rumbled evenly.

"Hungry? I don't feel hungry!"

"Well, here you don't feel it. Here, you look it. And believe me, you look it."

"I believe! I believe! What do I do!?"

"You do what any self-respecting cloud does. You eat."

"Clouds eat?" asked Tobbi dull-wittedly. "Clouds eat what?"

"Why, clouds of course. Here, try this pink one." The Head closed its mouth tightly.

There were a few colorful clouds floating within the inner

Ilya Simakovsky

space. Head's cheeks puffed up, getting bigger and thinner, stretching until they looked ready to burst. The Head squinted and cracked its mouth at the corner. A jet of white steam shot out with the force of a hurricane. It flung a small pink cloud at Tobbi.

Bull's-eye!" roared the Head, while the cloud, with Tobbi trapped inside, bounced off the walls like an enormous pink ping-pong ball. *What now?* he thought.

"Just eat your way out, hombre. What are you waiting for?"

"Well, here goes noth'n," Tobbi bit into the pink stuff. Strawberry! It tasted like strawberry. Suddenly he couldn't stop. Tobbi gulped and pushed with his hands and gulped again continuing until he broke through. He climbed out and said "A mole I am not, but if digging is this delicious here I'll become one!"

"You don't have to tunnel through it; just take a pinch," suggested the Head. Tobbi did just that and ate until he felt tight and inflated like a balloon. The cloud-stuff was swirling and filling his body as if a glass bottle with milk. He tried to pinch himself. His thigh gave a little, but fingers didn't go in. "That's more like it," said Tobbi, "and you! Didn't your mother...hmmm I mean, whoever, teach you not to throw food around? I can get it myself, thank you very much."

"You can fly! Forgive me; it's just that nobody else here can."

Well, duh, Tobbi thought. The Head said, "Well, I fed you and now about your job."

"What job? I'm underage; not allowed to work," Tobbi smirked.

"We, clouds, are ageless, and you're one of us now, so listen up; we've been waiting for you for a long, long time. We've high hopes for you."

"We? Who are we? I see nobody else—" Tobbi choked. A shrill voice yelled, "What about me?" Then others joined in, "and me, and me, and me...me...me ...me..." White, puffy,

48

marshmallow man-like figures began popping out of a giant circular cloud, hundreds of them, and immediately went to work. Some smoothed the edges of the cloudring; some went after the low-floating clouds; suddenly this uninhabited land turned into a busy place, like the Mall during the Holiday season. "Wow," Tobbi said.

"Wow-shmow," a raspy voice mimicked from behind. Tobbi twisted and saw one of the marshmallow guys standing right behind him. It had a round head, a round body, round eyes, round legs and a huge round stomach. Each of its hands ended in six long, thin, fuzzy fingers while the legs ballooned into enormous, flat, snowshoe-like feet with long curved-down toes. The Head was fuzzy-bold and its round gray eyes with spindle-shaped, golden, vertical pupils stared at him with unconcealed curiosity.

"You'd never find a pair of shoes for those," said Tobbi pointing to the thing's feet. "Shoes-shmooz! And why aren't you working? What are shoes, anyway?" Tobbi decided to stay on the subject of shoes. "Shoes are these leather things you wear on your feet to protect them—"

The thing laughed. Apparently, they did everything together, for within a minute all the occupants of the ring were laughing also. This was quite embarrassing: it's one thing to be laughed at, another—to be laughed at by hundreds of weirdos.

A weirdo at his side pointed at Tobbi's feet, laughing.

"What are you laughing at, you...you...steambrain!" Tobbi said.

"Steambrain, shpimfrain! You'd sure need protection for these ugly little feet, and somebody nibbled off some fingers from your hands. You look so funny, he...ha...he..."

"I look funny!" Tobbi bristled and then surprise, surprise chuckled himself; good thing there wasn't a mirror here, he probably looked hilarious.

"I'm thirsty," the Head thundered. The cloudies, as Tobbi decided to call them, started running. "Standby to receive!"

49

somebody shouted.

All of them spread on the side of the cloudring that the Head was facing.

"What's happening?" Tobbi asked.

"Happening-shmeppening," his cloudie answered, "just watch."

The Head twisted its massive lips to the left. Tobbi was astonished to see a long stone pipe protruding from the mists below. The lips encircled the pipe and the Head drew in; water roared and the Head raised its eyes to the sky in satisfaction.

"The mother of all straws," Tobbi whispered. The Head let go with a tremendous belch. A white cloud ball shot out of the Head's mouth and sped across the cloudring. The cloudies scrambled to catch it.

Tobbi's cloudie commented: "The ball comes out from the center and slightly off to the right. The forward defense misses but what a tremendous effort! The ball's in the midfield now; such a terrific shot, and plenty of spin on it, too. They go for it—another miss. It's up to the outfielders now. They gather...what a rush...it's a catch! The defense scores! Hooray!" A loud cheer spread through the cloudring. Tobbi hyperventilated, not believing any of it. A few of the cloudies towed the caught cloudball to the side while the rest got ready again.

"What? More?" asked Tobbi.

"Yep! The Maker is very thirsty; the fireheart must be hot tonight."

"Which Maker? What fireheart?"

"The fiery heart that gives us life lives deep in the cone of stone beneath the Maker of Clouds, who must quench it; least it erupts in anger and smites us all. And the Blue Yonder would forever be void of beauty," his cloudie recited this as if a prayer.

"The cone with fire...eruption," Tobbi groaned, "a volcano? VOLCANO! This Maker of yours seats on top of a volcano! What if it lets go? We'll all die. Let's get out of here. This is nuts."

Tobbi stumbled, seeing that his words seemed to leave more impression on the stone wall than on the cloudie. "Didn't you hear me?" he asked and pulled on the cloudie's arm. "Let me save you. Come with me we'll fly away; see the world—"

"When the time comes I'll take the journey," said the cloudie. "The thing you call volcano, what is it?"

"Well..., it's a big mountain with a pipe inside that reaches deep inside the earth. The earth's hot core sometimes pushes through the pipe and blows up everything; hot lava comes out and—"

"The fiery heart is quenched. It won't blow. It gives us life and will not take it away. The Maker will make sure."

"But you can't stop an eruption, it's—"

"The Maker can. He's been doing it forever. Don't worry. This volcano has a good fiery heart. Anyway, look! Ball two."

Another belch and a new cloud rushed across the cloudring. This one wasn't as fast and the midfielders caught it, cheered by all. "Is he done now?" asked Tobbi.

"I don't know, the Maker's mighty thirsty tonight. Your jabbering made his throat dry."

"My jabbering!"

"Jabbering-shmabering! Look, another one's coming. This one's going to be big. Oh-oh, this could go wild, oh my!"

An explosive belch produced the fastest and the biggest cloudball yet. It was hopelessly missed by infielders, helplessly watched by midfielders and furiously attacked by outfielders. A few cloudies were able to grasp it, but not enough of them; they were ripped from the cloudring and flown away toward the split in the rimwall. A loud wail rose from the cloudies. The Maker looked remorseful and Tobbi's cloudie was terribly upset.

"What's the matter?"

"A wild pitch. Our friends are forced on the Journey,

51

unwilling and unprepared. They will perish without purpose. They will not come back with knowledge. Their glowhearts are lost to us forever." The cloudie joined others in a sad, monotone but melodic wail, and waved goodbye. It was quite touching, but Tobbi just didn't get it.

"Why don't you go after them?"

"What do you mean?"

"Well, fly after them and get them back."

"Who do you think we are? The earthling's flying machines...birds? We are clouds! We can't fly!"

"Bummer! I'll do it then," and he took off like a rocket. The effect on the cloudies couldn't be more dramatic. The wailing turned into a cacophony. Meanwhile, Tobbi reached the runaway. The cloudies hung on that cloud with their mouths stuck open: they couldn't believe their luck. Tobbi plunged his arms into the cloudball and pulled. Nothing happened. He pulled again, harder and the runaway slowed down. Tobbi pulled even harder, if he were still human he would've turned red; here, naturally, he got white in the face but the cloud slowly reversed. A chaotic noise organized into a mighty cheer as Tobbi dragged his load to the cloudring. Deafened by all the noise—not least of it, the Head's thunderous laughter—he had to endure enthusiastic greetings and back slapping by the ecstatic cloudies. Things quieted down eventually when he came face to face with the seven cloudies he had rescued. These seven put their six fingered hands on their chests then stretched them toward Tobbi, as if giving something away. One stepped forward and started the chant echoed by everyone.

> *"The time of giving; the time of taking.*
> *The time of sharing; the time of caring.*
> *It shall come in the morning light,*
> *It shall make every glowheart bright.*
> *As is every cloudherder's right*
> *This glowheart of mine shall be yours*

52

For the new glow to ignite."

Tobbi didn't know what to make of this but obviously it was very important. Now they were expecting a response. The longer the pause, the grayer became faces of the rescued cloudies. Tobbi felt a nudge.

"Com'n answer them," his cloudie whispered.

"What do I say? What?"

"Tell 'em if you accept or deny. Tell 'em quick, or you'll offend everyone."

Tobbi glanced at desperate-looking cloudies. "I accept," he said.

Instantly the mood changed. Everyone cheered and the rescued positively beamed with joy. But he would be cursed if they didn't expect something else from him. Tobbi got frustrated to no end for he hadn't a clue. Again his cloudie helped: "Common, dummy, choose the one."

"Choose the one what?"

"What-shmot! Choose the one you like, oh quick-witted one!"

Here goes nothing, thought Tobbi and pointed to the second one from the right. "Her, I choose her," he said. He didn't know why he called that cloudie a her, but her round eyes were bigger then most, her body more slender, and her feet smaller. She just looked like 'a her,' that's all. The chosen cloudie turned solid white in the face as everyone cheered, and Tobbi's questions remained unanswered. Meanwhile, the sunlight was leaving the mountain well. The diminishing light drained energy from everyone including Tobbi. The crowd began to disperse and he was left with his helper and the one he chose. His cloudie yawned and said, "It's time to turn under for the night. Let's go." Tobbi was tired of asking so he just followed while they searched for something. They found whatever it was behind the large boulder protruding from the rimwall. His cloudie crashed onto the cloudring followed by Tobbi and his new companion. Tobbi asked,

"Listen, How come you all speak English? I find it incredible."

"Incredible, mikredible! Nothing to it! We, cloudherders speak anything."

"What do you mean? That's nonsense!"

"Nonsense, shmonsense! And what's wrong with nonsense, huh? It's as good as any other language; he bent forward and addressed the new cloudie, "Hvyoch naxkoo hihicappon xogahood ghoshasho (He looks like a whirlhead, when puzzled, doesn't he?)." To Tobbi's great surprise the string of gibberish from the right was answered by a string of gibberish from his left, "Shmicaboon taramochoo kalibo karaban tokee (He certainly does, but such a cute one.)."

"Palamaboo karamaboo taraboo bu-bu-bu-boo," pronounced Tobbi just to have the last word. This got him a slap from his cloudie who declared, "How dare you say that! You're not such a prince yourself!" and he turned away with an attitude. A giggle from the left.

"What did I say? What did I say? I was just saying nonse...I mean I had no idea I said anything. What DID I say?"

His new companion translated, "You said that he looks like a pregnant mountain picking warts off its nose."

"What!? There are no pregnant mountains...what am I saying?! This is pure nonsense—"

"Precisely!" said his cloudie.

"You listen good!" Tobbi declared, "I don't speak nonsense, okay?"

"But you just did!"

"Oh! Gosh!" Tobbi exclaimed. "I was just playing along; I didn't know what I said."

"Isn't that what nonsense is?"

"Yes! Of course! That's exactly right. But you understood, therefore it's not nonsense, yet...Oh, Gosh! Somebody shoot me! You're driving me crazy!"

"Say you didn't mean it."

"I didn't mean it." This was easy and true; Tobbi was

happy to comply just to stop this nons...oops—idiocy. "Hey, let's stick to English, so that we don't keep insulting each other, okay?"

"Well, okay. But you're the one that started with non-sense—"

"Enough! I'm tired, confused, and frustrated and if you don't stop this minute I'll fly you to the first cloud on the way out of here, got it!"

"Okay...okay, don't be mad. I was just trying to be precise; English's as good as any. It's okay with me. I don't like speaking nonsense. You have to make it up all the time. I can live with—"

"Quiet!" roared Tobbi. His cloudie grabbed a fold of the cloudring and stretched it over himself, disappearing completely from sight. His new companion vanished next. Tobbi looked around his new home as it rapidly submerged into darkness. He could barely make out the Maker with steam escaping from under his chin and from his mouth. The big eyes were closed. Tobbi shook his head and pulled the cloud blanket over himself, letting the darkness overtake him as well.

CHAPTER 12

Some Days It Just Doesn't Pay to Wake Up

A broad belt of white clouds ran endlessly before him, as if unwinding from a giant paper towel roll. It stretched tighter and thinner, as it streamed faster and faster past him. Tobbi's eyes jumped right and left, right and left, sore from the strain yet unable to keep up. Suddenly, in silence the belt ripped into small, fluffy fragments. Thousands, millions, billions of these now floated aimlessly everywhere, like snowflakes on a lazy Sunday morning, so quiet and peaceful. All at once the flakes exploded and then unfolded into rich, magnificent colors, like flowers in a speeded-up film. Their petals: red and blue, green and violet, yellow and purple began to flutter in a wind like wings, and then became wings. Myriads of butterflies filled the air now with a mosaic of radiant hues, vivid colors, and flashy shapes. The new butterflies pirouetted and swirled, sailed and dived, dancing with life. Only now, since he had flown himself, Tobbi could begin to appreciate their amazing grace and beauty.

A dark shape entered the corner of his vision. Danger! Intuition warned him. A flying thing, like a gray carpet with a giant black hole at its front edge, was moving in on his beautiful butterflies. Its vast, gray flaps-wings hoarded the fluorescent ocean to the front, where the creature's mouth gulped and gulped, snuffing the color out of the sky and leaving dark emptiness behind. The black hole grew with every second as if fed by the beautiful creatures. It moved closer, growing in size still. The mouth, a gloomy deadly cave, now swooped down on him....

Tobbi thrashed in the darkness and tore his eyes open. He trembled, still unable to see; murk...everything seemed murky, dark, and weird. With a terrific scream, he pushed through the murkiness and into the bright, vivid light of the morning. He tumbled in the air, howling. Suddenly—an outcry, then another and another. Little figures began popping out of the circular cloud. Each new cloudie saw its neighbors screaming and immediately joined in; soon hundreds were yelling. The pandemonium went on and on.

"Oops," Tobbi said. It was certainly too late for that. *How do I stop this mess now?* he wondered. The cloudies didn't show any inclination for quitting.

"Quiet!" the Head roared, twisting and turning on top of its mountain, overpowering everyone. White steam poured out of its open mouth. Its eyes, full of angry red flames, were opened wide in fury. This shut the cloudies up all right.

"What's the meaning of this?" the Cloud Maker barked, once it caught its steam. The tomblike silence contrasted wildly with the mad scene of a minute ago.

"Who started this outrage?" demanded the Head, turned detective. A cloudie asked another if he'd started it. He denied it, but questioned his neighbor. Soon, all cloudies were just as busy questioning each other. Tobbi chuckled, thinking what a great Duracel commercial this would make.

The Cloud Maker put an end to this one also. "Enough of this! Let the one responsible for this mess step forward and be quick about it. We've work to do."

No one did. Smoke started coming out of the Maker's ears and nostrils. *I hope he doesn't pop,* thought Tobbi as he lifted his hand. The cloudie below him did the same and, wouldn't you know, soon everyone pointed. The Maker, whose mouth was closed tightly in anger, started shaking like a cover on a boiling pot. Finally, its mouth popped open. A jet of steam exploded out and pushed the Maker into a spin. The whirling jet whacked cloudies off their big feet and rolled them like tumble-weeds across the cloudring. Tobbi was propelled backwards too, but bounced back off the wall.

He looked around in awe: cloudies rolling every which way; steam spurting across the well; clouds darting around like mad, air-leaking balloons, and in the midst of it the giant Head was spinning with a mad, bewildered expression on its face. The Maker hissed in frustration. Somehow, it helped it to stop spinning. Now it panted, spewing smoke rings.

"Well, oof...oof...I've never...oof!!" it thundered, "Someone...oof...better take responsibility for this...oof...or I'll... I'll...I'll blow everyone into the sky...you worthless sons of a cloud. I'm waiting oof...!"

None of the quivering, fearful cloudies dared to look at it. So, Tobbi flew forward and said, "Me. I did it. I'm sorry!"

The Maker stared at Tobbi hard. "Well, well, well...the young cloudtender took his time to admit—"

"It has nothing to do with—"

"Do not interrupt me, earthling!" the Maker roared, expelling so much steam that it had none left to speak with. While it closed its mouth to gather more Tobbi seized the opportunity and said, "If you didn't blow your top and fling us around, I would've spoken earlier!"

"If you didn't scream you wouldn't have to admit anything!"

"If I didn't see a bad dream, I wouldn't have to scream!"

"Well, if you didn't...a bad dream!" The Maker stumbled, and then asked, "What's that? Where did you see it? Is it dangerous?"

The cloudies, already nervous—nobody dared to talk to the Maker that way before—became even more agitated; they searched the skies for the scary thing called: a dream.

"What are you all looking around for!? Don't you know what a dream is?" he shouted. A chorus of "No's and Uh-uh's" was his answer.

"You can't see my dream, so stop looking."

"Is it an invisible danger, perhaps?" inquired one cloudie.

"Yeah, right! Gees! Get real! See, they are these...things inside my head. I can see them when I sleep. Sometimes they're good, sometimes bad. I screamed because I saw a bad, scary dream. That's all."

Tobbi felt a tug. Turning he saw his cloudie reaching, but ready to bolt if necessary.

"So, if it's inside your head, it can't get out and hurt us, right?" Totally phased out, Tobbi nodded.

"Do all earthlings have these invisible dangerous things called dreams, living in their heads? Is it normal or—?"

"Yes! NO!! Oh, gosh! Must you take everything so literally?! They are not living things, I tell you! Dreams arc something we, humans, imagine in our sleep. They're not real. Get it through your heads. Don't you ever imagine anything?"

A whole lot of blank expressions clinched it. Tobbi just threw his hands up in submission. How do you explain imagination to someone without one? "Never mind. What I saw can't hurt you, so don't worry."

The Maker spoke at last. "Describe your bad D-R-E-A-M thing so that we know what to look out for."

"But it's not the same every time," Tobbi hissed.

"Never mind that," commanded the Head, "tell us!"

"But—" Tobbi said and gave in, telling cloudies about the beautiful dream with the snowflakes and butterflies. The cloudies were avid listeners. Together they cheered, laughed, and hooted at every new detail. It was fun while it lasted, because the minute he described the dark devouring monster the effect on the cloudies and even the Maker was instantaneous and ghastly: everyone's face turned the same shade of translucent gray as if milk diluted by water. Some cloudies even backed away, their round eyes peering at Tobbi with a weird intensity. The Maker's mouth fell open, leaking steam.

Tobbi stumbled, and turned to his cloudie, but even this guy shrunk away from him.

"How do you know about the Shadow Eater?" the Head asked.

"I don't know any eaters, shadow or otherwise. All I know is there I was, a normal kid, and now I'm a flying, fluffy, crazy cloud talking to other crazy clouds and even worse—believing it! Is this nuts, or what?"

The Maker coughed a few times and explained, "What you saw in your...eh...dream is real. The Shadow Eater is one of the reasons you are here, but there's more."

"Finally!!" expelled Tobbi, relieved and worried at once: now he'd find out the truth.

"Not before we do several things," the Maker said.

"Not again!" Tobbi yelled and started darting to and fro like a madma...madcloud that is. "What is it with you?" he stopped and asked. "Every time you come close to making some sense of things, you choose to drive me bananas instead. Someone's paying you for this or what?"

The giant Head, known as Cloud Maker, considered the question, then announced, "I can't drive."

Tobbi chuckled and then poured all of his frustration into an uncontrollable, unstoppable laughter: He pointed at the Maker, laughing and imagining this enormous cotton ball sitting behind a wheel of a car, cursing at other drivers, steam flying out of the window. Then he envisioned the size of that car and nearly choked. The Maker was stumped: on one hand he was ridiculed; on the other hand this earthling's laughter was quite infectious. Its lips twitched. A mighty boom echoed within the well, bouncing a few dozen cloudies of their feet. The Maker looked embarrassed, but let go of another blast. Then, one after another these blasts merged into a continued roar of an ear splitting, mountain-trembling laughter. Gradually, the tossed around cloudies joined in. The mountain well began to look like a gigantic nuthouse full of mad cottonballs laughing, apparently at nothing.

CHAPTER 13

Ooops! I Didn't Mean to Do This

Nothing lasts forever. The cloudies quit laughing, looking shaken and thin. The Maker tried to say something but the train-size lips just flapped in silence, his steam was completely exhausted. He puckered the lips next and reached for his stone pipe-straw. Surprise! His eyebrows lifted, eyes widened: he couldn't reach it. The Maker mouthed something at Tobbi and flicked his eyes towards the pipe. Tobbi didn't understand. The Maker couldn't even vent his frustration because there wasn't enough steam.

"You want to reach the tube?" Tobbi guessed, finally.

The Maker barely accumulated enough steam to whisper, "Hurry!"

"What's to hurry for? I kinda like it when you can't talk. Life's safer this way."

The Maker's face contorted into a hideous mask. Tobbi crouched and looked back for support. Startled, he jetted up a hundred feet: the cloudies were sagging down in groups, looking gray, lethargic, and transparent. *What have I done?* Tobbi realized that they needed food. He looked around for clouds, but the Maker's mad laughter swept them all into the sky. Then he looked at himself and discovered the gray bands in his own body, although, he wasn't nearly as bad.

"So, now I'm a tough guy? What do I do?" he asked.

The Maker flicked his eyes again.

"What? I don't get it?"

The Maker grimaced.

"I could turn...?" Tobbi thought out loud and saw the Cloud Maker quake. "...turn you to the pipe!"

"YES!" mouthed the Maker, "HURRY!" He looked anxiously at the cloudies.

"But how can I move you!?" Tobbi yelled. "Look at you! Compared to you I'm an ant, a dot; how, on earth, can I move you?"

The Maker squinted and sucked his cheeks in impatiently.

"Well," whispered Tobbi, "let's be reasonably unreasonable here; if I were down on earth, would I seriously consider pushing a giant cloud with an ugly face? Nuh, no way! I might as well try, then." He flew up towards the huge dangling nose, noticing a certain sluggishness in his movements. It was now or never: in a little while his strength would also fail and then what? He reached the Maker, feeling like a mosquito about to sting Godzilla. The gigantic black and red eyes crossed hideously trying to keep him in sight. Tobbi warned the Maker, "Don't you hold it against me later!"

The Maker just rolled his eyes. Tobbi buried his hands into the humongous, bulbous, dangling nose and pushed. The nose bent, the giant eyes squinted, and that was that. *I hope there's no snot in there,* thought Tobbi and pushed again with all his might. The nose stretched and the Maker moved. Inch by inch it turned closer to the pipe. The Maker's eyes bulged; his lips extended impossibly long but didn't quite reach yet. Tobbi was out of strength and ready to give up.

"Look," the Maker hissed. Tobbi turned. All the cloudies were sprawled on the cloudring, barely moving, their bodies gray and nearly shapeless. His cloudie, his helper, his...friend (Tobbi realized with a surprise) stretched his hand towards Tobbi. Tobbi flipped around and pushed with new determination, using every wisp of his new body. It didn't even register when the colossal lips finally encircled the pipe, pulled, and sucked for a long time. A gurgle of a waterfall turned into a monstrous hiss somewhere deep inside the mountain. The Maker coughed and spouted a mountain of cotton, accompanied by a thunderous sigh of relief. "Ooof, I could drink up an ocean," said the Maker. "Don't gloat! Bring food to the people and after that straighten up this snout of mine. I sound like a plugged up bagpipe."

"You've got that one right, but what food?" Tobbi asked.

"The food I'm going to make, genius! Gang way," shouted the Maker and drew another river out of the pipe. This time instead of one giant ball he popped out a bunch of smoke rings. Tobbi snagged some and dived to the cloudring. He took a bite on the way. Strangely, it tasted just like cotton, nothing like the explosion of flavors he experienced before. It gave him strength, though. He passed the first one to his cloudie, who was barely able to tear off a piece. After the third swallow he was able to sit up; after the fifth he got up on his ski-like feet, grubbed some rings and started feeding his fallen brethren. Tobbi, meanwhile, kneeled at the side of the cloudie he had saved once before. Her round eyes followed his every movement, but she had no strength to move. She was so thin, barely a puff of gray fog contoured on the background of pure white. Yet, in a ghostly way, she was beautiful. Gently, Tobbi raised her head and put a handful of cloud into her mouth. She swallowed with difficulty. He gave her more and noticed happily her body filling in.

As soon as she was able to sit she said, "Please help the others, I'll be fine." Her eyes followed Tobbi with such admiration and gratitude that he felt embarrassed. He turned, but she tugged him on the arm and pointed, "Can you leave one for me?"

Tobbi winced and gave her one ring, handing the rest to others. The space inside the mountains by now was full of white balls, rings, sheaths, tubes of every conceivable shape. Looking absolutely magnificent in his swirling steam shroud the mighty Cloud Maker continued making food by dumping water cascades into thirsty volcano. The emergency was over. The cloudies could take care of themselves now.

Tobbi, however, was very curious about the stone straw. He flew over to check it out. Protruding through the cloudring there was a stone pipe. It was formed out of the wall of a volcano. Where did it come from? Tobbi tore into the cloudring. It was tough, much tougher than any cloud he encountered before, yet it parted when Tobbi persisted. How come the cloudies didn't try to eat it? He took a puff in his mouth and spat it out in disgust. It tasted worse then dirt, not edible. He dug through the whiteness much as he would through a dense snow pile. The cloudring was thick, fed continuously by the volcano. It took work. The whiteness ripped—he was through; Tobbi gasped and buried his arms deep into the dense cloud, grasping it with all his might as the space that opened up below was vast. Tobbi pictured himself plunging down to his death. Then he remembered who he now was and willed himself to let go. He didn't fall. The awe took over then: the sheer enormity and beauty of the landscape below was stunning.

The outer walls of the mountains spread wide on the way down. They seemed to grow into the earth rather than out of it. Behind him there was a wide canyon entrance where the light and life thrived in the richest. A dense dark-green jungle engulfed the ground between the outer walls and the central volcano. Its slender offshoots climbed up the sides of the canyon, like so many fingers. It seemed as if two gigantic green hands wrenched the mountains apart and clawed their way to the life-giving sunshine. The jungle continued halfway around the base of the volcano ending at the shores of a deep blue lake. This horse-shoe shaped lake fitted around a monstrous finger of a volcano like a dazzling sapphire ring.

Everything here is so...big, thought Tobbi eyeing the most spectacular sight of all—a tall feathery waterfall. In a joyous, long fall the water broke into many strands that splattered, sparkled, and splashed over rough, moss covered, stone ledges. Swarms of bouncing water droplets parachuted lazily in the air and painted the sun rays with rainbows.

"Far out! Tobbi whispered, forgetting his goal. The roar of gurgling water reminded him. "No way!" he said. The pipe went all the way down the side of the volcano and into the lake. "This is so cool," said Tobbi. The Maker sucked water out of the lake through the straw, a mile long. It fed the living, talking clouds with the food-clouds it made, using the volcano for a stove! Tobbi decided right there and then that if he becomes his old self again, he'd never be astounded by anything—ever! He wanted to go back now. Glancing over the magnificent landscape again, Tobbi climbed back into the tunnel that just begun to close. Soon he was back in the Maker's dominion armed with new respect and ideas, but cloudies had their own agenda. Gathered in several double rows they began cheering like mad the minute he appeared. Then he was dragged by his two...friends to the hastily made cloud pedestal and placed there. The Maker, more awesome then ever, yet somehow more friendly, cleared the excess steam from his throat, and thundered, "Dear friends, we are gathered here to welcome our new comrade who, surely can cause a jumble, and who has proven his worthiness again." Tobbi's objections were drowned by the cloudies' laughter.

"Yes," continued the Maker, "all of us would perish, if it weren't for you, Tobbi, and the beauty we create would be lost forever to the world below. So, let us celebrate!"

A weird procession appeared from behind the volcano. Everyone cheered. In front walked, well...not walked, wobbled one big cloudie. He was wider than taller and his feet were humongous; with every step he tilted in order to lift a foot off the cloudring. It was quite unnerving: it seemed that any minute the fatso would keel over and roll around the ring, like a colossal roulette ball. Tobbi actually forced himself not to fly to the creature's aid. Yet, he kept on, somehow in command. The cloudies fidgeted in anticipation. Perhaps, the swarm of multicolored clouds that the group was towing had something to do with it. Tobbi was left in the dark again.

"What now? A parade?" he asked, raising his eyes to the sky.

"Parade-shmarade. Food! That's what now," a familiar voice mimicked from the right.

Ilya Simakovsky

"I can't tell you how I missed your mocking me, you puffed up hairball. Haven't you had enough to eat already? Surely our top honcho, Mr. Smokebreath, made enough for everyone."

"Shh! Don't talk like this! The Maker will blow you to flufferings," warned his other cloudie, glancing at the Maker fearfully. Tobbi held back his most obnoxious reply. Instead he said, "I'm not afraid of him. I'm just tired of not knowing why I am here and I'd better find out soon or I'll make some...whachamacallit...flufferings of my own."

"Please be patient," she smiled, "all will be revealed soon, I'm sure." Tobbi's anger dissipated like smoke. She was just too cute.

His other friend found his breath again, "What you gave us before was sustenance. This is FOOD that's coming."

Turning to him Tobbi said, "Oh, yeah? What's the difference? A cloud is a cloud, doesn't matter how you cook it."

"Cook it-shmook it! And a rainbow is just a light. You'll eat your words once you taste the work of the Master."

"The Master is the skinny dude at the head of a food chain, I presume?"

"Hmmm...I'm not talking to you, until you quit insulting everyone. You try to figure out things on your own from now on!" He turned away, obviously upset. The other cloudie just looked at Tobbi with her huge eyes. Tobbi felt guilty as hell. Just like that—a complete turn around in feelings.

Sighing deeply, he tugged on his friend's shoulder, "I'm sorry, bro. I'll try your food and make no more fun of you guys (Tobbi crossed his fingers behind his back). Who is this guy? Some kind of cook or something?"

"Only the greatest Dresser of Foods this side of the Terra Firma!" The cloudie turned as if waiting for the opportunity, "Am I supposed to guess what a cook is?"

"Mad weird! A cook puts all these things like vegetables and meat on a fire and heats them until they are...rea...dy...." Tobbi lost track, for his friends turned gray and jumped away from him as if he skunk-sprayed them.

"You guys had better stop doing this!" Tobbi said tiredly.

"Fire and heat are death to us. A little too much and we are poof—gone."

"Oh, yeah, I can see why. Well, let me assure you. I'm NOT A COOK!"

"Okay." His friends came back. By this time, the food train made it to the agitated cloudies. *I've got to try those,* Tobbi thought. The Ronald McDonald of Cloudland was truly an immense guy up close. He looked like a huge walking earth globe with a little moon of a head perched on the very top. He had fat, puffed up cheeks and a bulbous, dangling nose. With thin legs ending in the biggest feet yet, long arms and fingers, and a gremlin-like face, he would scare the death itself. Yet, his smile was warm and contagious. Tobbi found himself smiling as well when the cloudie stopped and saluted.

CHAPTER 14

Finally, Some Answers

"Cloudtenders!" said the Maker, "Let us thank our distinguished guest for his bravery. Even though his greatest challenge may lie in the future, we must appreciate what he has accomplished already. Saving six of our cloudtenders was the smallest of his feats. In a true masterstroke he rescued us from peril, which he had inadvertently engineered." Cloudies laughed, not holding a grudge. It finally registered: Tobbi was amongst friends. He relaxed and smiled at the Maker's jab, then gave the thumbs-up sign to the audience.

"Yes," the Maker rumbled on, "he even rearranged my cute face in the process." Tobbi snickered remembering the Maker's nose job. Meanwhile, the attention of the crowd wavered. More and more the eyes shifted toward the colorful menu on display. Tobbi also anticipated a meal. He missed the hungry rumbling his human stomach would make. He shuddered at how alien this human memory was.

"And now for the thing you've all been waiting for. I learned from a confidential source that our beloved Master Decorator has outdone himself for this occasion. So, let the feast begin!"

The color clouds were handed out. Cheering and laughing cloudies tore into them and happily stuffed themselves. The foodclouds seemed to melt like butter on a hot skillet. Expressions of great delight were seen everywhere. But Tobbi's party, in the back, wasn't getting any food. At last, one remnant fell into his friend's hands. It was all torn up with holes, like a piece of a yellow Swiss cheese. Tobbi's friend divided it into three small pieces and passed them out. Tobbi bit in. It tasted like buttered corn—his most favorite food on earth. Tobbi wondered, *How come it was so incredi-*

bly tasty? Meanwhile, they had nothing left but a growing craving.

The feast was a blast; the cloudies had a terrific time sharing and plucking the clouds like cotton candy. The distinguished, but starving subject of the feast was forgotten completely. Puffing madly his cloudie pointed at someone and shouted, "Hey, you!"

"Who, me?" someone answered. "No, not you. Him!" Tobbi's friend pointed to another cloudie that was devouring a piece of a golden cloud. The guy tried to help and called, "Hey, you!" Yet, someone else answered, "What?"

"Not you, him!"

"Me?"

"Not you! That one."

"Who? Me?"

"No, him..."

"Oh, hey you!"

Round and round they went, endlessly.

"Who's this party for, anyway? Don't you guys have names?" Tobbi growled fuming. He saw blank stares and said, "Look here, me—Tobbi, you—?"

They still didn't get it.

"All right, listen. A name's something you call a person; don't you see what a mess you've caused? If you guys had names, all you'd have to do is call: hey, you, Barfbreath, and that person would answer."

His friends' eyes lit up as if they heard from a god of clouds.

Tobbi laughed, "What?"

"Why didn't we think of this before? Oh, the time we waste organizing things: nobody ever knows who's speaking to whom. Oh, this is incredible! Oh, oh! Where could we find these nn...ames?"

"What do you mean where? Look under those boulders...." Both of his friends bolted towards the wall.

"Stop, you two." Tobbi was bent over, laughing. "You

69

guys are unreal! I'm kidding; just come up with names, make them up."

"Make them up from what?"

"Oh, stop it! This isn't cool, man. You're messing with my head; words, dude, ideas—that's what it's about. Just make your name up."

"But how?"

"Man! You are a radical dude. If I didn't need you, I'd kill you. Just sit down, put your hand on your head, lift your eyes up and go—la,la,la,la,la this is a good name for me and bla, bla, bla—make one up."

The cloudie sat dawn, put his hand on his head and sat there looking up helplessly. Just as helplessly, Tobbi said, "Or, I just could give them to you." His friend straightened up and asked breathlessly, "You'd do such a great thing for me?"

"No sweat, for you, for her, for everybody!" Tobbi suddenly felt generous. "Here. You're "Pouch" and she's "Nelli." They are my friends below as you are here. See? Easy! You have names now."

The cloudie, freshly named Pouch, was shaking with excitement. "Pouch," he tasted the word; he rolled it in his mouth; he savored and digested it. Then a wide grin pushed his soft cheeks out, squishing them into bubble-like pouches; he looked like one ecstatic rodent. The name fit him to a tee. The newly named Nelli sat with her face buried under her arms.

"I like it. Pouch...I really like it. Would somebody please call me!"

Nelli yelped, "Pouch!" laughing into her fingers. The Pouch went into a weird leg bending dance and screamed, "Again!"

"Pouch," yelled Nelli.

"Nelli," shouted Pouch.

"Pouch," said Nelli and so they went calling each other names, laughing and dancing, forgetting food and everything else.

"Okay, kids, while you're insulting each other, I'm getting a little thin here; gonna get us some chow." Tobbi took off straight up and stretched his hands as wings. Screeching like a diving F16 he aimed for the foodstuff. "Tally ho!" He yelled as he snagged some remnants. When he got back he found his friends staring at each other, happy and oblivious to the world.

"Now WE eat!" he announced and bit into a brownish cloud, nearly choking on the rich, sweet chocolate-like flavor. "Man! This is Soooo...good. Here, you guys, take the others, while I work on this beauty. Mmmmm!"

For the next few minutes, they ate in silence while the rest of the cloudies slowly gathered with guilty expressions on their faces. One cloudie conveyed everyone's feelings, "We are sorry to neglect you like this. It's just that the food was so good and then we started searching for somebody; so...."

"It's okay," said Tobbi. "No harm done. We're tight as drums now, aren't we Nelli?"

"Yep, drums...tight now," she answered proudly.

A great agitation rocked the crowd. "What's a Nelli," someone asked.

"Pouch's my name and Nelli's my dame," said Tobbi's friend. The crowd surged.

Someone yelled, "What is this name thing?"

"Names are what earthlings call one another, and we are all getting them, Tobbi said so!" Pouch answered. Stunned for a second cloudies went wild, screaming and climbing over each other to get to the front.

"Stop it! Right now," bellowed the Maker ending this one quickly. "You've almost started a revolt but I must say that's a good idea, Tobbi. I never get anything done because I go through fifty cloudtenders before getting to the one I need. We must get to it later; right now I want to tell you why you're here."

"It's about time! I was beginning to think you were dissing me."

71

"Give them room, please," the Maker said. The disappointed cloudies spread into a wide circle around Tobbi, Nelli, and Pouch.

"As you might've guessed by now," started the Maker, "we make clouds that float around the earth and—"

"Get real now. All clouds?"

"Such heartburn I'd get if I even tried." The Maker thundered, "No, Tobbi, we're an artist colony. You see, under the direction of our incomparable Master Decorator, we create and sculpt the clouds in order to bring beauty to the world."

"I thought he was a coo...a chef, I mean," interrupted Tobbi.

"He's a sculptor, painter, designer, and project Manager as well."

"No wonder! There's got be a lot of him to go around."

"Yes, he's very busy, but he likes it, and he's exceptionally good at it." The globe-like cloudie took a proud bow, which looked like an impossible feat with all that girth. He even managed to straighten back up: his huge feet—a big asset.

"A long while back I had another Master Decorator. He was such a creative genius, but a crazy one; wild in ideas, unstable in attitude, and... so stubborn." The Maker posed. "He always knew better than anyone. Against my advice he took his Journey-for-Knowledge before he was ready. He came back changed; gone were the humor and the high spirit. He became a grouch, always screaming and complaining. Along with his disposition, his color had changed too. He began to look just like a storm cloud, gray and menacing. The evil smile had taken a permanent possession of his mouth scaring everyone, and worst of all, some cloudtenders found gray patches on their bodies too. As much as it displeased me, I told him to leave. He laughed at me!" the Maker roared, his eyes shot with red, angry sparks.

"So, what did you do?" asked Tobbi with a new respect.

"I blew him away!"

"You killed him for laughing at you?"

"Killed? No! I blew him away from this place."

The cloudies cheered, showing support for their leader.

"Oh, sorry," Tobbi said, "to blow someone away means something much worse in my world. So, what does all of this have to do with me?"

"Patience, earthling, patience! I thought...we all thought, that was the end of it. Storm clouds are known for their short life span. You know how the saying goes? Angry and gray turns the cloud into a water spray."

"Nope. Uh-uh. Never heard that one. Not a frequent topic among my friends," said Tobbi.

"Of course not. How silly of me! We soon noticed that not all cloudtenders returned from their Journeys; our beautiful creations often turned up gray and stormy. We didn't know why until one brave cloudtender escaped."

A thin, leaf-like cloudie got up at the insistence of his neighbors and bowed, while cheered by all.

"Houdini," said Tobbi.

"What?" asked the Maker.

"Houdini. That's his name. I've read about him. He was the greatest escape artist on earth."

"Why did he have to escape and from whom?"

"See, an escape artist is an...," Tobbi took one look at all the puzzled faces and changed his mind. "Eh...just take my word for it. He was great. Just call that brave one, Houdini, and don't ask any questions, P-lease!"

Another freshly named cloudie stretched his mouth—the widest smile yet. Tobbi expected those cheeks to burst any second.

"Hey, you," a couple of hundred cloudies reacted. Tobbi could truly see the Maker's problem now. Tobbi grinned, "Yo, Houdini! Sit down. Let me hear the rest of the story."

Hundreds of heads turned to the cloudie, who sat down proudly, then turned back to Tobbi. Hundreds of mouths formed a silent "Oh!" the advantage of having a name became painfully clear in that instant. The wave of cloudtenders surged forward.

"Stay where you are! All of you!" ordered the Maker. "Not just yet. Very nice, Tobbi, again you are causing a riot! What is it, a hobby of yours? First we finish with this, and then everyone may have their names."

"Okay, but I'm still not sure why you need me; just drink and make more clouds," said Tobbi.

Sighing torturously the Maker explained, "We need you to find the Evil Spoiler and...and...destroy him." The Maker struggled: despite much steam and thunder he was a peaceful creature.

"Why should I do such a thing?"

"Because, Tobbi, the Evil one is set to destroy us and bring misery to the world below."

"How?"

"He invented a potion with which he turns regular clouds into gray stormy ones. He's finished with small-scale experiments and getting ready to unleash his evil on a grand scale."

"Huh! Let me tell you something, there's no small scale anything up here; so, what I'd like to know is: how small is small?" asked Tobbi tapping his foot.

"Haven't your scientists reported the increase in hurricane activity lately?"

"No way! Now you're telling me he's making hurricanes? Not likely. I know they are caused by spinning air currents and...wait a second! If that is small, what's grand?"

The Maker looked so sad. "He wants to cover the whole sky with ugly and gray; to drown the world below in storms, beat it with hurricanes, and kill it with darkness."

Tobbi didn't think it was possible for the cloudies to be this quiet. "He can't do it. No one can. It's impossible...is...is it?

Silence.

"Look at me, you guys. I'm...I was an eleven year old boy turned a teeny-weeny cloud. How can I do anything? Why don't you try? You're much bigger."

"Oh, we've tried...and tried, many times. We've lost many friends this way."

"How?"

"The Shadow Eater—the creature of your dream—is his creation. It captures the cloudtenders for the master to poison and feeds on those that oppose it. Many cloudtenders perished in its vile mouth."

"But...but why? Why's he doing this?"

"Revenge. He wants to punish us...me for throwing him out."

"But why below, what did we ever do to him?"

"Nothing, but he knows we care about it. We want peace and beauty in the world and he wants it all for himself. Maybe I shouldn't have blown him away. Maybe I should've tried to help him, find a cure somehow...."

"No," said Tobbi firmly, "he was a disease; you had to fight it. If everyone just fights the evil within, the whole world would win. We must fight for our world now. I just don't know what I can do. I'm so small and weak."

"No, Tobbi, you're not weak. You are the first earthling to make it here. You've proven yourself. You have what we clouds don't have—determination, will, and...freedom of flight.We just go with the winds, usually."

"How else can you go?" Tobbi asked.

"Ah! But there are many winds: north winds and south winds, west winds and east winds; and we know them all. We choose the ones to fly with, and since some of them are friends—"

"What! Are you telling me now that winds have personalities? I've accepted clouds with minds. It was hard, but I did it. Now winds!? No freaking way. What's next—rocks with attitudes?" Tobbi shook his head, which was squeezed between his hands like a balloon.

"Don't be upset, Tobbi, winds aren't smart. They just go along sometimes if we ask, that's all. Winds are free. No one

Ilya Simakovsky

can tell them what to do, but if you know how to ask, they may listen."
"And how do you ask, I'm curious?"
"When the time comes, you'll see."
"Mystery again; I can't tell you how thrilled I am! Well, what now?"
"Now, we do it, if you agree."
"Agree—disagree! Who cares? How hard could it be to get rid of one dirty cloud? My father always says, 'The higher they fly, the harder they fall.' Let's do it!"

CHAPTER 15

Names for Dames and Gents

Tobbi dreamed. In his dream he roamed the sky, searching for a place. He didn't know what this place looked like but he knew he'd find it. He had fun though, flying around snowy mountains with Nelli and Pouch by his side until something dark and menacing appeared on the horizon. Evil emanated from the place. Tobbi woke up scared and sat up, piercing through his cover. He squinted at the bright blue sky then yawned more from the habit then a need. A gust of the fresh morning breeze brushed his back. He turned and jetted straight up as if propelled by a hot rocket. "What! What's happening!" he croaked, instantly awake. Behind and now below him a line of cloudies stretched all the way around the volcano and back. The most amazing thing was that they all stood orderly, without any commotion.

Then he saw Nelli walking towards him along the line, organizing the cloudies. Pouch did the same on the far end of the line.

"What the heck's going on here," Tobbi said, more curious by the minute. Nelli approached and said brightly, "Good morning, Tobbi. Are you ready?"

"Ready for what!? A mile long leap frog, a beauty pageant, free food, autographs—what?"

"I don't know about those, Tobbi," said Nelli, "but please get down. These cloudtenders have been waiting for you since dawn."

"But why?" Tobbi suddenly felt like crying.

"A promise is a promise."

"What, I'm afraid to ask? Money?—no. Candy?—no. Video games?—no. What else is there?"

"Names. You've got to give them names."

"Oh!" Tobbi exhaled with relief, "That's easy, why not?"
Two hours later he knew why, but by then it was too late.
He had been naming cloudies nonstop and there was still no
end in sight. The worst thing—he was running out of names.
He made some up and nobody noticed. Tobbi let his imagi-
nation run wild, a dangerous thing, indeed. But who else on
earth had Batman and Robin for real friends, Beethoven and
Mozart, Milky Way and Honey, Aladdin and Jafar and only
God knows who else. Of course, there was Snow White and
all seven dwarfs. One humongous cloudie won the appropriate name of Goliath and the smallest cloudie simply became
Smudge.

Now Tobbi wriggled his mind trying to name the cloudie
that was shuffling nervously on his snowshoe-like feet in
front of him. By some whim of nature one of his legs was
noticeably thinner then the other. The name of Captain
Silver sprang into Tobbi's head and the new pirate was born.
No treasures to find in these lands, thought Tobbi. Meanwhile, Captain Silver hobbled towards the sea of the newly
named cloudies. They were busy getting reacquainted by
mouthing each other's names back and forth—a noisy bunch
at that.

The next cloudie required special attention. The enor-
mously round Master Decorator was up. He stood there, a
mound of white, proudly looking at Tobbi but not quite able
to hide his nervousness. Tobbi scratched his head. He flew
around the Master Decorator several times and asked, "Why
should we name you anything else. Aren't you happy with
Master Decorator?"

"That's not a name. That's a job description."

"So? It has a great sound to it."

"Yes, but it's not mine. There were Master Decorators
before me; there'll be others after. I want to be the first with
a personal touch. It's important to an artist."

"Okay, okay, I've got it. Michelangelo, that's it. He was a
famous painter and sculptor a long, long time ago."

"Michelangelo...hmmm—long. I like it," smiled the big guy. "Only if he was good—"

"Yep, very famous, very—"

"Was he a good...cook, too?"

Tobbi scratched his head again. "Well, I don't know, but even if he wasn't, you're simply going to add this to his list of talents. So, Master Michelangelo, go create something special with your name on it."

"Perhaps I will, perhaps I will. Thank you, Tobbi! Master Michelangelo, it really has a nice weight to it. Good."

The happy Decorator turned and, amazingly, started skipping away with his bulky body shaking, quivering, and twirling. The Maker watched his Master Decorator with a happy smile.

"I've never seen him so happy," he rumbled, "you have definitely got a good thing there, Tobbi. Maybe it'll make him less grouchy when we get to work. Go ahead, finish with the names already or the rest of them will have—what you humans say—a crow?"

"A cow."

"Yes, yes—a cow."

Tobbi faced the remaining, impatiently fidgeting cloudies. Thankfully, he was almost done.

"Okay, you mutants, let's finish this. Next."

"You be Chip. Next. You be Bip. Next. You be Skip. This is fun! Next."

Instead of one, four similar looking cloudies stepped forward and arranged themselves in a line. All had long necks and barrel shaped chests. Tobbi squinted and said, "What! Quadruplets? I've noticed you kids before. You always hang together. So you want one name or four?"

"Four," the group answered in unison.

"It figures. Hmmm...oh! That's easy. You," Tobbi pointed at the first one, "are Uno, he's Dos, next are Tres and Quatro, all to be known as a Spanish Quartet. Who knows, may be I can teach you to sing."

"Thank you," sang Uno.

"Thank you," sang Duo, two notes higher.

"Thank you," sang Tres, two notes higher yet.

"Thank you," harmonized Quatro. Then they vocalized together, "Thank you, great Tobbi," in a perfect harmony. Tobbi swallowed his tongue.

"Okay! Maybe you can teach me to sing, all right?" The Spanish Quartet nodded as one and got ready....

"Not now," cried Tobbi. "Let me finish with your friends here. Go sing to your compadres over there, before they wear out their new names."

Totally in sync, the Quartet marched over to the naming melee and started warming up.

"la-La-LA-La-la," sang Uno.

"la La LA LAAA LA La la," sang Dos.

"LAA LA La la laa," sang Tres.

"LA la LA la LA laaaa," finished Quatro.

Their unusual behavior attracted everyone's attention. *Thank God*, thought Tobbi, and turned back to the last few cloudies in line.

"What, they always sing to you guys?" he asked, "They are good."

"No, never sang before," said the cloudie in front, not surprised one bit.

"But, but... how come they can sing?"

"You told them to sing. So they sing."

"But who taught them?"

"Nobody."

"Oh, my! Natural talent. You guys never cease to amaze me. You can speak anything, you can sing anything, but the natural thing you should be able to do—fly—you can't. Go figure! All right, you'll be known as Professor since you know so much. Next!"

In ten minutes he was finished. He added Scarecrow, Dorothy and Oz, as well as Darth Vader and Luke Skywalker (how appropriate) to the list of names. The last two cloudies were short, roughly oval, and plump with feet as long as flippers; they were so clumsy that Stumble and Fumble became their names, seemingly all by itself. They commenced walking away from Tobbi, tripping, as usual, over their own and each others toes, like two drunks on a stroll.

The job was finished at last. Tobbi looked at tireless cloudies with envy, but even they were becoming quieter, all but the four new singers who sang their hearts out as if they had been doing it all their lives. They did it well, too.

CHAPTER *16*

The Seat of Evil

It was tall, the mountain of gray mists. Protruding high above the busy and noisy city that draped the valley below like an old, lumpy blanket, its triple peaks were forever shrouded in gray clouds. Like a devil's fork they plunged into the sky and stirred the gray misty brew into turbulent mess. The wild unruly winds reigned on the top. They swept the stone slopes clean of debris and life, discouraging people from climbing the mountain. Oh, some tried, of course, but a few who claimed to reach the top spoke of a perilous, unrewarding climb. The summit wasn't beautiful; it was ragged and stormy, and inhospitable. So, people intruded less and less, which suited its self-appointed landlord just fine.

Those disgusting humans, he often thought, *sticking their ugly hard noses into somebody else's business, but not for long. Soon they'd have other concerns. Ahh, what a plan! Worthy of a true genius, indeed.* The Evil Spoiler cackled viciously and scanned over his domain. Situated in a giant cavern carved out of the central peak by the ancient volcano action, his factory of cloud poison was humming. The gray workers were shuffling back and forth, cautiously avoiding the center of the cavern. An ugly jagged crack was there; like an old festering wound it boiled over with bubbling red mud. Now and then, the mud sputtered and extended a torrid, bright tongue up to leak the bottom of a giant stone bowl. It hung suspended from the ceiling on the end of a massive, icicle-like stalactite. In the bowl a filthy, greenish-black broth was boiling. Over the countless eons Nature had created this incredible setting, and presently the red and black shadows twisted and slithered on the walls, filling its evil occupant with glee.

Yeah, the Spoiler thought, proudly inflating his chest, *that puff-brain isn't the only king of the skies; he thinks he is hot stuff, blowing me away like a defective cloud. Well, I'm hot now and getting hotter. This sky's too small for two kings. In a little while they'll all slither on their bellies, asking for mercy. But no! No mercy for the dudhead and his cronies. Well, I may let some of them work for me; after all I'm not without compassion, but the rest—into the soup.* He got distracted from his happy thoughts. A gray worker, who was filling a small clay container with the thick and stinking brew out of a stone trough at the side of the bowl, spilled some on the ground. Like a hawk onto a helpless rabbit, the Spoiler descended on the poor unfortunate who stood there shaking at the knees.

"You incompetent fool," screamed the Spoiler. "It'll take me weeks to replace the potion you've just spilled. I should destroy you right now."

The gray cloudie shrank away in fear, causing a small smile on the Spoiler's face. A nice smile it wasn't; it turned his face into a malicious mask. The worker didn't look up, that's why he believed that the worst was over when his master addressed him in a surprisingly soft voice, "Well, it wasn't a deliberate action—just a mistake, was it now? It can happen to anyone, right? I should forgive you this time." The worker nodded and bowed. Grinning ugly, the Spoiler commanded, "Carefully pick up the spill and we'll consider the incident closed. See—I'm fair. I know you'll NEVER do it again, but the stuff must be picked up."

The worker hesitated, but there was no way out. Many others were now watching, not expecting anything good to happen; and it didn't. He bent and scooped the gooey substance. Bringing his hands carefully over the clay container, he opened his palms and tried to empty the fluid into it. Nothing happened. The fluid had stuck to his hands. The worker began to shake his hands frantically, looking up at the Spoiler and back at his hands, whimpering. Finally the Spoiler's smile became happy. The fluid was seeping into the hands of the unfortunate. Dark streaks spread from his hands up into shoulders, neck, and down his legs; they meshed into a spider web, then blended in. The worker stretched his hands toward the Spoiler, begging for mercy. Then the darkness reached his head and his eyes became dull, lifeless; the movements—slow, robotic. In a few more seconds the worker became a tar statue, frozen forever.

"Let it be a lesson to you all," roared the Evil Spoiler. "Nobody messes with my plans! Nobody wastes my poison. I am your master. Do not disobey me or this will happen to you."

The Spoiler grabbed the petrified worker and threw him into the bowl. The statue dissolved into the liquid and only a small puff of vapor reminded everyone of the perished cloud-tender. The Spoiler rubbed his hands and said, smiling, "All's well, we are back where we had started from; nothing's wasted. Back to work now, time is of the essence." Without emotion, the gray workers went back to their duties, less one.

The Evil Spoiler stretched happily: nothing perks up one's spirit like a little evil deed. He went through the tunnel to the mouth of the cavern and called out, "Where are you, my ugly. Here, here pet; time you came to papa. Where are youuu...?" He stood there searching the skies, while the winds whipped past him. Evening was fast approaching, and the Spoiler felt his energy recede. As if by magic, a small crystal flask appeared in his hand. He gazed lovingly at the dark liquid inside.

"You'll make me feel better, won't you?" he asked the bottle. "Give me the strength and power to accomplish my plans, won't you my darling?"

He stroked the bottle and gently unplugged the top, carefully tilted the bottle over his face and let two drops fall into his mouth. He shuddered. The gray wave swept down his neck, up into his head, down through the chest and into his legs. "Yes!" he screamed into the sky, "what a rush!" The echoes reached deep into the cavern making the workers hunch their shoulders in fear. "Yes!" the Evil Spoiler repeated spreading hands wide. "I don't need the sun; I don't need the light. Darkness and fear are my friends; hatred is my power. Everything will be under my power when my friends conquer the world. Soon! So very soon." And he laughed insanely into the graying skies.

CHAPTER 17

The Workers of Doom

There was a disturbance in a cloud layer slightly below and to the right. The Evil Spoiler peered intently then leaned back with a remarkably friendly smile.

"Here comes my ugly. Come, fly to Poppa," he whispered. The endless cloud layer around the gray peaks erupted in that spot, spawning a hoard of cloud whiskers. These were immediately torn apart by winds, as if by a pack of wild dogs. Out came the thing that had made the Evil Spoiler so uncharacteristically mellow. The Shadow Eater flapped its wing-like edges like some gigantic gray manta ray pulling its bulk out of the clouds. At long last a round tail came out. A ball of a white cloud was hooked on its end. The Shadow flapped to a stop in front of the Spoiler wiggling the tail like some poodle with a fancy hairdo.

"Here you are my Shadow," crooned the Evil Spoiler. Incredibly, he looked more like a mother hen now than an evil mastermind. He patted the Eater under the slit of a mouth and scratched the darker gray circles around the creature's tire-sized eyes, two above its mouth and two below. The Shadow Eater shuddered at his touch, unclear weather from pleasure or hostility.

"Here, here my ugly; you like that, don't you? You big gray flounder you! Now, what have you brought Poppa? Give it up. You have something nice for me in that big mouth of yours, don't you? C'mon, open up!"

The creature wiggled its roof-sized mouth and sent the Evil Spoiler flailing backwards. The Spoiler's eyes flared darkly in anger, but he laughed instead, ran back and jumped on top of the Shadow Eater shouting, "What if I ruff you up some, you big flat-top bully, huh?"

86

He began scratching the surface of the Shadow, making it fluffy like poodle hair. The Shadow Eater just buckled its back and the Spoiler tumbled all the way into the mouth of the cave. When he came back out he was all business—playfulness gone.

"Enough games! Let me see the catch of the day. I need more bodies. The progress is too slow, and I lost one worker yesterday and one today. Drop the food-stuff into the tunnel and let me see what you've got; quickly now!"

The Eater flapped away from the entrance and whipped its tail. Like a stone out of a sling, the cloud ball flew into the tunnel. Some gray workers pulled it inside, others went out to the ledge and now inched their way toward the Evil Spoiler, their heads bowed.

"Well, we're ready. Let's see what the Shadow dragged in."

The Eater drifted closer and opened its giant mouth. Five cloudtenders sprung out. They looked around with hope until they saw the Evil Spoiler. He stood in the mouth of the cave wrapped in an ominous red shroud by the emerging fire glow. They huddled together in fear. Savoring their reaction, he glared at cloudtenders as a hawk on its prey. The cloudies huddled even closer, except for one, who stepped forward and yelled, "Who are you!? Why have you brought us here? You don't scare me. You'd better let us go or—"

"Or what? You little unspoiled thing. What can you do?"

"Maybe nothing, but the Maker will hear of this, then watch out!"

"That buffoon! He can do even less than you. All he could do is blow his top, but that would leave him with...what? No! I...AM...the Evil Spoiler! And I control the sky! You will work for me. I may even let you be there when I spoil the famous Cloud Maker himself and make him my slave."

"Never! I'll never work for you, traitor! I'd rather die," screamed the cloudie while the others shrunk back in horror. He ran to the edge attempting to jump into the wind.

Ilya Simakovsky

The Shadow Eater moved in and blocked him. The Spoiler giggled when the cloudtender ran back and forth; finding no exit he turned and sprinted at the Spoiler. "Grab him!" the Spoiler yelled, stepping behind the wall of gray workers that caught the brave cloudtender in the many handed grip. The rebel looked at the gray cloudies with surprise. "What are you all doing? Let me go. Let's take him. there are many of us and he's only one. We can do it. Common! Are you cloudtenders or what!?"

"My, oh, my!" said Evil Spoiler, "you've got spunk, but you're wrong. They're no longer the cloudtenders you knew. They had been spoiled. They are mine, as you are now. All I want is to spoil you a little—or maybe a lot." He was speaking like a kindly grandfather now, "As the matter of fact, I'll make you a foreman. Yes, yes—you've got energy and initiative; maybe even a Project Manager. The old one's too slow for my liking. Common, bring him to me. I'll spoil him first."

Kicking and struggling, the cloudtender was brought to the Spoiler and forced to the ground. The unfortunate stared defiantly at the Spoiler while his hands and legs were pinned down.

"Hate's such an invigorating feeling, isn't it?" the Spoiler said. "Soon we'll hate together, you and I. Aaaah...spoiling is such a delight. Open your mouth. It won't hurt one bit."

Seeing the crystal flask appear in the Spoiler's hands the cloudtender tried to get away in a last ditch effort; too many hands held him and only his eyes shouted his defiance.

"Common, feisty one, open your mouth; it'll be faster this way."

The cloudtender refused.

"Okay, have it your way. It's all the same to me; either way you're mine." He allowed one drop to leave the flask and smiled one of his awful smiles. It fell onto the shoulder of the unfortunate, who had finally succumbed to fear and watched with horror the drop seeping into his body. Within seconds, a gray spider web began spreading from the spot like cancer.

The cloudie was indeed brave, for just before the web reached his head he looked up and his eyes lit up with defiance. The Spoiler took a small step back, but then smiled; the web had reached the cloudtender's face and the fire in his eyes snuffed out. The grayness blended in; another obedient gray worker was born.

The Evil Spoiler joyfully ordered the new worker released; he could now complete the spoiling unopposed.

"Come here!" he commanded. Something—a speck of free will must've remained somewhere inside; the new worker hesitated. The Spoiler winced: this was unthinkable. Then the worker bent his head and stepped forward. Smiling with ease the Spoiler let another drop fall onto the rebel's body. His grayness deepened and expression changed. The head came up and, and like an eager dog, the spoiled cloudtender looked into his master's eyes waiting for his command.

"Ah, that's better. Why fight? We're friends now, aren't we?" The new worker nodded with an artificial, robotic smile.

"Should we keep you like this, or make you something more?"

"By your command, Master."

"But of course. Okay, I've decided; to my new Project Manager." The Spoiler lifted the flask in a toast and spilled another filthy drop into the cloudie's mouth, who swallowed it readily. The change happened quick this time. The darker gray wave swept through the cloudie's body. As it reached his head, he took a deep, spasmodic breath. Now his eyes changed too. They gained a darkly evil sheen, turning his face into hard and merciless mask.

Watching it all, the remaining cloudtenders shriveled together so close that, but for their shifting horrified eyes, they looked like another bulbous cloud. The newly promoted Project Manager glanced over his former friends without recognition or compassion. The Evil Spoiler nodded his approval. He asked, "Well my evil doer, how do you feel?"

"Great! I feel strong; hard...my body's hard. I hate these

weak things and their Maker. I feel like I could do things...evil things." He bent over and put his dark gray hand on a small stone and picked it up. "Look, what I can do!" He threw the stone at the group of cloudies, and when they scattered out of the way he bellowed a harsh, rude laughter.

The Spoiler laughed also, "Now you understand: hatred makes you hard. You can do anything when you hate; none of these distracting concerns—friendship, compassion, safety. Can you see how strong you can be?"

"Yes, Your Evilness. I can do anything. I will conquer these weaklings and—"

"Whoa, whoa! Hold it there my ambitious friend. Don't forget who's the boss here. I'll do the conquering and you'll do the helping. Is that clear!?"

"Of course, my Spoiler. I'm at you service."

"Ambition's a fine thing when kept in check, or there's always room in my pot for a few more drops of poison. Remember that! And now we'll see to your education."

The Spoiler walked over to the cloudtenders. Frozen in terror they didn't even react when he carelessly dropped poison fluid on each of them. After a few, short, ghastly moments, a fresh bunch of docile gray workers awaited orders. The Spoiler ordered them inside, then stretched and said, "This work makes me hungry. Unfortunately I've got to feed them too. The darn thing, though, if they don't eat, they just vanish. Common, Project Manager, let's get started."

They went in but a little whimper made the Spoiler pause. He turned around and smacked his lips. "How could I forget my pet, my ugly Shadow? Get over here!"

The Shadow Eater edged closer to the entrance. The Spoiler scratched under its mouth and the Shadow Eater wiggled its tail again.

"Have you eaten already, my ugly? You look too pure for my liking."

The Shadow's front edge folded into an accordion-like wave which ran across its mouth a couple of times—the yes sign.

"Well, well, well and you didn't tell daddy. A little spoiling is due or you'll get too good for us. Here you go..."

The Spoiler dropped eight drops of filthy fluid into the Shadow's mouth. It shuddered as the gray net flared all over its huge body and blended in, darkening its color. When the Evil Spoiler reached to pet it again, its mouth snapped. Jerking his hand back the Spoiler smiled. "That's more like it. Go! Bring me more workers."

With a shrill whistle the Shadow Eater took off into the sky. The Spoiler turned sharply and went inside with the new Manager in the tow.

The crowd of Gray workers waited inside the cavern. Their desolate, hollow eyes devoured the food-cloud, placed near the wall by the entrance. The Evil Spoiler climbed a small ledge above and set down on the highest in a row of the several stool-like stone stumps. The puzzled Manager set on the next one.

"What now?" he asked.

"Now we eat and watch a show." Pieces of a food-cloud were served to them by two workers. Like a movie director the Spoiler raised his hand and shouted, "Everyone for himself! Go!" In silence the horde of gray workers fell onto the cloud. It shook and quivered violently, shrinking by a second. There was no order, politeness, or care as workers grabbed as much food as their frantically working mouths could store. The Evil Spoiler burst into maniacal laughter— the only sound to be heard.

"See how they hate each other. My poison works so well," he said.

"The stronger ones get more. Others get enough to last till the next meal and some won't—into the soup with them." He laughed again—horrible, demented sound. "Learn how the natural selection works." He continued, "The strong work, eat and go on; the weak, well...they exist or they don't—who cares!? Thanks to my Shadow Eater I get new

91

ones all the time...look! They're finished. Let's do some spoiling first, and then I'll show you my Factory of Doom."

They climbed down and walked towards the line of workers whose grayness was diminishing from all the food filling their bodies. Since the ones in front ate the most they changed the fastest. The clouide in front was looking around as if awaken from a deep sleep.

"See how they need my spoiling," the Spoiler told the trailing Manager.

"You, in front, come here!" he commanded. The worker hesitated; he appeared to be thinking—a terrible offense in this neck of the woods. The Spoiler fell on the offender grimacing with hate. The worker recoiled in fear.

"You ate too much, fool! So, here, and you better be worth it." He allowed two drops of poison to fall on the shivering worker. The effect was instantaneous and ghastly. His grayness deepened and shivering stopped. The new foreman was born. All signs of independence vanished and he faced his master with doglike attention.

"Splendid," exclaimed the Spoiler. "Now! Bring the rest to me."

The new foreman pushed the next recovering cloudie to the Spoiler. One drop was all it took this time. Before long everyone was done except for the last two. These unfortunates looked so thin, nearly transparent. They barely had the strength to walk up to the Spoiler, despite the constant, merciless nudging from the foreman.

"My, my, my.... Didn't get much food, you poor things, did you?" asked the Spoiler. The workers nodded. "What a pity. You can't work then?" Another weak nod. "Well, maybe I'll let you rest, or find something to eat or something...." The no good, awful smile disfigured the Spoiler's face again.

"Please take good care of them," he ordered the foreman and threw a dark stare at the Project Manager. A simple nod from the foreman sealed the unfortunates's fate.

Another gray worker shuffled up to the Spoiler. Grayer

than the others, he was lightening up even as he spoke. "What about me, great Spoiler? Don't you need to—"

"You are demoted," the Spoiler said offhandedly.

"But why?"

"You don't push the foremen enough. The project needs to move faster."

"But—"

"But what?" roared the Spoiler. Be careful or this will happen to you." He pointed. The new Manager and the foreman just reached the boiling pot of poison. Each grabbed a worker and, over their weak cries, threw them in. Two puffs of steam rose slowly to the roof and vanished in the darkness there—gone like yesterday's memories.

"You see...oh, well..." The Spoiler turned, but the former Manager was no longer interested in anything but servitude. The demotion to gray worker was completed.

"Oh, well," repeated the Evil One, "go to the collection station and harvest the basic solution. And remember, production is all that counts—no spills."

CHAPTER 18

The Weapons of Doom

The Evil Spoiler put his arm around the new Project Manager—an unheard of gesture—and steered him towards another tunnel which led deep into the central mountain. They walked a while, fighting a rising wind. A couple of gray workers fought their way past them, staying as far away as possible from the Evil Spoiler. He paid notice only to curse one of them as the worker faltered against the wind: small clay containers they carried were fragile. Eventually they reached the end of the tunnel where it emptied into a curved side of a large, sausage-shaped chamber. The wind went mad here. It entered the chamber from the outside and bounced off the walls in different directions looking for exits. Finding one in the chamber's deep end the wind gathered its energy in a furious twister and exited the cave moaning like a wounded giant. On the way it whipped past the tunnel's mouth, where the observers now stood.

"Here's where it all began," the Evil Spoiler screamed into the Manager's ear, over the steady howl of the wind. "As you notice, the wind in the chamber is loaded with dirt and fumes. The humans in the valley below make it; the stupid humans are producing my poison for me; huh! How do you like that!? Their cars, their factories, fires and chimneys—all contribute to my basic solution. This invention of mine captures and concentrates the smoke into goo that serves as basis for my cloud poison."

The Manager was already eyeing the dense, thick, dark, curtain-like thing that covered the upper half of the tunnel's mouth. "So, what is it?" he asked.

"Ah, that was a stroke of genius on my part. Come closer and look."

94

"Spiders!"

"Yes, my Manager. Spiders are the key to everything."

"I hate spiders," uttered the Manager backing off, "...too many big spiders."

"Wrong emotion, underling! Change it or the soup's on. Spiders are essential to my plans and they are beautiful. Understood?"

The Manager nodded uneasily.

"Now, my yet, untested Manager, go back and play with them while I explain." When the Manager hesitated the Spoiler bellowed, "Now!" the Manager hopped to the giant web and touched it. Immediately two of the ugliest, biggest, hairiest spiders jumped on and ran up and down his arm, looking for something, their monstrous, hooked jaws wet and dripping. The Manager shook and shivered but stood his ground.

"Good. You might make it yet. Yes, we feed them. That's what they are looking for. You wouldn't have a couple of bugs on you, by any chance, would you? Ah...huh-ha...ah...huh-ha!" the Spoiler laughed loving his Manager's distress.

"Okay. That's enough. You can put them back."

The Manager exhaled and lifted his arm. Precisely at this moment, the sun peaked into the chamber highlighting the curtain. It took all the self control the poor Manager could master not to run. The curtain was a spider web; but what a web! It was crawling through and through with hundreds, thousands of spiders. Nearly a foot thick, the dark membrane seemed alive as it writhed and twisted under millions of hairy legs. The adult spiders were monstrous, but there were also millions of babies that couldn't wait to grow into their parents' repulsive likeness. Paralyzed, the Manager watched the spiders jump off his arm biting it a couple of times for good measure. Finally, he jumped back gulping air like mad. The Evil Spoiler was roaring, of course.

"Well now, listen up!" The Spoiler turned serious. "Here's how it works; the winds brush by the web and pollution

95

sticks to it. Somehow the spiders and their web change and concentrate the pollution turning it into my poison. That liquid drips down onto the small ledge, where I collect it for further processing. It's as simple as that."

The Manager just noticed one of the gray workers squatting in a dark corner, replacing a filled-up clay container with an empty one, very, very carefully. He spilled not a drop.

"See, they know what happens if they spill my poison," said the Evil Spoiler. "Anyway, we feed the spiders; spiders make the web; the web makes the liquid; we collect the liquid. Ingenious, isn't it? Oh, we also collect the excess web and spiders. Nothing! I repeat, nothing, must interfere with my collection procedures. Is this clear?"

The Manager nodded and scowled. He had realized at last that he was to be in charge. He liked it.

"Looking good there, project Manager. Keep that thought. Now let's go back and I'll show you the rest of it. You, two...," the Spoiler motioned to the busy gray workers. "I need more spiders and web. It grew too long on the bottom. Harvest it and bring it along."

Just then another couple of workers arrived. They brought a pear-shaped container with a flat cover.

"Ah, good!" exclaimed the Spoiler. "You'll be able to see everything. Take a look at what they've brought." The Manager crept to the container and lifted the cover, just a tad. His head swung back as if punched; out sprung the biggest, ugliest, and slimiest of all cockroaches. The Spoiler went into a fit of laughter again because the Manager's face quivered with gray rifts and mounds.

"Cute, isn't it?" tormented the Spoiler.

"What?" the Manager whispered.

"Spider-food. That's what. There are bugs, cockroaches, slugs, mice and other beautiful but unlucky creatures in there. I feed the spiders and they in turn help me. Watch!"

The workers laid the container in the niche next to the web. The spiders knew what was coming. The web rippled and twitched under their agitated feet, but it was nothing compared to what happened when the container's lid was removed. The spiders that were piled up on top of each other at the edge of the web went still and then...and then.... The panicked insects and mice streaked out of the container and found gaping jaws and grabbing legs waiting for them. The web shook violently as wave upon gray wave of multilegged, stinging death descended onto the hopeless prey. In seconds they were all gone, except for one brave mouse that somehow managed to evade the spiders and escape. The workers hunched their shoulders as if it was their fault: the Spoiler glared at them, but even he couldn't blame them for the bravery of the mouse. Just the same, they quickly faded into the darkness of the tunnel. The web became as still as the death it had just unleashed. Eyes feverish and ablaze, the Evil Spoiler asked, "All yours to command. What do you say, project Manager, can you run it for me?"

The Manager nodded and grinned slowly. "Done!" exclaimed the Spoiler. "We go back now. You're committed. You will not fail! Now, I can show you my greatest invention and my deepest secret."

Walking back was easy; actually, it was fun. All they had to do was jump and the wind carried them ahead. The Evil Spoiler took a big leap and, as he rose to the roof, he screamed. The Manager stumbled; it sounded as if his master was in trouble. He looked up but the Evil Spoiler seemed to have vanished into the darkness. Then he saw that a swirling cloud of bats was ripping into the helpless Spoiler. For a second, the Manager was content in letting them do it, but then he leaped up into the melee hitting and kicking. This was too much for the bats. They scattered. The wind carried the winners a little distance and deposited them near the bend in the tunnel. The Spoiler found a calm spot near the wall on which he leaned and closed his eyes, looking positively mauled.

"Bats. I hate bats!" he whispered. Then he skipped forward and snarled with venom, "I will catch them all, twist their necks, rip their wings off, gouge their eyes out, feed them to the spiders I'll...I'll...." He just stood there, curling his fingers, growling, oblivious to everything. The fretful Manager cleared his throat. The Evil Spoiler jerked around and squeezed through taught lips, "Don't you ever, ever tell anybody about this. Do you hear?"

"Yes, Master, nobody," the Manager cringed.

"That's good. You'll go far, underling. You did good back there; real good. Just stick by me and you'll do all right. We'll rule this stinking world...hmm...I'll rule, that is, and you'll administer."

"Yes, the Evil One."

The Spoiler smoothed out the rough spots the bats had left behind. A couple of gray workers flew around the bend just then, not noticing their master. They carried a piece of the web.

"Okay. Let's go," the Spoiler said. They completed the rest of the way in silence. Needless to say, there was no high jumping anymore. When they walked into the red, dimly lit main chamber the Spoiler finally relaxed. Two workers were waiting by the boiling bowl. He nodded to them. Instantly, they threw the web in.

"Watch!" commanded the Spoiler. The web stuck to the simmering fluid and began to dissolve. The poor spiders crowded at the top, trying to escape but to no avail. They died in agony and disappeared one by one, until nothing was left. the Manager turned to his boss, puzzled.

"Yes, they're among the ingredients; there are dirt, soot, bugs, tar and other things, nothing you need to concern yourself with. I'll tell you what to do, and you see to it that it gets done. And now, let's see the rest." The Evil Spoiler turned and went up the narrow stair-like ledge. Manager hurried to catch up. They went through a bunch of passageways and narrow creepy tunnels on the way to a hidden cave.

Although smaller than the main chamber, it was even

more spectacular. Tall and narrow, roughly cylindrical in shape, it was filled with magic.

First, there was this noise: a soft, surging, menacing hissing. The Manager searched for its source, but it seemed to come out right from a hazy mist that swirled everywhere. Steam was escaping out of every crack and vent; it rose in tortured columns toward the roof of the cave where it poured out into the sky through a large opening, while the morning sunlight poured in. Sunrays speared the walls and reflected in glitter; some kind of embedded crystals discharged laser-like beams that cut through the steam in colorful bursts.

"Wow!" said the stunned Manager.

"Wow is right, underling," the Spoiler rumbled, standing on the nearby ledge with hands on his hips. "Look, Manager, that's where the poison hits the fan. You're now in the heart of the project. There's no way back. Look at this...this ...magnificent thing."

The Manager couldn't help but look; delicate spiral ledges wound up the cylinder's walls. Several slender stone arches spanned across the inner space. Naturally ornamented by lumpy minarets, spikes and towers, they seemed to float on air. Light, glitter, shifting haze, everything seemed unreal, magical. The Evil Spoiler finished gloating and said, "Let's go up and see it."

"See what?"

"What you'll see."

They climbed up one of the spiral ledges, coming in and out of the steam. Suddenly a steam vent let go with a mighty whoop. Were they a few steps ahead, they would've been swept off the ledge like snowflakes. The Spoiler snorted, while the Manager sprinted past every little crack in the wall from then on. At last, they reached the top. Their ascent ended on a wider ledge that led to the cave's opening. Several gray figures were working there, unhindered by the especially thick fog which made it difficult to see.The Manager twitched with every whistle, whoop, hiss or sputter.

"Wow!" the Manager exclaimed again.

"That's rather a limited vocabulary you're demonstrating, underling. You'd better have more to say after you've examined this." The Spoiler moved ahead signaling for the Manager to follow. The Manager stepped through the curtain of steam and saw it. This time he just froze with his mouth agape.

"Frankly my dear," hissed the Evil Spoiler while savoring his Manager's reaction, "I had hoped you'd have more to say about this."

Whoop!...a mighty steam head exploded bawling the Manager off his feet and out of his trance. He jumped up and, whirling his arms around, run out of the steam. The Evil Spoiler just kept lecturing oblivious to it all.

"See, I had a dilemma. I made a weapon—my poison. I had an enemy. I had an army. I had the ammunition—these clay containers (a mountain of them was piled against the wall), but I had no way to deliver my weapon to my enemy. I had searched and searched, getting desperate, until I found this place. And then I knew I was destined to rule the sky because this...this incredible creation of mine makes it all possible. So, do you know now what this is, underling? Do you...?"

The Manager shook his egg-shaped head, a sheepish smile peaking from the puffy lips.

"Hua!" exclaimed the Spoiler, "did I make a mistake here? Are you fit to be my Manager? Should I demote you or...?"

"No, Your Evilness. I am your Manager. I'll do what it takes, but won't you tell me, what is this...thing?"

The Evil Spoiler turned sharply away. "All right!" he barked, "I can't expect everyone to be a genius. This is a cannon, designed and manufactured by yours truly, the Master of Gray Mountains and soon the whole earth!" he ended in a roar.

The Manager's eyes were glued to the thing. "Of course, a

cannon!" he whispered. "What's a cannon, master...how ...you made it or...? How does it work? This is incredible! You're a true evil genius, Master."

"Indeed, underling," allowed the Spoiler, "trying to get on my good side, aren't you? I can see where this would overwhelm an average mind. Even for me it was an exceptional flash of brilliance. Oh! To convert this freak of nature into a weapon that shall impose my scourge onto the sky...was glorious, simply glorious. See, here the steam pushed its way through the wall to the outside. To me it looked somewhat like the strange pipes on wheels I've seen humans use below; cannons they call them; there is usually an explosion, a lot of fabulous smoke, then humans seem to fall and never move again; seemed evil enough for me! Anyway, it cost me five foreman and scores of workers to widen and polish the vent. I can't tell you how it had slowed me down. It was the most time consuming and frustrating operation."

The Manager still stared in disbelief. The Evil Spoiler went on, "Anyway, after I plugged the holes, I needed to create steam pressure for a shot: the steam was going through the barrel in a continuous stream, like a smoking pipe. Oh, how I twisted my brains to come up with the answer. Sorry was a worker who got in my way; I had no mercy then. I was so close...and then I had it; a big flat stone slab was hanging over the opening of the barrel. I had my solution! I widened this chamber in the wall behind the barrel—"

"How? It is a stone!" asked the Manager trembling with awe.

The Spoiler's forehead crumbled, "What's that?" he snorted.

"How did you cut the rock? It's hard!"

"Of course it is, stupid! I...workers did it with these strange stones which seem to grow on walls here. See how brilliantly they sparkle in the light? They appear flimsy and useless, but they are hard, harder than anything. We've got a whole pile of them—look in the corner behind you."

The Manager observed a pile, twice his height, made of the peculiar clear, sparkling rocks; many were as big as his hand. With his no good, wicked smile the Spoiler continued, "No interruptions now, underling. That overhanging piece of rock was cut and dropped into this chamber; see it lying below the opening of the barrel? Yes? Good! Do you want to see how it works?"

The Manager nodded. The Evil Spoiler waved his hand and waited, hands on hips, chest puffed out. A number of workers hobbled toward the contraption. The Manager's anticipation grew. They seized a shaft of rock, protruding out of the wall like a hitchhiker's thumb. Steam was whooshing out of every slit and crack around the shaft. With great difficulty they pushed the shaft in, twisting it at the same time. It shuddered and rattled, then locked into place. Instantly the hissing stopped. It got quiet. This stillness was like the calm before storm, not the hush of the evening. The workers backed off and the Spoiler's chest deflated. His fingers started twitching and he leaned forward like a runner waiting for a starter gun. The Manager hunkered down, just in case. So when a loud screech pierced the silence the Manager jumped, looking around like mad. He missed his landing and ended up on his rear watching the big slab begin to move. "What magic is this?" he shrieked. Slowly at first, then faster the stone rose, scratching the walls of the chamber. It came level with the opening of the barrel and a little higher.... There was a loud blast. The stone dropped down like a stone it ought to be. After a pause, the whole process began again. The Evil Spoiler signaled the workers, who twisted the stone shaft. It came out of the wall all by itself, accompanied by a cloud of steam. The hissing returned.

When the Manager looked back at the Spoiler there was a holy fear in his eyes. The Spoiler enjoyed it for all it was worth, then said, "No, it's not magic, my simple-minded friend. The shaft redirects the steam. The steam builds up pressure under the heavy stone, lifting it. As it reaches the opening, the steam pressure blows out the barrel and whatever is in it. Simple, isn't it? We can do it again and again. I assume you noticed that there is a short pause after the stone drops. In that time you will learn to load the barrel. I will not accept failures. You must practice day and night until it becomes flawless. You'll supervise the foremen as well. Daily quotas must be filled. We'll be ready soon! Nothing will stop me now!"

Indeed, shrouded in a coat of steam the Evil Spoiler appeared larger then life. To those beneath him and to himself he was God, a frequent delusion of those who try to master others, while failing to master themselves.

CHAPTER 19

Catching Clouds

The sun, brilliant in its magnificent golden shroud, posed at the zenith as if to enjoy the beauty it created below. Inside the mountain well everything looked spotlessly clean, pristine even, under such relentless illumination. The dazzling white contrasted wildly with the gray and brown of the mountains and everything appeared sharp, in focus. The Spanish Quartet, encouraged by the undivided attention, wasn't showing any signs of weariness. Their music, sometimes with words and sometimes without, soared over the audience, almost visibly, as hot air wavers over the scorched pavement. Tobbi listened to the exotic, yet soothing melodies. It was nothing like the music he loved, with its hard, rhythmic beat. *"Metallica" wouldn't make it here*, he thought.

These tender colorful harmonies intertwined into soft melodies that broke into separate clear voices that united again for tender highs or the harsh lows. Somehow, it made Tobbi think of sailing. On a bright sunny day, like now, Tobbi and his father would float over gently rolling waves, pushed and pitched by the playful wind. Tobbi's heart would flutter with each sway of the boat, just as it did now with this enchanting music.

"I hate to be a party pooper," a mighty basso intervened, "but we're way behind in work. This music is wonderful, but it's not going to make clouds dance in the sky, if you know what I mean. Besides, I'm thirsty."

The Spanish Quartet was the last to catch on—the show was over. One by one they stopped singing, looking lost. Noticing this, the Cloud Maker smacked his lips and announced, "All right you four. I can't see why you couldn't entertain us while we work. The Spanish Quartet singers are now official. You're allowed to sing any time, as much as your little glowhearts desire. Hold it! Before you celebrate, this excludes nights, rest time and communal meetings. Agreed?"

The answer was a resonant: "Yes!"

Tobbi, meanwhile, again asked himself a question: why was it his fate to fall in with a bunch of rooting, tooting, talking, thinking, and now singing clouds with a war on their hands?

"Let's get to work then," cried out the Maker, shaking and rattling the cloudies with his enthusiasm and...shock waves.

"Now, what do I do?" murmured Tobbi under his breath.

"Do-shmoo," a familiar but not exactly missed voice mimicked from behind.

"Copycatting again, Pouch? Be creative for once—take the lead. What do I do?"

"Do-shm...I said this already, didn't I?" snickered Pouch, rolling awkwardly off his ballooning midsection and onto his flat feet. "I don't know; are you good at anything except causing trouble?"

Tobbi frowned and stepped toward Pouch. "What do you mean!?"

"I mean what I say. Trouble's trouble and you look like one," said Pouch and slammed his awesome foot on the cloudring. The cloudring buckled and backward went Tobbi yelping, while Pouch and Nelli were having a dandy good time. Tobbi rocketed high into the air, flipped over and dived at his friends. Far too late, the pair attempted to scatter. Snatched and whisked up by the flying ace Nelli squealed as the cloudring dropped off to the side. Tobbi was surprised at how easily he was able to carry his friends, so light they were. He laughed, taking them for some wild spins and hearing their yelps.

"He, who laughs last, keeps on laughing," he finally pronounced with sweet revenge. "You want to go down now?"

"Yea, yeah, yeah..." moaned Pouch, while Nelli's face sported this huge grin.

105

"More, more; I want to do more?" she yelled. Just as Pouch began to whimper again there was a rumble of rushing water followed by a hearty belch. A big cloud shot across the cloudring. A team of cloudies managed to snag this one, barely. The next belch was even stronger. Speeding like an out of control bus, the new cloud evaded all the defenses.

"Sorry," rumbled the Cloud Maker guiltily, "I'm afraid I can't quite control myself; I'm—belch—so thirsty. Sorry." He reached for the stone straw and drew in again. Meanwhile, Tobbi had made a decision.

"Okay. Enough games. We're going to catch."

"We?" asked Pouch.

"Yes, we! You, copycat! I knew right away that flying is your thing. I mean, you're enjoying it so much." Tobbi darted towards a small cloud.

"Nooooo," Pouch cried, "I can't fly...I...I."

"Really?" Tobbi asked, "You fly with me then."

"Stuck in your armpits?" Nelli asked.

"Fear not, I've got something better than deodorant here." Tobbi said and deposited his friends onto a small flat cloud. Without another word he proceeded to mold a big loop-like harness at the edge. He climbed in it and turned to his friends as if expecting applause. His companions hadn't a clue.

"What? Never seen a horse carriage?"

Silence.

"Bummer! Of course not. What am I thinking? Listen, just grab and pull."

The makeshift contraption worked. The towing team pulled a visibly giant load toward the cloudring. The Maker was beaming. A cheer erupted from the awaiting cloudies; it got out of hand, naturally. Belch—and out of the smiling mouth came an artistic treasure. This cloud was elongated and shaped like a sixth of the moon—beautiful in its own right. It was missed by all celebrating cloudies but the ever-watchful Michelangelo, who sent a team after it. Tobbi, meanwhile, looked for someone to hand down his load to; who could remember all their names?

"Ahoy there, Captain Silver! Stand by to receive."

"Ready here, Tobbi," answered the Captain proudly. Little did he know that being hailed here had nothing to do with fame: he was easy to remember, thin leg and all. Captain squinted, estimated the load, and called out, "Hey! Chuck, Plum, Stringbean, Knobbs, Tootsie, and Buttons come give me a hand,"

After the transfer Tobbi got ready to go after another runaway.

"Thanks again, Tobbi," Nelli said.

"For what?"

"Didn't you see how easily Captain Silver organized the cloudies? All because of the names you gave us."

"Oh, that. Good thing he knew their names."

"What do you mean?"

"Well, he called them just like that...I mean, he didn't have to say: hey, what's your name, come here. He remembered their names. That's what I mean. I can't...."

"I still don't get it. Do you Pouch?"

Pouch shrugged and asked, "Didn't you give us these names?"

"Yeah."

"Well..."

"Well, what?"

"What-schpot...don't you know them!?"

"There are a couple of hundred of...THEM! Are you out of your mind? Who do you think I am? A computer!" exploded Tobbi.

"No, you're Tobbi and who's Com-p-uter?"

"Thank you very much, but I'm not—repeat—not explaining computers to you; don't even ask."

"Okay."

Tobbi sighed, started to pull, and then stopped. "Correct me if I'm wrong," he addressed his friends, "are you saying that you know all of your friends' names?"

Nelli and Pouch nodded nonchalantly.

"From the one-time introduction!?"

They nodded again.

"Ah...Huh! Sure...Baloney! You're full of it!" Tobbi spun around and jetted along the cloudring towards another group of working cloudies. His friends hung on for dear life. He dived to an abrupt stop startling the poor cloudies who jumped back like jack rabbits, tearing pieces out of their treasured tow.

Pouch spoke first. "Tobbi, if I liked myself shaken, not stirred I'd be called a martini. Take it easy! You're gonna make me lose my lunch."

"What are you talking about?" sneered Tobbi. "You are your lunch, besides—a cloud with motion sickness? Gimme a break."

"Okay. Maybe not, but I think that you should clip your neurotic flying. What's gotten into you, anyway?"

"Don't get off the topic, Pouch. You said you could remember all of the names. Here's your chance to prove it. What's that name of the guy in front?"

"Why, that's Crane, of course." Everyone stared at a tall cloudie with a long, furry, forward bent neck and a protruding conical nose. Crane, unnerved by all the attention, twisted his neck around, looking for support.

"Well, are you?" prodded Tobbi.

"Me?" asked the anxious cloudie. "What did I do?"

"Nothing. You did nothing. Just answer the question!" Conversing with cloudies was proving to be the hardest aspect of his heavenly experience.

"What question?" Crane whispered.

"Oh! Fart-rap! You guys are too much! Why are you all getting bent out of shape whenever I ask you anything? All I want to know if your name is Crane. Are you Crane?"

"Yes...you said that I was...ah...but if I'm not, you can change it; I don't mind."

"No, I don't want to change it. Gosh, I just don't get it...."
Nelli's had enough. "Why are you doing this, Tobbi?" she
asked sternly.

"Doing what?" he snapped back.

"Scaring our friend. That's what!"

"I'm not scaring him; I just asked a simple question and
look where it's getting us."

"No, Tobbi, not us—you. Perhaps if you were a little more
patient and kind, your simple question would get a simple
answer; and why is it necessary, anyway?"

"You said that you can remember all of the cloudies
names, and I wanted to check."

"Why? Don't you believe us?"

"No...I mean...yes...I—"

"That's just it." Nelli interrupted, her big eyes burning
him like lasers, "You don't believe us and don't trust us, yet
you call us your friends. How could that be? Friends are
trusted; at least here they are. I don't know how it is below.
Let's go Pouch."

Nelli jumped off and started walking away. Pouch looked
at Tobbi with sadness, shrugged his shoulders and followed.
Tobbi was left literally hanging behind, scrutinized by many
scornful stares from the cloudies and feeling like an idiot.

The commotion was also observed from above. "Well,
Tobbi, what do you think?" asked the Cloud Maker, as softly as a cruise ship's horn. Now everybody was looking. Tobbi
itched all over. "See, Tobbi," the Cloud Maker continued,
"clouds are like your elephants, we never forget. We also
never lie. It's not necessary up here and just complicates
things. The truth can always be handled but lies multiply
like thunderclouds until the storm crashes you when it hits."

Tobbi took a deep breath and said loudly, "I'm sorry
everybody and..."

The cloudies picked up their choirs where they left off,
the hustle and bustle returned to the cloudring. Yet, Nelli
and Pouch were still walking away. Tobbi caught up with

them. They kept walking. It wouldn't be as easy, Tobbi realized. "Hey, guys stop, please." First Pouch, then Nelli stopped. Both turned around. "Listen! I do believe you, I do. Sometimes you just say things that at first are difficult to accept for a human. We're not as trusting and direct as you clouds; we should be, but we're not. I'm trying, though; I really am. Be my friends and help me. That's all I ask."

Pouch glanced at Nelli and said, "Okay, let's catch us some clouds, shall we?" They reclaimed their cloud carriage.

Tobbi hesitated and begged, "Before we go couldn't you do one thing for me, please? Just to make me happy."

"What?" both answered.

"What is that cloudie's name? The one on the right there." He looked so sheepish that his friends had no choice but to laugh as they screamed back: "That's Boomerang. Can we go now?"

Tobbi took off, shaking his head in amazement.

They worked as a celestial tow truck for the next hour and then one smart aleck suggested to exchange riders. From that point on, Tobbi felt like a pony ride attraction: he worked his fresh cloudie behind off giving rides to his new friends, but somehow he didn't resent it. Finally—the last runaway. The original pair was back. The first-ever cloud tow operation was bringing this cloud home. Now Tobbi's wondered where they all went. His friends eagerly agreed to take him there and directed him to the section of the wall located directly across from the entrance canyon behind the volcano. As he flew by, Tobbi waved to the happy Cloud Maker, who finally had enough to drink. Soon a peculiar opening became visible on the rear wall. From somewhere high up a thin, dark crack descended the rim wall splitting wider near the cloudring. It ended there in a black swelling of a cave. The whole thing reminded Tobbi of..., "It looks like something...I...I...ate!" he whispered, trying to capture the illusive image. "I got it!" he yelled out.

"What did you get?" asked Nelli the curious.

"You got something to eat?" asked Pouch the ravenous.

Tobbi ignored them. "It looks like...a Hershey's Kiss!" Indeed, the teardrop-like swelling of the cave with a pointy upper edge leading into a thin gash was reminiscent of the famous candy's shape.

"Wow! A Hershey's kiss the size of the Empire State Building. What a concept! If it were only silver or g...o...l...d." Tobbi stumbled because just as he said "gold" the slightly protruding edges of the cave were splashed with golden rays of the descending sun.

"A gold Hershey's kiss; how about that?" repeated Tobbi.

"Who's Hersh?" Pouch asked.

"What's a kiss?" inquired Nelli.

One can always count on a girl's intuition to ask the most embarrassing question. Tobbi explained: "Hershey's Kisses are my favorite candies on earth. It's chocolate."

"What are candies?" asked Pouch,

"What are kisses?" insisted Nelli.

Tobbi looked at her and shook his head, smiling. He explained, "Candies are these sweet things kids love to eat. They taste something like that brown cloud we ate at the cel-ebration, remember? Except they are small."

"I like big," commented Pouch.

"But what's a kiss?" drilled the pest at his side.

"See, Pouch, candies are much smaller than clouds, but they are very dense and so rich you get a lot in every bite."

"Mmmm," moaned Pouch, smacking his lower lip, "I like rich; I like dense."

"I bet," said Tobbi, ignoring Nelli. Nelli squirmed a little, but she wouldn't be deterred.

"And kisses are what?" she rephrased.

Tobbi was pinned down. He gave up.

"It's just the shape of these candies reminds us of...it's just a shape. That's all."

Nelli, attacked sensing the writhing of her pray, "The

111

shape reminds you of what?"

"Well...of a kiss."

"So, what's a kiss?"

They couldn't seem to get away from this damn question. Even Pouch got interested. "Yeah, what's a kiss?"

"What's this!? A police interrogation!?" Tobbi gave up. "Never mind that. Kissesarewhatsomepeopledowhentheylikeeachother," motor-mouthed he.

"Is this some kind of a code?" inquired Pouch.

"Whatpeopledowhentheylikeeachother?" fired back Nelli.

With murder in his eyes, Tobbi answered, "Well, they kiss each other."

Here was the cursed question again: "What's a kiss?"

"All right...ALL RIGHT!! I'll tell you. A kiss is when- ...you...take ...well...her and come close...your mouth sort of pouts like this...and ...and...you take, and...kiss and that's all; you see?" Both calmly observed Tobbi's torture and shook their heads, very clearly not seeing what he was explaining. Contemplating an immeasurable evil Tobbi took a deep breath and said, "here goes nothing." Quickly he freed himself from the harness, streaked to Nelli's side and stifling her outcry, pressed his lips lightly to her cheek. Into a blessed silence he announced, "That's a kiss. Satisfied?"

Nelli's face became translucent—a ghost's face; her eyes grew huge. Then just as quickly it turned white and puffy while a transparent stripe traveled down her entire body, bounced off the soles of her feet, shifted up again and finally dispersed in the stomach. Tobbi, on the other hand, was surprised at the softness of her cheek; he, too, felt strange: embarrassed but pleased.

"Wow!" exclaimed Pouch, energized by Nelli's reaction. He turned to Tobbi and offered his plump cheek. When nothing happened he stepped back, regrouped and tried again.

"What?" asked Tobbi

"Now me."

"What?"

"A kiss."

"Not on your life, dude."

"But why?" asked Pouch, shaken a bit. "Don't you like me?"

"You might say that."

"But before you said—"

"I know what I said. Didn't I show you how to shake hands?"

Pouch nodded.

"Well, some people you kiss, and some people you shake hands with. Here, let's shake hands." They did. Yet, Pouch obviously wasn't satisfied, he asked, "But why—"

"Why—shmai," retaliated Tobbi. "You're going to have to live with it, dude. I'm not kissing you. That's just the way it is."

Pouch looked hurt. Tobbi was hugely pissed that he ever got on this topic, but Nelli, was sitting with this stupid look on her face as if she had won a lottery or something. Tobbi threw an evil stare at her and said, "Look, Pouch, you only choose one to kiss. Nelli looks like a girl, so I chose h...er! Stop! Don't ask me what a girl is, Okay? Just listen. You, I shook hands with, her I kissed—same thing."

"It didn't look the same."

"Pouch! Friend. Drop it." Suddenly Tobbi had an idea. "Pouch, I know what we can do."

"What?"

Tobbi came around to Pouch and demonstrated. "This is a special handshake." They went through the complicated motions of touching palms, thumbs, fists, elbows. Of course, it was instantly memorized. Just to be sure Tobbi asked, "You got it? Let's do it again." They went through it once more, fast. At the end Tobbi threw his hands around Pouch's fat chest and squeezed once. It was Pouch's turn to turn see-through.

"It's called a hug, dude; first a shake, then a hug, how about that?"

A big smile brightened Pouch's face.

"So, I get two things and Nelli gets one, huh?"

Tobbi decided that the end to this torture was too near to reveal anything else.

"Yes. You've got it, bud. It's all yours. Can we go now?" Tobbi strapped himself into the harness, not looking back. While they talked, they drifted upward quite a bit and the contraption became flimsy. It held while he darted toward the Hershey cave but came apart just before the entrance. Yelping like puppies, the riders tumbled into the cave. Tobbi pulled back to organize his thoughts. More than anything now, he wanted to avoid explaining human relationships to cloudies; the thing was too messy even for him. After a couple of minutes he followed his friends.

CHAPTER 20

Artist's Paradise—Food Coloring Explained

To Tobbi's surprise, there was no one inside the cave. Where did they all go? He moved farther in and discovered a short tunnel that led into another large chamber, also empty. There was another passage to the next chamber and one more to the next one. It was as if a giant air-filled sausage was strung through the mountain. In the third chamber Tobbi began to hear a faint noise that turned into cloudie chatter deeper in. Apparently, this crack in the mountain wall went all the way through to the other side: there was some light and the air was fresh and moving briskly. At the sausage's end, quite a view opened up. A final "link" or chamber split into three caves: right, left and a center. It was busy in there, noisy too; the cloudies chattered loudly but he couldn't understand a thing. Then he realized why and laughed hard: they were talking in different languages. In the biblical story of the tower of Babel, God made people talk in different tongues and they couldn't finish the tower since no one could understand one another. *I suppose,* Tobbi thought, *God would have to be more creative with the cloudies because they understood everything.* The minute they noticed Tobbi, everyone switched to English.

The central cave had several outlets to the outside. In the roof there was a big chimney-like opening to the sky. The front wall had a horizontal, bean-shaped slit which curved around a peculiar bulge. Tobbi couldn't quite make out the details: it was masked by shadows. He, however, noticed all the actvity. The cloudies zipped in and out of the side caves. The one on the left was dark; the one on the right seemed to have interior lighting. Tobbi heard his name. Pouch was waving at him from the entrance to the dark chamber. Tobbi flew

115

there quickly.

"What is this place?" he asked.

"Place-shmace. That's where it's at, whirlhead. The happening place, the heart of hearts, the master chambers, the artist's paradise. Yo! That's where we rock and roll, bro, twist and shout; bump and grind—you know what I mean?"

"No, not a clue." Tobbi said, "Cut the crap. You're not up on a lingo as much as you think; Gimme a short version."

Pouch rolled his eyes and mumbled, "Didn't this sound cool? I mean..."

"Look. Humor me. Don't try to be cute."

"You want, I should be ugly?"

"You're already ugly. Gees! Why is there no short conversation with you?"

Pouch's face melted. The puffy eyebrows oozed over his round eyes like boiling milk over the brim; the meaty lower lip swung down in a garage door style, plump cheeks sagged: he looked like one unhappy basset-hound-cloudie. Tobbi swallowed another sharp remark.

"Pouch, you're not ugly. I'm just—"

"Okay," Pouch recovered instantly, "let's go inside."

It was dark, but Tobbi could see, somehow. The cave was long and tall, and it was filled completely with clouds, sentient and not.

The cloudies were paired up and stood in rows, facing the exit. Each pair towed a floating cloud. Tension leaked into the air. Everyone was edgy and ready for action. Tobbi turned to his friend and asked, "What—" Only to be interrupted by a high-pitched, squeal of the Master Decorator. Michelangelo was not happy. "No...no...no! You're in the wrong line, darling. You're breaking my glowheart. This is not, I repeat, not a food material. Look at the texture, the density, the softness...ah; this is a masterpiece not an entrée. Darling Dingdong...," he whined patting a bell-shaped cloudie on its pointy head, "do me a big, huge favor. Don't mess with my art!"

The berated Dingdong looked up sheepishly.

"Oh, you're such a delight," said Michelangelo, "such a wonderful conversationalist you are. See, we talked, reminisced, discussed issues, and came to a decision together. That's what I love about my job, everyone's so agreeable. Now, Dingdong and Beehive, as we have decided, go to the front of this row and be good cloudtenders—stay there. Ah! You look marvelous," he praised someone else as he darted between the rows like a nervous director before a show.

"Bonzai," he said from the left side now, "you take those six adorable little fingers out of your cute, but not so little mouth and pay attention. It's almost time, everyone. There you are, Bonzai, you look so much better with your hands as hands, not mouth openers. Get ready!" Michelangelo was off running again, muttering something.

"Was he swearing?" Tobbi asked Pouch. No answer. Tobbi turned to ask again and came nose to giant nose with Michelangelo, who materialized behind him as if beamed by a *Star Trek's* transporter.

"Yes, I was swearing," said Michelangelo. "I'm stressed out and now you are here."

"How do I figure into this?" Tobbi asked. "What did I do?"

"Nothing yet, but you will if you keep standing where you're standing."

"You don't like this spot, I take it?"

"Precisely! Everyone's so bright today. So, you need to be moving, because....?"

"Because...?" Tobbi mocked back watching Michelangelo gulp air and puff up in agitation.

"Because, genius, you're blocking the exit and if you don't move this instant I'll start swearing again. Remember, I can do it in 133...no, 134 languages. I got an inexhaustible supply. What I don't have is time. So..."

"Keep your shirt on, Gees! All you have to do is ask," said Tobbi, but he was speaking into empty air. The Master Decorator was gone, his voice ripping somebody else apart in

117

the rear of the cave.

"Pouch," yelled Tobbi. "Where are you? You'd better explain what's going on here. Pouch!"

"Don't strain yourself. I'm right here." Pouch walked back in after escaping the raging storm named Michelangelo.

"Some friend you are, leaving me alone with this mountain of fury. Why is he so worked up?"

"He is an artist! Besides, I wanted you to get the flavor of the moment, I've seen it before."

"I did—a ton of it."

"Ton-plon. We'd better move. It's time."

"Time for what, for goodness sake?"

Pouch just grabbed and dragged him out. Tobbi blinked: light exploded suddenly, soundlessly. Rich colors flared on gray walls; the white dancing sparks splashed onto the roof of the middle cave. "Far out," Tobbi whispered. The sunlight was pouring through the kidney shaped hole, and there, imbedded in the bulge, he now saw a huge, magnificent crystal of perfect clarity; it shone with amazing, blinding power. Some light reflected off its top sending sparks to the roof. He had to squint to watch the river of light pour out of the crystal and cover the entire length of the back wall with thick bands of red, orange, yellow, green, blue, and violet. That's diffraction, Tobbi remembered his physics; the crystal fractured the white light into its component colors. "This is awesome," he said.

Pouch was astoundingly brief, "It sure is."

A thousand questions sprung into Tobbi's head: Where did the crystal come from? Who put it up there? What's it for? There was no time for that; a loud shout startled him.

"Reds! Go, go, go..."

The red band of the spectrum was now draped over the dark cave's entrance highlighting its edges in a red frame. A cloudie pair sprung into the frame from the inside and flung the cloud they towed into the light. It flared red and soaked in the color. Immediately after exposure, it was taken back and replaced with another. Tobbi began to understand and as fantastic as it seemed, he didn't dare not to belicve his eyes. Shortly the band at the dark chamber's entrance shifted from red to orange and the command was issued: "Oranges! Go!" And so it went for a while, as the sun moved across the sky the colors of the spectrum shifted as well. It got complicated when, in between the pure colors, specific mixtures were called. Only cloudies with their perfect mcmories could manage to keep it all straight. Now Tobbi could understand why Michelangelo went nuts. Then it was over. The sun moved beyond the mountain and the central cave got turned off like a bedroom light. It seemed so...wrong; one minute colors and sparks, the next—dusk and shadows. Something akin to a depression hit Tobbi. He sagged to the ground—fat chance! Pouch pulled him up saying, "It's not the time to rest, Tobbi. Got work to do; create things! Let's go."

"Yeah, yeah, yeah! More mind boggling stuff still to come and I've got no mind left," growled Tobbi. Inside the 'photography' cave the cloudies were still divided into two groups. Michelangelo was still in hyperspace, of course, for the reasons only known to him. Suddenly Tobbi felt like a parade: the dark chamber was filled with colorful floats, someone just needed to switch the lights on and the party would begin. For everyone else, however, it was just work.

"So, why are you standing here, Ping?" Michelangelo flared up somewhere to the right. "Can't you see you don't belong here? And you, Pong, should know better. Look at this thing! In no shape or form is this art! Must I do everything myself? What are you waiting for, Ping!? Pong move it! To the food line—on the double!" The group parted and the chastised pair moved their cloud to the other side. Michelangelo trailed them, plowing into the group on the left like a bowling ball into pins. Soon he was mauling someone else.

"Marilyn, my darling Marilyn, are you counting stars again, even where stars don't go? You're on the wrong side

119

again, dear. Yes, cutie, just look at the treasure you're holding. I don't expect the Professor here to know the difference; he's a braniac, but you! You should see that this...this stunner isn't for eating; uh-uh, no sir. Look at these curves, the texture, and the hue. Let's move it to the other side, love, gently, gently; one foot in front of the other and don't bump it. Good. Well, this about does it. Everyone get ready to move out. All set? Let's go!"

They began to file out of the dark chamber.

"Where are they going?" Tobbi found himself whispering for no good reason.

"To the other side." Pouch whispered back.

"What other side?" Tobbi whimpered, fear tightening his chest all of a sudden.

"The cave on the other side."

Tobbi breathed easier: he was thinking Poltergeist somehow.

"Why are we whispering?" he asked. Pouch pointed back at Tobbi.

"What now?" Tobbi asked louder then he had to.

"We follow and stop acting strange."

"Okay."

Now the dark cave was more than half empty, while the line of colored clouds stretched across the central chamber turning it into a spring garden full of plump multicolored flowers. Michelangelo, who inspected every cloud, cried out suddenly. Everyone stopped except for the last pair that staggered through the exit in a drunken sort of way. Tobbi soon had an explanation: Stumble and Fumble. Not too graceful to start with, they had a doubly difficult time walking with an extra load. Michelangelo watched in horror as their prized haul came close to a sharp wall protrusion. With their feet crossing and uncrossing seemingly all on their own they continued on, giggling in embarrassment. The fact that they took steps didn't necessarily mean they progressed forward. Tobbi offered them a ride. The offer was immediately accepted, to everyone's relief, none greater than Master Michelangelo's, who even ventured forth a smile—such a ruckus it caused.

Tobbi got ready to airlift the dynamic duo.

"Wait a second," he said, "what happens with all the rejects?"

"There are no rejects. Those are food." replied Michelangelo resentfully and went back into the dark cave. He rumbled from there, "I'm about to spice them up now. Everybody will be wasted after all this work. I must feed them."

"That's cool. I'd like to watch."

"Sure, why not? Leave the two graces there and come in. Fumble and Stumble you stay put!"

The pair was only too happy to wait. Walking wasn't their favorite activity, but they hoped to find one someday.

Tobbi followed Michelangelo toward the back wall, where he saw several niches. Michelangelo explained: "The white clouds are dull and tasteless, but add a little color and flavor to them, and....delicioso; ahh, magnifico!" He touched his lips with cropped up fingers. "The taste, the texture—like beautiful music—so pleasing; add a little sweetness here, a touch of bitterness there, a smidgen of saltiness and create a symphony of tastes—so fun to eat. Of course, mixing flavors right helps, but that's mostly luck and...and a little talent," he added, modestly.

"Just a little, I'm sure." Tobbi laughed. Michelangelo glanced impishly at Tobbi and blessed him with another smile.

"So, how do you do it?"

"Do what?"

"A smidgen of sweetness, a bunch of bitterness...whatever—"

"A touch of bitterness and smidgen of saltiness—"

"Yeah, yeah, whatever—"

"No, not whatever. It's very specific. You put a little too much and no one eats it. I can't tell you how capricious these cloudtenders are."

"Sure you can. You're one of them. Look, Michelangelo, can the philosophy. Let me see you do it."

Quite deliberately Michelangelo touched his huge head with the back of his right hand and mumbled, "Such disrespect. No one appreciates me; all the hard work I do."

Tobbi rolled his eyes and said, "Of course they do; everyone does. They just adore you!"

Michelangelo perked up. "They do?"

"Immensely."

"Really."

"Well, are you going to show me, or do I need to butter you up some more?"

Michelangelo pulled one of the clouds over. It was tinted green with yellow highlights around edges.

"Taste!" Michelangelo ordered. It tasted slightly sour, palatable but blunt.

"You like?"

"I could eat it."

"Huh! He could eat dirt if he could eat this! Let me see, now...," Michelangelo stroked his cheek. He reached first into one cubbyhole in the wall, pulled something out and sprinkled it onto the cloud, then went into another and yet another.

"Taste!" he ordered again. Curious now, Tobbi took a pinch. Since he saw nothing fall onto the cloud, he expected little difference, but it was as if a taste bomb exploded in his mouth. He first smelled and then savored a green forest after a morning rain with a tinge of cut grass scent; its lemony tartness tingled inside his cheeks and playfully released the hidden sweetness that further teased his abruptly aroused hunger. He felt alive and playful inside. "Wow! Wow! This...this stuff's great!" Tobbi stuffed more of it into his mouth.

Michelangelo wriggled his huge bulbous nose proudly and asked, "So, my young cloudtender, could you eat this as well?"

"Could I? Could I!? You bet your megabelly I'll eat this. How'd you do that? I didn't see anything. What did you put on this?" Tobbi could still feel the freshness a few bites created inside. He proceeded to stuff his face, neck, belly and any other available space with the delicious food.

"Whacht djid yooou pfuhct in zhis?"

"Oh, stuff."

"Stuff-shmuff. *Why am I talking like this.* What stuff?"

"I don't know if I should tell you. You're not a regular cloudtender, you know."

"Define regular. What do you think I'll do? Steal your recipes? Then what? Take them home!? I have a surprise for you, but clouds aren't considered a delicacy where I come from."

"Of course, how silly of me. Okay, I'll tell you...." Michelangelo's face relaxed and became dreamy. "The morning's east winds bring us the freshness of the forest, the mustiness of marshes, the tangy odors of grasses, and scented pollen of wild flowers. The afternoon south winds carry the frothiness of waves, the spicy salts of the ocean and the bitter dryness of sandy beaches. The evening north winds are full of glacial coolness and the burning tingle of ice crystals. But the night's west wind—ah! The night winds bring us the softness of the moonlight mixed with the aromas of the sleepy earth and night blossoms—"

Tobbi, who on earth couldn't tell poetry from pottery, was moved by these images. He saw the mighty ocean with giant rhythmic swells of waves; a hundred-year-old forest swaying in the wind, dark green and full of life; moonlit lakes and meadows giving up stored heat of the day in wavering mists—all crumpled into tiny specks and poured into his mouth. Tobbi choked and snapped out of it. "Man, that's weird stuff. Michelangelo, what did you do to me? Hypnosis? Don't bother! I'm at the point where I'd believe anything you guys tell me. Just like this, (Tobbi tried to snap his fingers—

a futile attempt of course.) you say this and that and you know it, your trusty neighborhood dork—Tobbi—is right behind you, cheering." Michelangelo shook his head and said, "I must say that for the first time in my long life I don't understand what someone's saying to me. Anyway, that's how I make food. Are you satisfied now?"

"At least my body is," mumbled Tobbi. "I've got to get out of here. I don't think I feel well, excuse me." He flew back into the central chamber, found a small ledge and set there, cradling his head in his hands. A noise coming out of the lighted cave on the other side reminded him that there was more to see, so he scooped Stumble and Fumble together with their haul and flew there. Suddenly Nelli stepped out of the cave with her arm outstretched.

"Stop!" she said.

PART TWO

THE BOOK OF DESCENT

CHAPTER 21

The Shaping of a War

Tobbi veered to the side barely avoiding smacking into her. "We have a surprise for you," Nelli announced coyly.

"Oh! Finally a surprise!" Tobbi sneered.

"For his heroic services to Cloudland, we, the Cloudtenders, on this day commence forth a tribute to our honored guest and friend, Tobbi."

Nelli stepped aside and out marched the Spanish Quartet in full swing, singing something rhythmic, loud, and important. Tobbi stepped back, anticipating anything but a large pink cloud shaped like a head. It was turning... turning....

"Oh, my," Tobbi whispered staring at his own enlarged face with the ever present clump over the forehead. Cloudies poured out of the cave too and like so many chicks surrounded his detached head in a swirling, bobbing mob. It was placed beneath the chimney-like opening in the roof and released. Slowly, majestically it rose; its blank eyes seemed to stare at him. Tobbi shivered and rubbed his neck, feeling creepy. Then it was gone.

Everyone looked at Tobbi now. *What do they want, isn't losing one's head traumatic enough?* he thought. But this time, there's no one by his side to give him a clue.

"Amm...ahmmm," Tobbi cleared his throat, "thanks everybody, I—" His next words were drowned in an uproar, as he was rushed by smiling cloudies, who patted him on his shoulders, back, head.

"Great speech, Tobbi, wonderful words...terrific...very eloquent...magnificent...so touching...hooray for Tobbi—"

Tobbi surrendered, smiled, and then laughed with these adorable but forever perplexing folks. Later he inspected the chamber where his head was created. It was filled to the roof with cloud sculptures. Here, a tall white ship with beige sails was ready for the winds. There, a mighty tree spread its many gnarled branches. Further in, a mystical many-armed beast was being completed, while a long curved cloud was pulled toward the exit. *"Moby Dick" lives again,* thought Tobbi, watching a big white whale rising into the ocean-blue of the sky.

The forever grouchy Michelangelo dashed about like an air leaking balloon, making last minute corrections, refinements, and delivering a swift kick in the behind here and there—verbally, of course. There's no violence in these beings. Later, when all the creations were gone a deep sense of accomplishment settled in. Tobbi finally felt like he belonged when in a big happy group the cloudies walked back to the Cloudring. A delicious feast followed and after that everyone settled for a well deserved rest as night approached. The shadows of mountain peaks spread across the cloudring like a puddle of dark paint, closing in on the cloudies that clumped together like a bed of barnacles. This was one of those rare moments when these fidgety beings were totally at rest. There were quiet conversations and even the Spanish Quartet, which hadn't shut up since its naming, fell apart into four individuals who didn't utter an identical word for five whole minutes. Tobbi felt homesick all of a sudden. He missed his parents; he missed his friends; he missed his school, and he even missed his sister. He stopped just short of missing his wheelchair on account of the incredible rush of flying.

The Maker, for all his size, didn't miss much and presently addressed Tobbi with a deliberately hushed voice. Noise suppression, like everything else in Cloudland, was a relative thing; He'd still make a pipe organ jealous.

"What's the matter, Tobbi? You're not happy."

"All this (Tobbi swept his arm widely) is phat but it can't be real, man. My home, my family is real this...this...I don't know."

"Huh, here we go again—a doubting Thomas," the Maker said with concern. Two figures disengaged themselves from cloudies and walked over to Tobbi.

"Reality," the Maker said, "what is it? We all dwell within the limits of our perception. If our perceptions match we experience same things; if not, we live in different realities. Some lucky beings break through the limits and make amazing discoveries. You, Tobbi, entered into our world. All you see is real to us. Deny it and we all may perish."

Nelli looked deep into Tobbi's eyes and took his hand. "Does this feel real to you?" she whispered. Tobbi looked around, taking in Cloudland with its mountains, volcano, the Maker, and the cloudies.

"It's time to decide, Tobbi! Will you fight with us and keep this place pure, or will you let the darkness win?" Cloud Maker's voice wasn't so steady. Hundreds of eyes stared at Tobbi now; everyone was suddenly aware of the importance of this moment.

Tobbi sat up straight. "Gosh, I really like you guys; this sure is real enough. Count me in—no more doubts."

Happy screams arose from hundreds of throats, but they were overpowered by the Cloud Maker's bellow. "Quiet everyone. Rest is in order. We'll start our war tomorrow."

Cloudies dispersed and disappeared into the cloudring, just as the night's shadows gulped the last of it.

CHAPTER 22

To Eat or Not to Eat—That's the Question

For once Tobbi didn't dream. He slept until brightness aroused him and he climbed out to see cloudies running about, as usual. The Cloud Maker was on a drinking binge again. Many clouds were being hauled to the caves. Others were just floating around. Everything appeared crisp, bright, and in focus.

"Good," Pouch drawled from behind, "the sleeping beauty's up. Hold everything...."

"Stuff it, Pouch!" Tobbi felt a charge building up. The energy was for free here. It pierced the air in a pure light and made everything clear, possible, and attainable. Tobbi stretched, noticed his flimsy arms and inquired, "Is there anything to eat?"

"Huh! Does lake have water? But for YOU there's no food. You're late!" Tobbi jetted, straight into Pouch, knocking him off his large feet. Pouch squealed, rolling like a fat beer keg. "See, Pouch, now I have a problem." Tobbi climbed onto Pouch's round stomach, pinning the poor cloudie to the cloudring. This sudden development made Pouch loose his cool. His huge lower lip started to tremble, but Tobbi, struggled hard not to laugh.

"I looked at my arms a minute ago, bud, and they didn't look so good. Thin and scraggy they are, see. I was told this means hungry. Like, I think this to myself, my friend, Pouch, says that there's no food left for me. I've got to believe him, see, he's my best buddy here. But, if I don't eat, I'll just disappear, you know? Like, I've got to find me a cloud to nibble on. Then it dawns on me: Pouch is a cloud! So, here I'm sitting on top of you, struggling with a dilemma. See, I still look kinda sickly, so to speak, and in my human way of thinking

130

this plump little finger of yours looks a lot like a sausage. So, like I said before, I've got me a problem, dude. Since you are telling me that good food isn't available, I don't know if I should restrain myself. I mean, since you are my best buddy here, in this whole Cloudland, you wouldn't mind sharing, would you? I mean, what's the big deal, you've got five others. It's just a finger!"

At this point Tobbi started to wonder because Pouch's eyes were flooding up with horror. Pouch squirmed a little, and even tried to smile, but when Tobbi opened his mouth and leaned forward, Pouch howled, buckled his mighty abdomen and threw the aggressor off. He staggered to his giant feet and, panting madly, shook his finger at Tobbi. That's how Nelli found them.

"What's the matter, Pouch?" she asked. "You look like you saw the Shadow Eater."

"I...I...he...he...," Pouch gulped. Nelli turned to Tobbi.

"I...I...he...he...," Tobbi hiccupped, unable to speak also, but for a different reason entirely; he was laughing too hard.

Nelli raised her eyebrows quizzically. "You guys rehearsed this or what?"

"He almost bit my finger off!" Pouch snarled.

"Why would he do such a stupid thing?"

"I told him that there's no food, so he said he would eat my finger. Don't look at me that way! He did, he really did!"

"Now, Tobbi were you really?" Nelli inquired dubiously.

Tobbi, still laughing madly, squeezed between spasms, "NNNNoo...o," gave up and just shook his head.

Pouch's shoulders drooped. His eyes shifted right and left looking for an exit.

"He...He...really...th...thought...I could eh...e....eat his finger!" Tobbi whined with the last of his air and then sat down gasping, "oof...oof...oof" Pouch had been had. He knew it, so he laughed too, but only for show. Tobbi looked at himself again, or rather through himself and stopped huffing. It was weird, no organs or anything, he just saw through to the brown-gray stone on which he was leaning.

"Seriously, Pouch, is there anything to eat, like right now?"

"Yeah, I saved you some. If you look behind that boulder you'll see. Remember, it's with these fingers I carried it for you."

"It's okay, Pouch, you still have them all."

"I wouldn't if it were up to you."

"Come on, Pouch, don't start that again. Take it like a man."

"How could I? I'm not a man!"

"Stop it you two!" Nelli had had enough. "Tobbi, go stuff yourself, we've got work to do," she ordered. And so he did, on something orange and summery, realizing that being told to get stuffed wasn't an insult here but a life-saving advice.

"So what's happening?" he asked when finished.

Pouch said, "Work's happening, that's what."

"So what do I do?"

"Help is the word that comes to mind." Pouch was still grouchy.

"I'm glad that your mind is so busy since your body isn't doing much work either."

"It would if Michelangelo hadn't sent us to get you, Mr. Slumber Allday."

Tobbi's had it. "Put it up, fatso. Let's see who's sleeping now and who'll be sleeping later. Put them up!"

"Put what up?" asked Pouch, while Nelli watched with suspicious eyes.

"Your fists, dummy, what else?"

"Why?"

Stupid, that's how Tobbi felt, standing there like Mohammed Ali posing for a photo.

Nelli came alive, "Fists like in...hitting, fighting! What is this, now? Cloudtenders don't fight. Fighting solves nothing, all you get is holes."

"Well, maybe it's time you learn, you've got a war on your

hands."

Pouch, meanwhile, experimented with his fists bringing them up and down and imitating Tobbi. Next, Pouch tried to mimic the punches Tobbi threw while talking. He did all right with a jab. Then he threw an impressive hook and lurched after his fist; with a wild, puzzled expression he spun to the ground and landed on his belly at Tobbi's feet.

"Spectacular!" Tobbi's anger morphed into guilt, as he watched Pouch rock on his belly trying to get up. Nelli drilled into him, of course, increasing his misery, "What's wrong with you, Tobbi. You were going to hit Pouch! How could you?"

"But I—"

"You can't do it here, you know. That's not allowed!"

"But he—"

"There are other ways, more cloudlandlike—"

"But I—"

"It doesn't matter. Make up now. That silly thing you taught him...a shake. Do it now!"

"No!"

"Do it!"

Pouch, who had managed to get up at last, swung his round, puffy fists around and said, "Okay, I'm ready. Let's see who's who here. Let's do it."

Under Nelli's stern gaze, Tobbi stepped over to Pouch mumbling, "Yeah, all I need is a pillow fight!"

"How's that?" asked Pouch and Nelli in unison.

"Never mind. Let's just shake. Simmer down, bro! I wasn't about to eat any fingers of yours, I swear."

Pouch stopped swinging and looked at Tobbi's hand for a second. "Okay," he said, "it's six on one and half a dozen on the other hand. All fingers are accounted for. Shake!"

After their elaborate handshake Pouch demanded a hug too. Tobbi rolled his eyes but went through it; anything to end this. "So what did Michelangelo want with me."

"Oh, he wanted you to get a couple of runaways he liked."

"Which ones?"

"Those big ones," Pouch pointed at the very top of the ring wall. Tobbi got ready.

"Take me," Pouch asked.

"No," answered Tobbi, savoring his revenge. He took off under the wistful stares of his friends. *How do you like that,* he was thinking, *clouds that don't get enough flying time?* The incredible exhilaration of flying improved his mood quickly. He brought the two largest clouds down, feeling like a genie: an enormous celestial towing power in a teeny weenie package. Together they moved clouds into the caves where Michelangelo inspected the big wavy clouds, smacking his fat lips and mumbling excitedly. Then he personally moved the prides of the fleet, as he called them, to his side of the cave. Tobbi watched the cloudies work for a little while, and then went outside.

"So, how're things in there?" the Maker asked in a strange, horse whisper. He even looked wasted.

"I don't know. Looks busy."

"Good," Maker hissed.

"Hey, you don't look so good." Tobbi was suddenly concerned: the Maker's cheeks were thin and scraggly, showing the gray of the volcano walls behind. His eyes, giant and still richly black, seemed to be floating within a fog and there wasn't much steam coming up around him.

"Are you all right?" Tobbi asked again.

"Nothing that a little steam bath couldn't fix."

"So, go to it. Suck up!"

"I can't just yet, Tobbi."

"Why not?"

"I overdrew a bit, got to wait for heat to come up again."

"So, what now?"

"We wait."

"Patience is a virtue my mother says, usually when she strips the skin off me. But I wouldn't stake my life on it. There's got to be a way to fluff you up some." He looked at the Maker. The gigantic eyes were crossed hideously, focused on the monstrous nose. The nose wasn't well. Previously bulbous and intimidating, it now looked old and shriveled like a rotten cucumber. His eyes uncrossed and bored into Tobbi. The nearly lipless ghost of a mouth shaped one word, "Help!" Tobbi felt sick. With the Maker gone, the cloudies were doomed, as were his chances of getting back home. Besides, he developed warm and fuzzy feelings for the big head.

"Oh my!" he cried out, "you're a cloud, aren't you?"

The Maker grimaced; this wasn't the time for statements of the obvious.

"Of course you are! You must do what all the other clouds do. Eat!"

The mighty Cloud Maker was puzzled at first. Then a ghost of a smile formed on the ghost of a face. Tobbi took off like a rocket. He brought a big shapeless cloud back as quickly as he could and deposited it into the cavernous mouth. It appeared as a mere speck there but still caused a white band to shoot up into the Maker's forehead.

"It works!" shouted Tobbi and took off again. *This is for the birds,* he thought, as he fed the colossal Maker with big, heavy clouds that were but tiny morsels for him. Yet, even morsels make a meal when there are lots of them. There came a point when the Maker's eggplant-like nose inflated back to the size of a blimp. Then Tobbi had to gag on tasteless cloud as well to restore himself. It was all worth it. The Maker, still without steam, mouthed his gratitude to Tobbi. Now, that was especially good. Gratitude or else, he needed to be flung around by his steam blasts even less than a fart in a crosswind.

CHAPTER 23

Truth & Lies

For the first time since he got here Tobbi felt spent. He and the Cloud Maker stared at each other in silence. There was neither cloudie chatter nor hissing of steam, whistling of a wind nor thundering of Cloud Maker, and Tobbi had never enjoyed quiet this much. Of course, it didn't last long, a crowd of cloudies piled out of the caves. Chattering and giggling, they fanned out across the cloudring and broke the silence like a dusty old mirror. It wasn't long before Pouch and Nelli found him. Pouch, noticing Tobbi's somewhat transparent state, said, "I swear I've never seen a cloudie who wasted more steam by doing nothing than you, Tobbi."

"Oh, yeah! Trust me, doing nothing is hard. Find me something easier to do, won't you?" Tobbi grabbed his confused friends and took off, twisting and shouting with joy. Suddenly he felt good, happy to be alive, happy to be here, happy to have saved the day...again. His friends rejoiced with him, always ready for a good time. It ended as soon as Tobbi asked, "By the way, Pouch, is there anything to eat?"

Pouch curled his fingers. "Must you ask ME all the time? Didn't we exchange words about it before? Feeding you is risky, and I had learned through that delightful experience not to deny you food, ever. Where did it all go, anyway?"

"You know, dude, short answers to simple questions just isn't your thing. Do you fly for a living, Pouch?"

Pouch shook his head.

"Then how do you know how much stuff it takes to fly?"

Nelli finally intervened, "You guys are impossible," she said. "In all my time I've never seen two cloudtenders more at odds with each other then you two. Why do you even float together? You can't get along, so why bother?"

Tobbi and Pouch stared at Nelli like she was a bad TV commercial.

"We're getting along fine," said Tobbi.

"Yeah, we're cool," echoed Pouch. "You just don't understand—"

"Oh, Yeah! I speak every language there is and YOU, I don't understand. As if!"

"It's not a speaking thing. Butt out!"

The look Nelli gave Tobbi would've frozen a fire pit. "Huh!" she snorted and turned away. Tobbi instantly regretted his words, but food was a priority.

"So, Pouch, how about it?"

"It ain't here, that's for sure. Go to the caves. There should be some leftovers there. It'll be stale and disgusting, but in your case, bon appetite!"

Tobbi flew there feeling sluggish and slow. He panicked when at first he didn't find anything inside the first cave. In a dark corner of the third cave, he saw a blot of color and, to his relief, found a couple of food clouds swaying under the ceiling like helium balloons. He grabbed one and gobbled it up in a hurry, barely noticing its bitter, dry, cracker-like taste. As his strength returned, he slowed down and tried to discern the mild flavors of the deteriorating meal. He caught a scent that vaguely reminded him of something from the past—some precious memory—something familiar, yet elusive. Perhaps it smelled like a little gravel-covered playground behind a decaying yellow church, where he played with his grouchy but loving grandfather when he was four or five years old. He missed his grandpa and this memory felt so good that he ignored the taste and just relished it. So preoccupied was he that a hard working group of cloudies with a huge cloud in tow walloped him. Tobbi recovered and got run over by a second group pulling hard on another cloud; a third followed, then a fourth. Enough of that, he got out of the way and counted eight groups altogether. He followed, first making sure there weren't others. Something was up again.

In the daylight, the eight clouds turned into the magnificent skyships which Michelangelo had personally designed. In the lead was a large elongated cloud. Its many flat decks, like so many shelves, were adorned by scores of sail-like flaps. The whole thing looked like an old dried pinecone. Another cloud loomed like a tall sailing ship Tobbi once saw in the Marsh Harbor festival. Yet, another reminded Tobbi of an insect with a dozen yellowish wings. Near the end there was a beautiful ship that looked like a crimson flower with scooped petals arranged around the circular flower head. They were all awesome. The last ship, however, was very simple. It was a raft; something akin to what Huckleberry Finn and Jim must've traveled on—a big flat cloud with a single giant square sail rising in the middle. Tobbi loved that story and many times fantasized about drifting on that raft for days and weeks. *Maybe I'll get my chance yet*, he thought.

The ships slowly advanced toward the entrance canyon. It would take some time. Tobbi was too curious to wait, so he flew over to where he'd left his friends. Only Nelli was there. She sat with her round head resting on plump arms crossed over her bent legs. It looked weird. Her limbs just bent in an ark without any sharp angles, yet it looked graceful somehow. She was cute, Tobbi decided.

"Hey, Nelli, what's going on? What's with all these clouds?"

Nelli just turned away.

"Come on, tell me."

"No! I'm butting out, as I was told."

"That's a thing of the past, Nelli."

"I'll decide what's in my past and what's not, thank you very much."

"Look, Nelli, I was hungry. Sometimes a guy says dumb things when he's hungry. Just forget it."

"Forget!? How's that? Memory's our greatest trait. Everything we see and hear stays right here in the sky; forgetting isn't my thing."

"Gosh, all I do is apologizing here, and I can't find a way that works. Nelli, come on; don't make it hard for me. I'm sorry. We humans aren't as considerate as you clouds. We tend to abuse each other a lot."

"Well, you shouldn't—"

"Yeah, I'm learning, Okay? Nelli, how about it?"

"I suppose I could ignore your comments—"

"Yes, oh yes! Ignore! That's the word I was looking for. NOW can you tell me about those clouds?"

"I don't know—"

"That's it. I'm asking someone else."

Tobbi got ready to go.

"A race," Nelli said quickly.

"A what?"

"A race between the contenders."

"Whoa...how...?" Tobbi struggled. Competition between clouds was a hard concept to accept. "What for?"

"The contenders will run against each other. The fastest two crews will take the Journey and fight against the Evil Spoiler."

"How come I'm the last to know? Who decided that we needed two ships or whatever you call them?"

"Skybergs," Nelli said.

"Yeah, whatever! Who said we needed them at all? I mean, if I have to go and fight that Evil guy, shouldn't I know what's going on?"

"I took the liberty to arrange everything with Master Michelangelo, Tobbi." The size of this argument took the fight right out of Tobbi.

"Somebody could've told me."

"Somebody just did. See, Tobbi, you're just a visitor here. Even though you can fly as you wish, which none of us can do, you still don't know the nature of things in Cloudland; its dangers and its traditions. This competition will show us who is ready to take the Journey. You and I will choose the crews at the end."

"Are you telling me I can't be in it?"

"It wouldn't be wise, Tobbi. Things happen sometimes and you can't interfere. This is a true test of a cloudtender's skill and determination. We'll have to go on without you some day."

"Wise! Who's wise? I won't interfere. I promise. I want in."

"Well, Okay. If you just observe and do nothing, you may stay on the skyberg of your choice."

"All right! A race!" exclaimed Tobbi. He didn't notice the somber glance that the Maker threw at him. Tobbi turned to Nelli and said, "Let's go, I'll take you to the starting line. You can watch from there. Man, this sounds like fun, a race, cool!"

Nelli round face remained passionless. "I'm not going to be watching, Tobbi," she said.

"Why not?"

"Because I'll be racing. I'm ready for the Journey."

"Oh! But...but isn't it dangerous?"

"Yes."

"But I don't want you to get hurt. You don't have to go."

"I must. You're my friend and I'll be with you in your fight...our fight; win or lose." Nelli's big, luminous, round eyes peered into Tobbi's. He shivered. There was strength, concern, and admiration there. He found nothing to say; instead he hugged her tightly thinking that he'd protect her at least, if he couldn't prevent her from going.

Nelli looked up at Tobbi with a puzzled expression on her face.

"What!? My armpits smell?" he asked.

"Huh! You really know how to make someone feel special!"

"Sorry, but why are you looking at me like this?"

"You hugged me."

"So?"

"You said that hugging is for Pouch, a guy thing—remember; I mean, and for me is—"

"Oh, for heaven's sake, Nelli...not again...I lied. I can hug anyone I wish."

"Lied! I know the word, I think, but doesn't it mean not telling things as they are?"

"Yes, so?"

"But why?"

"Sometimes you have to."

"No, I don't. Why?"

"Man! Are you telling me you've never told a lie?"

"Never."

"Not even a little teeny weenie one?"

"No."

"That's bull."

"What does the animal have to do with anything?"

Tobbi threw an exasperated look at Nelli and gave up. What choice did he have?

"Nothing," Tobbi responded, "It's just an expression," and handed her another lie. "It means that's great." What possible harm was in it? It's not like there would be a cloudie-human cultural summit any time soon.

"Oh, okay."

"Nelli, do me a favor, don't tell anyone about the hugging thing."

"Why? It's so nice."

"Because I'd have to do it with everybody!"

"That's nice."

"No! It's not nice! It's awful! I'd die. I don't want to...anyway please don't."

A horrified expression came onto the cute face. "You mean, you want me to lie?!"

"No! Not lie. Just don't say anything."

"But that's a lie!"

"Look here, if you tell, I would have to kiss everyone, too."

A girl's a girl anywhere you go. Nelli was impressed. An uncommon resolve took hold of her face.

"You mean, if I don't tell—a kiss is just for me?"

"You've got it, babe!"

"Do it!" Nelli ordered.

"What?" asked Tobbi, fearing the worst.

"A kiss! Right now!"

"Just shoot me!"

"No! A kiss would do."

Tobbi was pinned down, left without escape, trampled by an overwhelming force. He walked over and performed the ordeal with the eyes shut tightly. Secretly, almost deniably so, he enjoyed it. Nelli, on the other hand, was enjoying herself openly.

"I like this more than a hug."

"Is that so?"

"It's a deal. I'll not say anything, but you kiss no one else."

"You mean you are going to lie?"

"No! I just won't say anything."

"Ahhhhh," Tobbi exhaled not pressing his luck further. A vision of hundreds of cloudies lining up for a hug or, even worse, a kiss was the ultimate nightmare. One has got to take one's losses and move on.

"Satisfied?" he asked.

"Oh...yeah," sighed Nelli, "more later. But now let's go. The skybergs are ready."

Tobbi shrugged, not even entertaining the thought that she'd forget.

142

CHAPTER 24

The Race

Tobbi flew very, very fast giving Nelli enough thrill to take her mind off the previous line of thought. It worked. When they landed Nelli bubbled with joy.

Pouch jumped them as soon as they landed, "Where have you two been? Everyone's ready."

A light flared in Nelli's eyes. Tobbi cringed.

"Tobbi gave me a ride," said Nelli. She didn't even blink. Tobbi exhaled. Quite suspicious, Pouch squinted with his left eye and bent his right leg. Then he shifted to his right eye and left leg. To no avail, his friends patiently waited for him to come out of his detective mode.

"Let's go. We're ready to call winds," he finally said.

"Some kind of group farting exercise?" asked Tobbi.

This earned him blank stares from both cloudies.

"Never mind. Let's go call winds, or whatever!"

They walked over to the cloudies that were separated into two groups, one at each vertical edge of the canyon. Entertainment was provided by the ever harmonious Spanish Quartet. They listened for only a short time when the mighty voice of the Cloud Maker demanded their undivided attention.

"Hear ye, hear ye, hear ye the gathered sky dwellers:
Venture forth with the united voice.
Make your song of the wisdom flow.
Hail the wind that roams the void
May it become a friend not a foe."

The cloudies snapped to attention. As one, they all turned and faced the open sky. Tobbi's questions remained

143

ignored. Obviously, some kind of ritual took hold of the cloudies as they began to chant:

> *"The south wind our mighty companion*
> *Leave your reckless ways behind.*
> *Swoop down like a mighty stallion*
> *Spur our ships on; may the fastest we find.*
> *Free and abundant in the endless sky*
> *Enter our land in the circle of mountains.*
> *Then those that are ready will be able to fly,*
> *And seek their wisdom with your mighty alliance.*
> *Journey...Journey...Journey!"* Then silence.

The low chanting followed: *"Who's ready...who's ready...who's ready—?"*

"I am!" a shrill voice pierced the chant. A cloudie, far bigger than his voice, stepped forward.

"I accept," the Cloud Maker announced.

"Hail! Goliath," cheered the group from which Goliath came out, while the other group continued with the chant.

"I am!" came another yell, and Panda stepped out—a cute bear of a cloudie with dark and light patches running down the length of his body. He got accepted also. Many more cloudies volunteered: Ding and Dong, good old Captain Silver, Buttons, Nelli and Pouch, even Smudge, and all were accepted. Finally it seemed that everyone who wanted to go had spoken. "Cloudies," started the Maker. But a shrill voice interfered, "We are...we are ready, too."

"What now?" bellowed the Maker.

At the far edge of the split a commotion started. In confusion cloudies jumped back and forth trying to let some cloudies through. It was messy but at last the confusion had an explanation: Stumble and Fumble. A collective sigh swept over the crowd.

"Oh, you," said the Maker.

A cloudie next to Tobbi said, "For the third time they try. If not accepted, that's it."

"Now, you two, why do you come forth again?" asked the Maker. "You can hardly walk on the level cloud. How's it going to be in the skies unknown? We've been through this before. You can't go."

Stumble deflated. Fumble, however, stuck his chest out, puffed it up with air and yelled, "We can do it! We must go! It's our right." Stumble perked up, but the Maker looked dubious and, frankly, so did everyone else. Yet, Tobbi saw what everyone was missing: against the overwhelming opposition they were defiant. That took courage. Tobbi pushed his way through the hushed crowd.

"Excuse me, Your Honor."

His attempt at sarcasm was totally wasted. "But how do you know that they can't do it?"

The Maker looked down and his eyebrows gathered. Red flecks began to dance in the dark eyes. He wasn't used to being opposed.

"Stay out of this, Tobbi. You still aren't familiar with the cloudie's ways. Your input isn't requested."

Considering the matter closed, the Maker looked at the pair. But Tobbi had no intention of quitting, yet. The eyes of the rejected cloudies were on him asking for help.

"Excuse me but—" started Tobbi only to be blasted by a roar of now really angry Cloud Maker. "I said no interference." The big guy was pretty scary: steam exploding, eyes flaming with red. Yet, Tobbi stood his ground. "Well, I disagree," said he.

The cloudies moaned and collectively grayed out. Someone close to Tobbi whispered "Oh—oh, duck!" The Cloud Maker was stunned for a second and then released a mountain shaking, cloud shattering roar, "What?"

Anyone standing went flying. Tobbi, who heeded a cloudie's warning, got up from his sprawled position and continued as if nothing had happened, although inside he

145

was quite shaken; he was dealing with one powerful dude here.

"You know if I hadn't interfered a couple of times before, some cloud boys we both know and love wouldn't be around now."

The Cloud Maker who had gathered another steam-head to better blast the insolent, choked on it instead. He coughed out several enormous, shapeless clouds and with them his anger. The cloudies looked at Tobbi with new respect.

"Speak," said the more civil Maker of Clouds.

"You know, the dudes want to see the world. Yeah, they're sort of skewed, so what? They aren't like the rest, that's all. Maybe they can do what the others can't. How would they know unless they try? When I got sick back on earth...I mean below, I...like, sat in this chair with wheels and, sort of, became like them—couldn't move all that well. But, man, sometimes I could do things: I kind of gave rides to the ladies of my choice sometimes...ah! You wouldn't understand but were my friends jealous when I got these girls.... That was so cool...hm...hmm.... Anyway, sometimes I could ride downhill and do other tricks. So you see? You've got to give the awkward homeboys a chance. Otherwise what are they left with? Shame, that's all. No way to plow these clouds, man. See what I mean?"

"No, but the presentation's interesting." The Cloud Maker looked uncertain, but he was thinking.

"I'll be there. I'll watch over them," added Tobbi. For the next minute the Cloud Maker kept looking back and forth between Tobbi and the pair, and finally said the only thing he could, "You win."

Cloudies roared. Stumble and Fumble looked around and their eyes were full of pride and happiness. They wanted to join the group of volunteers immediately. Try hard they did, and only stumbled once on the way. They paused near Tobbi and thanked him quietly but with such warmth that Tobbi turned transparent in patches.

The Cloud Maker smiled when he said, "We'd have to skip the rest of the ceremony. We've wasted too much time. Man your skybergs before it starts."

Cloudies took off, scuffling their big feet in a hurry, which was funny enough to watch.

"What now? What's going to start?" Tobbi got exactly zero answers because everyone was rushing so. Even Stumble and Fumble were shuffling in hyper speed, using each other for support. Then he noticed that the non-competing cloudies were concealing themselves behind walls on both sides of the split. Suddenly Tobbi felt the urge to hide too. He turned and bumped into Pouch.

"What are you standing around for?" asked Pouch. "Think you're invincible? Think again, bozo. It's coming, follow me, fast."

"What's coming! Why can't I get one answer here?"

"There's no time, Tobbi. We've got to get to our 'berg and get ready. Then you'll find out; believe me, better there than here."

"Mystery! Always a mystery. You're all nuts. Which 'berg is ours?"

"The big flat one."

"All right! Let's go then. Talk, talk, talk is all you do."

"Wha...?" Pouch yelped as Tobbi grabbed him and flew to his skyberg. Once there, he waved to Nelli, winked at Captain Silver, nodded at Buttons and elbowed Pouch in his side, feeling giddy. All were working but him. He expected fun. A race ought to be fun, yet cloudies were way too serious for that. Nobody returned his greetings except Pouch, who nailed him back with a right cross to the stomach.

"It didn't hurt," exhaled Tobbi.

"Too bad. Stop clowning and get tethered."

"Teeth!? What?" Tobbi agonized, then noticed how each cloudie grabbed the edge of the big sail and began to pull it back. The folds of the sail began to elongate into cables; as cloudies stepped back they stretched longer and thinner. The further back the cloudie was the higher portion of the sail he controlled. The sail began to look more like a parachute. Each cloudie chose the place and buried his big feet into the deck crouching low and waiting. Tobbi finally accepted that something extraordinary may, indeed, be happening. His problem was that the concept of ordinary got stretched to such enormous proportions that a very idea of extraordinary was a zany thing. He chuckled: didn't they look silly pulling hard on a still sail. Pouch backed into the spot next to Tobbi, yanking on a particularly thick cloud-cable.

"Listen," he puffed, "you don't have to steer, but grab onto something."

"I thought you'd never ask. I'll play. Where's the horsy? You guys are really paranoid. It can't be that—" and then he felt it. The big skyberg lurched as a squall hit them. Tobbi fought hard to keep from bouncing off his feet. "Crunchy butt crack," he exclaimed, a bit shaken. Then he smiled at Pouch. "See, it was noth...ing...." He noticed fear in Pouch's eyes; they grew impossibly big staring at something behind Tobbi. Tobbi turned and ducked on reflex. A dark force was invading; a whole enormous mass of air inside the mountain well was seized and crushed by this livid wind. Its wild head squeezed through the narrow canyon and pushed in madly.

"Oh! Boy!" Tobbi whimpered and dropped right to the deck, burying his fingers, his toes, his nose and any other available part into the cloud deck. And then it was upon them—a wind—a hurricane of wind. It rolled over the skyberg as if it were a massive tidal wave, whistling and moaning like death itself. It plucked the gigantic skyberg like a dry leaf, and carelessly flung it forward. Tobbi heard screaming and lifted his head, fearing that this simple act would fling him into vortex like a mote of dust. He saw that Pouch, Nelli and Captain Silver were slipping forward in one group. Another few seconds and they would be taken by the wind, lost forever. Somebody had to do something, except there was no one, only himself. Tobbi crawled toward Pouch, who fought bravely but was loosing ground. Tobbi pushed against the insane force of the wind and grabbed onto the cable, he got up, barely holding his own. Now he knew the advantage of the big cloudie feet—superb anchors. For whatever it was worth, he added his strength to his friend's. The slippage slowed, but it wasn't enough. All would be lost. Even he couldn't fly against wind like this. Tobbi looked across the skyberg and saw with disbelief as Stumble nodded and buried his enormous feet deeper into the deck, while Fumble let go of the rope.

"Noooooo!" Tobbi screamed. Nobody heard him in the wild roar of the wind. Fumble's long toes and fingers clutched at the cloud as he half walked and half crawled across the wide deck of the skyberg. This was an incredibly courageous thing to do, as Tobbi found out later nobody had ever done it. The pair's great feet turned out to be a tremendous asset. At last he made it across. Grabbing onto Nelli's cables, Fumble buried his fabulous feet and held them like an immovable anchor. They conquered the sail and the enormous skyberg accelerated. As it picked up speed, the force of the wind lessened. The sail filled out like a pregnant whale's belly and suddenly it was thrilling, marvelously exciting, and fun.

"Yahooo!" Tobbi screamed, and for the first time saw smiles on his friends' and shipmates' faces. It was time to run a race. "Remind me not to ignore your warnings, ever again," Tobbi yelled into Pouch's ear. Pouch nodded and pointed to their left. Tobbi gasped in awe. In a long line, stretched across the entire volume of the Cloudland, the eight magnificent, pastel colored ships were flying all out. Their inflated sails projected grape-like, lobular shadows which flickered and jumped over the rough mountain wall protrusions—the vivid indication of their neck-breaking speed. Multi-winged insect and flower-like ship pulled ahead. The cigar-shaped 'berg ran third, and their raft—fourth.

There was a lot of skill needed in steering here. The winds bounced off the walls, creating sheers and whirlwinds that either slowed you down or spurred you on. Under the expert directions from Captain Silver, the right and left side either pulled or released their cables, turning the sail into the fastest wind. For Tobbi's crew the biggest danger was in the beginning, since their sail was exceptionally large. Once they took control of it, however, their speed increased rapidly and they began to catch up. They neared the Maker in the middle of the course. The Cloud Maker had acquired the shape of a sock being sucked up into a vacuum cleaner. He didn't look all that comfortable. Tobbi was far from comfortable himself and, therefore, not very sympathetic. He had received a sharp blow in his side from Pouch, a reminder that he was supposed to pull, not ogle. Only minutes remained and the flower 'berg was winning. Either its sails and the skill of the crew were superior, or they were simply lucky—who knew?

The insect, the cigar, and their raft were in the fight for the all important second place and they were in dead heat. Tobbi desperately looked for something...anything. Then ahead and above he saw a stone outcropping extending out of the ring wall. It curved down forming a natural channel. The cloud-laden wind rushed into its wide opening, accelerated through the narrowing channel and shot from the smaller exit as if from the muzzle of a gun.

"Captain Silver—starboard...look up!" Tobbi yelled. Silver glanced up and back with a big question mark on his face. Tobbi let go with one hand and indicated what he wanted to do. Captain Silver understood, but hesitated. Pouch yelled, "We're losing. Let's do it! It may work."

"Yeah! Do it," Fumble yelled grinning like mad. He was having the time of his life, moving remarkably fast without taking a single step, what was there to worry about? "Rear, pull!" ordered Silver. The top of the sail tilted and like a stubborn horse the skyberg reared up. It quivered, held as if deciding whether it had enough, and bolted up like the obedient ship it was. *What a rush!* Tobbi thought. They nearly flew out of the well, but took control and dived into the pipe's outflow. The sailors from the other skybergs observed this wild move and thought that it was over for *The Raft* since it seemed to fall behind. The leaders on *The Flower* were all smiles. Screaming wildly, Silver's crew plunged into the accelerating air stream and nearly lived through the start of the race again when the wind smashed at them with the force of an explosion. It strained to tare the ropes from their tired fingers; Tobbi held on by sheer will only, wishing he had six fingers, like everybody else. *The Raft* jumped forth like a mad bull shedding cloud scraps from all sides. In the very last seconds of the race it sped past everyone, reached the far wall first, leaving the other crews with their mouths open. At the end all cables were released. The sails tore off. The irresistible wind met the immovable wall. In frustration it veered up and escaped the mountain well bringing along a trophy: a horde of ripped cloud-sails that continued their rivalry in the sky like a flock of young birds in the wake of a dying gale.

CHAPTER 25

A Tribute to the Heroes

All competitors were stunned into silence, but it didn't last long. A faint cheering reached them from the other side of the cloudring. That's all it took to ignite the crews; they swarmed onto the raft, like an army of ants, and found its crew sprawled on the deck in exhausted disbelief. The cloudies stopped and looked from one rafter to another. Buttons pointed and the worked-up cloudies descended onto the horror-struck Tobbi, who expected to be turned into a mashed cloudie by their fabulous elephant-size feet. Instead, he was hoisted up and shaken with a loving abundance. The Cloud Maker laughed thunderously, rejoicing at, among other things, the return to his own comfortable shape. Tobbi's protests were either not heard or totally ignored. Resigned to the fate of an ice cube in a cocktail shaker, he suddenly was enlightened by an idea. "Speech!" he shouted. Predictably, within a minute everyone chanted: "Speech, speech, speech." Tobbi was released. Cloudies gathered around quiet, but not calm. Their feet tapped the deck, their hands twitched, and the energy was gathered for the next outburst. All Tobbi had to do was redirect it.

"Amigos," he started and winced at the flurry of Spanish that came back. Mistake! "Sky dudes!" he restarted. "Well before our lucky finish, we were in trouble." He ignored the objections of his shipmates. "The wind was too strong. We were loosing ground, about to be flung into the wind. But wow! A cool thing happened! Two awesome dudes came to our rescue, our two brave shipmates. One held on like a rock, the other crawled across *The Raft*, in that murderous wind, and anchored us. It took real guts to do that. They are the real heroes. These cloudboys are sure special and they have what it takes!"

"What...what do they have....tell us." Cloudies took the bait.

Tobbi waited a calculated second or two and said, "Shipmates! I give you...Stumble and Fumble and their fabulous feet!"

The crowd gasped, then over their half-hearted protests Stumble and Fumble were picked up and tossed around. Their feet were greatly admired. In short, they enjoyed all the attention while Tobbi relished in the lack of it. He sneaked over the edge of the raft and sat down.

"Slickly done," a voice came from above. Tobbi jerked, expecting a crowd to fall on him. Instead a pair of slender (by cloudie standards) feet smacked onto the cloudring, followed by the rest of the body. Nelli sat next to Tobbi.

"Oh! You!" he exhaled.

"Yeap, just me. You've gotten rid of everybody else, quite inventively."

"What, you don't think they deserve the praise?"

"Of course they do, they did a very brave thing and frankly no one else could've done it. But they are with us because of you. We've won the race because of you, and...and—" Nelli looked at him with such admiration in her gleaming eyes that Tobbi suddenly wanted to hide. "And you were the first one to help us. We wouldn't have lasted otherwise. So, thank you, Tobbi."

"Oh! It's nothing. Forget it." Tobbi mumbled examining his toes.

"Sure I'll forget. Sure thing. Nothing to it!" Nelli said. Tobbi chuckled. Obviously the expression had no practical use in Cloudland.

"Anyway," continued Nelli, "the thank you is from the crew, but this is from me."

"Wha—" started Tobbi, but the monster he'd created landed a clumsy kiss on his lips. Embarrassment came in a transparent band that slid from the top of his head to the bottom of his feet. Nelli giggled, thoroughly enjoying the effect her little stunt produced. But the worst thing was that Tobbi couldn't muster an ounce of anger toward her.

"Don't do that," was all he said.

"Why?"

"Others will see."

"So?"

"It's a secret. You know what'd happen if everyone knew."

Nelli nodded. Tobbi did, indeed, create a new kind of cloudie here; he also dug himself a hole. Her secret would stay a secret only as long as she could exercise her privilege in private. There had to be a way out of this. Tobbi fidgeted because Nelli was gearing up again. The Cloud Maker called his troops back and the cloudies spilled over the edge of the raft. Regret clouded Nelli's eyes when Tobbi slipped into their midst.

The rest of the day was a blur of celebrations, feasts, story telling and more feasts. Lead by the inexhaustible Spanish Quartet cloudies also danced until sunset put a stop to it all.

CHAPTER 26

Broken Glowhearts

For once Tobbi was first to pop up. Peace and tranquility reigned over Cloudland but for the undulating rumbling that came from the sleeping Cloud Maker. Tobbi chuckled: this snore could wake up a city. The sun peeked over the rim of the mountains painting a yellow half-circle on the dark cloudring. As if curious, this brilliant spy lifted its eye further over the wall. The yellow part grew and soon the entire cloudring ignited in gold. Tobbi laughed. It felt good to be alone in the midst of such richness and beauty.

Next to Tobbi the cloudring exploded as Pouch popped out grumbling, "What...what's happened? What was that?"

"Simmer down, Pouch; I was just laughing," Tobbi sighed. Solitude was in very short supply here.

"Who at?"

"Nobody"

"What at?"

"Nothing."

"Are you sick?"

"No, why?"

"Why else you'd be laughing at nothing and nobody?"

"Go back to sleep, Pouch."

"Buh! He's the one laughing at nothing and nobody, and he tells me off. You should see a stinck."

"What's a stinck?"

"Isn't that what you earthlings call a head doctor, although I don't understand how they get inside your heads? Aren't they hard, like stones?"

"Man, are you thick or what? First, it's a shrink not a stinck. Second, they don't get inside the head literally; they talk to you and rearrange things inside, that's all."

"Wow! Powerful stuff! I don't think I'd want my head rearranged. Why'd you ask if I was thick? Do I look hungry to you?"

"What is this, morning of a thousand questions? Look how beautiful everything is."

Pouch opened his mouth. Tobbi gave him a stare. Pouch choked on it. Suddenly cloudies began to pop out like mad, instantly filling the cloudring with chatter. Everyone looked transparent. The guilty Cloud Maker, who had also overslept, puffed out some clouds that were easily caught and transported to Michelangelo for flavoring, who also saved a couple to start the repairs on the winning skybergs. Then everyone quietly ate. Tobbi was puzzled by all the hush-hush but didn't ask any questions recalling previous frustrating experiences.

"Friends," said the Cloud Maker as soon as everyone had finished, "there comes a moment in every cloudtender's life when he's called to search—a search for the meaning of one's existence—a search for wisdom, maturity if you will. A cloudtender has to see with his own eyes the vastness of our world, its divergence and its harmony. Happiness is a place where we truly belong, where everyone can be himself. One simply has to find it. So, Cloudtenders, go seeking. Take your Journey. Into the vast blue yonder you go naive and fresh, but come back to us as teachers. This quest isn't easy. Danger awaits you but as cloudtenders you will persevere. You will find the Evil Spoiler who threatens everything we love. With the help of our new resident flying ace—the brave Tobbi—you will win."

Tobbi cringed, but bowed when cheered. The Cloud Maker winked and thundered on, "Know this, cloudtenders, no matter how hard things are, or how long you're away we'll be waiting for you. So, go forth the chosen ones! Long live the Journey!"

Everyone chanted: "Journey, Journey, Journey."

All chosen voyagers walked in pairs toward the portion of

the wall directly to the side of the Cloud Maker. The rest followed at a respectful distance. Of course, the whole party was led by the appropriately pompous Spanish Quartet. Walking next to his friends, Tobbi asked, "How did you guys ever manage this before I named the four big mouths."

"Very, very quietly," Pouch answered. It took a while but the procession reached the wall. They went around a massive, weathered, vertical ridge and stopped. There was a long horizontal gash in the smooth, black, and shiny granite wall. It seemed strangely alive and moving under a silky sheath of water that slithered from above like a broad shimmering snake. Through many cracks water seeped inside and fell to the bottom of the gash in rows of fat slow drops.

The group of travelers turned with their backs to the wall and faced the staying home crowd. Somebody pushed Tobbi in the back so he stumbled forward, joining the travelers. Tobbi was too curious to protest, besides he found himself nose to spongy nose with Captain Silver, who crossed his eyes in a surprise. Tobbi shrugged and turned around.

"Who are the ones with the curious minds?" asked the home group.

"We are," answered the travelers.

"Who are the ones that are staying behind?" asked the voyagers.

"We are," answered the home group. They continued together.

"Let's unite for the very last time
Letting a friend go is terribly hard
But the Journey calls and I'll not be crying
'Cause through all the adventures that'll hold us apart
Home's a place that will always be mine.
I see wide planes to cross and skybergs to climb.
As I'm ready for the Journey to start
A small but important part of me I'm leaving behind
In waters of Cloudland a half of my glowheart

Stays and grows till a way home I shall find."

Each departing cloudtender suddenly acquired two companions. The ones in front placed their hands on chests of their departing friends, the others supported them from behind. Tobbi, so intent on observing, didn't realize that a hand was touching his chest also. He jumped aside. It's a good thing he did because at the nod from each traveler the companion's hand penetrated the chest. Tobbi flinched in horror; his head snapped to the front to find a hand reaching for his chest again. Tobbi flung himself back, knocking over the cloudie behind him. He shook his head and stuttered, "N...o, nnnn...o freaking way—" Tobbi's companion, a thin flat cloudie appropriately named Slice, stopped, looking lost. Meanwhile, all hands withdrew, each holding a warmly glowing object. Tobbi was beside himself. He learned to trust these creatures, but now his faith was tested to the limit. The change in the cloudies who had lost their glowhearts was gruesome. They became mere statues, robots without life, cotton dolls and he panicked when he saw Nelli and Pouch in the same listless condition.

"What're you all doing? Put them back this minute. Put it back, I said!"

Completely ignored and about to do something drastic, he was stopped by the Cloud Maker. "Tobbi," the big head hissed, "don't worry. Everyone's going to be fine. Don't interfere."

Tobbi objected, "I wish for once that I was warned ahead of time so I wouldn't feel stupid and scared. Is it too much to ask?"

Ignored again, Tobbi stumped his foot and continued to observe, but out of the corner of his eye he noticed Slice inching in his direction. He pointed a finger at him. "You stay away from me! You're not pulling anything out of MY chest!" Slice lost his nerve and just stood there.

The Cloud Maker said, "It's okay, Slice. Tobbi's home

isn't here. His heart belongs somewhere else. Let him be."

"Yeah! Let him be!" echoed Tobbi.

Meanwhile, each Glowheart was broken in two. One half was placed into the crack, so that it received a steady drip from above, the other half was placed back inside the chest of its owner who instantly gained life. All cheered. The Cloud Maker bellowed, "Let the Journey commence!"

CHAPTER 27

Departure

In a big messy crowd cloudies moved toward the exit from Cloudland. The departing cloudies were getting all the attention. The buzz of conversations filled the air. Tobbi pushed his way through the tangle until he found his friends. "Tobbi!" exclaimed Pouch and hugged his friend. "Tobbi!" cried out Nelli and repeated the hug. They both seemed drunk with energy. "Wow! Guys," said Tobbi, "I'd no idea you had these things inside of you."

"Things, shmings!" Pouch bristled "I had no idea you had no ideas. It's a Glowheart, not a thing and it makes us who we are."

"I thought I was going to pass out when they pulled them out. What was that about?"

"Are you thick or what?" retaliated Pouch. Tobbi swallowed this one: if you can dish it out you'd better know how to take it—a universal survival principle. But he got riled.

"I see your point, smokebreath. Now explain."

"No way, stonehead. Ask nicely."

"Not on your life, puffbrain!" Pouch and Tobbi faced each other nose to nose like sea lions at play. Nelli forced herself between the opposing noses. "Not again you, hormone freaks!"

Nelli gloated at their bewildered expressions.

"I think it's safer for me to explain, Tobbi," she said. "We cloudtenders don't have little ones to continue the line like you turf pushers do. Instead, when we depart on dangerous tasks, we leave half of our glowhearts behind. While we're away our hearts grow back to full size. If we return we get the full glowheart back, if we don't a new cloudtender gets our glowheart and we continue this way. See?"

160

Tobbi nodded, thinking of how cool this was. The crowd moved to the edge of the cloudring. It's time to go. "Now what?" asked Tobbi, "You don't expect me to tow everyone, do you?"

"Not quite," Nelli replied.

"But how—?"

"Here they come," somebody said. Tobbi twisted around, nearly unscrewing himself at the waist. The two skybergs, *The Raft* and *The Flowerhead*, arrived, towed by Michelangelo's repair crew. They looked magnificent and new, all sails gleaming crimson now. The crews started lining up along the sides of their respective 'bergs. Tobbi looked on proudly at his shipmates. He suddenly felt like he belonged. For the first time, he looked ahead with hope. They'd find and take care of this Evil guy. Impossible-to-ignore coughing rattled everyone. The Cloud Maker spurted out a couple of monstrous cloudballs, clearing his throat.

"Friends, let's say goodbye to our brave voyagers. They go into the great unknown to find and defeat the monster that threatens us all—the Evil Spoiler. Let our sky once again be free of evil. So go, cloudtenders, and remember your glowhearts are with us. You'll never be lost."

Tobbi shivered. He didn't have that safety net. Captain Silver bellowed, "Ahoy, Cloudtenders!" Everyone boarded.

Tobbi turned to follow but paused and said, "Wait a second." Everyone instantly froze. "Ssstop reacting like this," Tobbi stuttered. "Mad weird, all of you! Where are we going to find this Evil guy? That's all I wanted to ask."

"I was coming to that. Let them have it," said the Maker.

"Let us have what?" Tobbi asked suspiciously.

"Your navigation system, of course." A square cloudie (Rubex Cube, Tobbi remembered) brought in a white, nearly transparent globe.

"This device contains a piece of a contaminated cloud matter. It's hard to get, so take care of it. As you know evil attracts evil, so that little piece of...hmm...it will always point in the direction of the greatest concentration of evil and up here that would be the Evil Spoiler's lair. That's how you'll find him." Now Tobbi noticed the gray blob stuck to the inside wall of the larger white globe. He carefully took the globe from Rubex's hands and turned it. As if by magic the dark ball shook and then rolled around the perimeter of the white globe to point in the same direction it had before. Tobbi laughed. "This is so neat—the detector of evil. Man, can I take one of these home?" Now everyone laughed.

"So," said Tobbi, "all we do is follow the little dirt ball around the earth. So simple, yes? Let's go right, then left, a little up—no problem, just start your engines."

Captain Silver spoke. "Tobbi, you just leave the steering to us, okay?" Tobbi looked into the Captain's calm eyes and nodded. "Let's go!" shouted Silver. The remaining cloudies got behind the skybergs and pushed. As regally as magnificent ships should, the skybergs moved out and up. Once above the ring of mountains they were pushed by the wind towards the huge, red sun that was already sinking into the horizon. The ships soon blended with the rich crimson painting that the sunset brushed onto the herds of sleepy clouds which were creeping sluggishly into the night.

CHAPTER 28

In Search of the Evil Spoiler

Glittering clouds darted crazily above him. They seemed artificial—man made blotches on a blue wall of heaven. Tobbi struggled to open his eyes and chase the heavy sleep from his mind. Slowly a sleepy fog cleared, and Tobbi saw that light patches, not clouds, were dancing across his face. The light bounced off many shiny airplane models that swayed underneath his ceiling and these agile light-spots whirled and waltzed on blue walls, coming together for brief, chancy meetings only to streak away the next second. A sharp thought cut through his mind like a razor blade: he was home, in his room! In his bed! The familiar, ordinary, solid world surrounded him. Oh, brother! Right below were his parents. He missed them terribly. How he wanted to see them and tell them about his remarkable experience. Nothing could replace this feeling of belonging, of being home with people who loved you. *It's a pity that you truly realize it only after you lose it.*

He flew up and right out his door, but not quite. His legs felt like lead, they were stretched unmoving under a white sheet. He couldn't fly! He couldn't even walk! The contrast to the unbelievable freedom he got used to in Cloudland was horrifying. He pushed with his hands and rolled off his bed, screaming in frustration. The floor rushed up into his face, then rushed again, and again.... Every time, as he was about to hit it, the floor dissolved and a new floor materialized below aiming to smash his face. Tobbi fell through endless floors and screamed. His eyes tore open. A blinding light hit him as good as a solid uppercut. He was drifting in the blue and boundless sky, all alone. Panic tightened his chest. Wasn't he just home or was that a dream? Is this real? He

163

Ilya Simakovsky

was frightened and to his surprise a little...relieved!? He still could fly. Where were the skybergs...his friends? He remembered turning in for the night soon after leaving Cloudland. He must've drifted off *The Raft* somehow. What to do!? What to do? He had to search for his friends. Let's see: we flew out of the Circle of Mountains and to the right of the sunset. The wind seemed steady. So, assuming that it held true overnight, he would search due West, Northwest. He looked at the endless expanse of clouds and nearly freaked. How does one find an ice cube among hundreds of other ice cubes, a twig of straw in a straw pile, or a particular cloud among thousands? He was lost. But worse than that, his friends had little chance without him. He must find them. So determined, Tobbi glanced at the rising sun—the East; his back to the sun—the West. He took off due Northwest. Flying a broad search pattern, he advanced forward. Many times he thought he saw the familiar forms of his skybergs only to be disappointed again and again. Yet, he refused to give up; too much was at stake.

The solid sheath of clouds broke. Below, the edge of a great land mass rolled into view. Funny how it seemed, that he hung still and it was the earth that rolled lazily under a hot sun like an enormous whale. The land extended as far as his eye could see. To his right, high mountains treaded through a white haze like bathers in a Turkish steam room. To the left, the blue-gray of the sea was all there was. Tobbi tried to remember his geography. From his home he flew south all the way. Considering the starting point on the east coast of the United States, and the fact that he flew over the water for a while before coming over land, the Cloudland was located in South America somewhere. Now he had to be flying along its western shores where Chile, Peru, and Ecuador were situated, Tobbi remembered. That would make the mountains on the right the Andes, and the endless ocean on the left, the Pacific. *Wow*! Tobbi thought, *I read so much about travelers and explorers of this continent and now I'm flying over the exotic lands. If only I could look around a bit. No! I need to find my friends first!* Yet, every now and then he threw curious glances on the landscape below.

He's searched for hours. In dark engulfing tides the desperation came and went. Resisting it became harder with every hour. For a couple of minutes now something has been bothering him, something tiny, trivial and easy to overlook. He stopped. What was it? Tobbi scanned around slowly. There! There, far away a strange cloud swayed in the sky above others; it slowly rotated as a model in a fashion show. Why did it attract his attention? Excitement surged within him. Could it be...?

The cloud turned. It looked just like...a hand; yes, yes a hand that seemed to wave at him. Was there a palm and fingers? Fingers! "Hooray!" Tobbi screamed and took off like a speeding bullet aiming right at the middle of the palm. He found his friends; or rather they had hailed him. See, the hand had five...FIVE fingers.

Faster than one could say "out of this world," Tobbi was upon the strange cloud, and sure enough, a cloud rope was attached to it. On its other end Tobbi's friends were jumping and cheering looking a lot like popping popcorn. Tobbi kinda felt like popping himself from the enormous relief he experienced. He stopped thinking, lest his friends would jump out of their cloudie skin, and rushed down to be immersed in warm hugs that ever-friendly Pouch managed to teach the whole crew. When his shipmates were satisfied he had to fly over to the other skyberg, where he was lavishly manhandled also. Eventually it came down to telling tales. Tobbi described his surprise and worry at waking up all alone in the sky and his desperate search, while the cloudies explained how at first they weren't concerned, thinking he was out for a morning stretch. In time, Nelli raised the alarm; something went wrong. Tobbi got lost somehow and they had to figure a way to help him find the skybergs.

"It was my idea. I made it up. My idea." Flat topped

Ilya Simakovsky

Buttons was doing knee bends and beaming an enormous smile. "I thought to myself," Buttons continued, "how'd he find us among all the clouds? We must make ourselves visible. We must make—"

"A beacon," butted in Goliath. "We decided to capture a cloud and shape it into something that'd catch your attention. We argued for a long time but—"

"But it's ME! Me, who came up with the hand idea," Pouch puffed up with pride. His rumbling, low tones amplified in the spacious stomach and easily wrestled the attention from Goliath. "I thought that a hand with five of those silly little fingers of yours would promise a certain success and here you are. Was I right or what?"

Everyone jumped in then, shouting that they'd all participated in Tobbi's rescue. Soon the inflamed argument raged on the raft while Tobbi was ignored as thoroughly as he'd been welcomed. Tempers flared, especially when the sailors from the other 'berg joined in, claiming that capturing the hand-cloud-in-a-raw earned them an important place in the rescue effort. The Raft cloudies instantly switched their personal rivalry to a rivalry between ships. There's no indication that anyone heard what anyone else was saying. Tobbi shook his head and smiled.

"I thought we'd lost you," Tobbi turned and blinked at two bright little suns burning in Nelli's gaze.

"You weren't the only one."

"I'm so glad you're back."

"You aren't the only one," he said, feeling kinda dumb, but glad, more than he cared to admit, to see Nelli. "Stop looking at me like that."

"Like what?"

"Like...like...I don't...I feel...I don't know. Just stop."

"I can't."

"Well, look at other clouds then; it's not as if there's a shortage."

"You're the cloud I like."

166

"Common, Nelli, a cloud is a cloud is a cloud. Tell you what! Instead of wasting energy quarreling lct's stop these kids from tearing themselves into pieces on my account."

"Okay, but who's quarreling?"

Tobbi winked at her. "Stop it!" he screamed. Nobody paid him any attention. That got him upset. "Let's go." Tobbi took off with Nelli squealing under his arm; still cloudies were too busy claiming the leading roll in his rescue to pay him any mind.

They flew to a group of clouds where they each grabbed a medium sized round one. When he explained what he intended to do Nelli's eyes lit up again but differently. Mischievous and playful she looked, and very attractive, one might add. Tobbi accelerated towards the 'bergs, aiming at the narrow gap between *The Raft* and *The Flower* where the arguments still raged on.

"How long can they go on like that?" he asked.

"I don't know," said Nelli, "with no Cloud Maker to stop them—till the world ends or they get hungry, whichever comes first."

"Oooo'K! Let's make it the end of the world then."

They flew really fast now. At a calculated moment Tobbi released his cloud and a second later Nelli launched hers. They stopped to watch.

"Strike one!" shouted Tobbi.

"Strike two!" echoed Nelli, banging her soft palms together joyfully.

The speeding clouds slammed into Raft first and next into *The Flower*. The screaming instantly died. Most of the cloudies got caught inside the cloud balls—spike balls now with the cloudies' hands and feet sticking out in all directions. Nelli hiccupped with laughter. Tobbi was delighted. Slowly at first, then more frantically the cloudies freed themselves, but did they look scrawny and guilty. Suppressing smile with difficulty, because Nelli snickered behind his back, Tobbi said loudly, "Well, then, let's eat, you look hun-

Ilya Simakovsky

gry." Nobody moved. "Yo, somebody, spice these up some." The long-bodied cloudie came to life and sprinkled some fla- vorings out of a stash provided by Michelangelo onto the torn cloud resting on *The Flower's* deck. Tobbi transported him to *The Raft* for more of the same. Still in silence, they ate. Finally, Buttons expressed what everybody was thinking. "Will you forgive us, Tobbi?"

"For what?"

"For, you know...ehh...well for...not paying attention and arguing about...you know...we were so happy you came back...well—." Buttons grinded to a halt.

Tobbi waited a wicked second or two then said, "No sweat. Everything's cool." They still looked weird; action was needed. He hailed the Captain, "Yo! Captain Silver! I think it's time to stop going wherever the winds blow. Look at the evil finder; the dirt's pointing that-a-way and we're drifting that-a-way. Could you do something about it, maybe?"

The finder pointed northeast, but the winds were blowing them northwest and unless cloudies invented a cloud-pow- ered engine, Tobbi just couldn't see how they'd ever reach their destination by more than a mere chance.

The captain walked to the edge of *The Raft*. He looked, he tasted the air, and he listened. *And the Oscar goes to....* Tobbi thought. In a few minutes the captain seemed to have found what he'd looked for. He turned and shouted, "Ahoy there! Man your sails."

Everyone jumped to it. All were happy to get busy and even Tobbi found a job; leaping out of everyone's way. Finally everyone was ready but Tobbi. He asked Pouch, "What do I do?"

"Nothing."

Tobbi really felt left out now. "Why should you have all the fun!?" he objected.

"Fun-shmun!" Pouch puffed, "This is work and we know how to do it."

"Knock yourself out then. I happen to love work; I could

168

watch it for hours. I'll fly a patrol to...you know...watch for trouble."

"I wouldn't do that if I were you bec—" Pouch was speaking into empty air.

Tobbi flew up and stationed himself above the giant sail observing Captain Silver's work. "Thirty degrees incline!" shouted the captain.

The ropes were pulled until all the sails were bent the same way.

The Raft and *The Flower* began climbing. Slowly they emerged out of the cloud layer. *Fascinating,* thought Tobbi following *The Raft* closely.

"Quarter turn to starboard!" ordered Silver. The cloudies on the left side took up more of their ropes, twisting the sails. *The Raft* shifted to the right, while *The Flower* turned its head like a giant sunflower in pursuit of the sun.

"I wonder why—" Tobbi said when, suddenly, his body acquired a mind of its own. His lower part continued to go forward while his upper part insisted on going right. "Whoa...!" he screamed. His body stretched at the waist like a chewed-up gum. It happened all too quickly, no time to think, just scream. Like a cork out of a bottle, his lower part finally popped up and chased after the rest of him, smacking into the upper part and sending Tobbi tumbling head over heels.

"I'm not a cartoon!" Tobbi screamed summing it all up.

Meanwhile, the skybergs made a rather abrupt but well prepared for turn. Tobbi returned to *The Raft* wearing a chagrin smile. Everyone seemed to be busy securing the 'berg after the turn, but he knew—he just knew they were hiding smiles on his behalf. One face was particularly annoying: Pouch's bulbous cheeks seemed a little fuller, his round eyes rounder; his large mouth with its thick sarcastically inflated lips, appeared more provoking than ever. Better now than later, decided Tobbi, and walked over. Pouch looked at him kinda strange and opened his big, fat mouth....

"I don't want to hear it!" exclaimed Tobbi.

Pouch breathed in and again Tobbi cut in, "I know I didn't listen! I should've stayed here but I didn't. So don't bother with pointing it out, okay?"

To Tobbi's dismay the pain-in-the-neck-stove-top-stuffing-stuffed lips wagged again and there wasn't a darn thing Tobbi could do about it!

"As I was saying: you don't look all that good."

"What?"

"What-campot! Check out your shoulder, that's what!"

Tobbi's head snapped over to his right.

"Nothing's wrong."

"Wrong-shmong, the other one, dummy!"

Slowly this time Tobbi looked left and his eyes tried to take over his face then: his shoulder and arm were twisted in a coil.

"Hhh...hhh...o...wuuuuu...wh...what hap...pened?" Tobbi whimpered. "Help me, please!?"

"Nice of you to ask." And Pouch screamed using all of his considerable air capacity, "Flight surgeon!!" His yell was picked up by several other throats until a faint response came from *The Flower,* "Ready!"

By this time everyone on *The Raft* had gathered around the wounded. Cloudies sympathized loudly but to Tobbi's relief nobody laughed. Smudge slunk his way in between legs; being small had its advantages, but not when gawking in the crowd.

"Oh, wow, first casualty, great!"

"Oh yeah!" Tobbi barked, "How would you like to be a second one, Smudge?" Smudge vanished back into the forest of legs. Nelli pushed her way through next. She sat, or rather gracefully folded her body next to his, easing Tobbi's irritation immediately.

"Oh, my," she sighed with worry, "How're you feeling?"

"Twisted, sister," answered Tobbi, embarrassed by the

acute need to see his mother just then.

Captain Silver hobbled in, pushing everyone aside. "What's this!? A cloudtender's injured and nobody's doing a thing." That got them moving all right, which meant a bunch of agitated cloudies running every which way. Before another cloudie got injured, Captain Silver yelled, "Stop! Stop, I say! Let's lash up the ships."

Sails were turned and 'bergs began a slow process of approaching each other. It was taking too long. Tobbi took off, but surprise, surprise; instead of going straight his body flung him sideways, right into the hard working cloudies, knocking them over. *The Raft's* giant sail flapped ruining the mating of two ships. Captain Silver hopped over, mad as hell. "What's wrong with you? Well of course...hmmm...sorry. Want to stay warped, then? I can't have a berserk cloud bouncing around my ship. Stay put."

"Your ship!?" fired back Tobbi, but Captain Silver was back at the helm directing the crew. "Boy, do I feel uncool," Tobbi said.

"It'll be fine as soon as Stitch gets here." Nelli said.

"What makes him so special?"

"He's a flight engineer, surgeon, and Michelangelo's understudy."

"Understudy!" exclaimed Tobbi, "Why's it my luck that I end up a laboratory rat again."

"Don't worry—Stitch's good."

"Yeah, who says?"

With a slight bump, the ships touched. Immediately the cloud ropes were stitched through both sides and, for the time being, the two 'bergs flew as one. A thin graceful cloudie came to Tobbi's side. "Oh, you," Tobbi exclaimed, remembering this cloudie for her thin graceful fingers, supple arms, and fluid, precise movements; his grandma used to move like this when she sewed and knitted. Had Tobbi known that he would be the subject of his nominee's attention, he would've named her Doctor Stitch or something. She (this was another cloudie that came across as undeniably feminine) started to bend over his maimed arm.

"Wait a second here," Tobbi said, "Let me ask you something."

"Ask" said Stitch, with the air of someone being annoyed by a fly.

"Where'd you learn your medical stuff?"

"Medical stuff—who?"

"Oh, boy," Tobbi whimpered, now thoroughly depressed. Stitch went to work. Tobbi tried to see but his view was obstructed by several cloudies—Stitch's assistants. He felt tugs, something akin to ache. Then something went missing and, indeed, for a second he saw what appeared to be his arm, his detached arm, in somebody's hands—a perfectly good reason to go bonkers. Tobbi wound up....

"Freaking out, huh?" Pouch placed his considerable bulk right over Tobbi, looking down with an all-knowing grin. Tobbi wouldn't be caught dead admitting fear to Pouch. So, he perked up and answered, "Me? Not even close. This is child's play. I've had worse." Inwardly he kept praying for this medical experiment to be over. It was. Pouch was disappointed; he'd almost gained the upper hand. Tobbi was allowed to see his arm. "Wow!" he exclaimed. There's no sign of damage, except for a slight discoloration at the shoulder. A few punches and swings proved that the arm worked fine. Tobbi took off and flew around his 'berg landing hard behind Stitch's back. Stitch jerked and hopped around.

"Thanks, Stitch," Tobbi said. "Everything works fine. You can be my doctor anytime,"

He then hugged Stitch sending her into nervous shakes and transparency.

"Get ready to park," Captain Silver ordered. Everyone perked up. Tobbi found himself next to Buttons. "I hope we park next to a mall, I miss shopping," Tobbi shared.

"Yeah, I miss schlepping, too."

"Right," Tobbi sighed, "what's your favorite spot then?"

"Well, any big cloud will do. It'll be good to stretch our legs a bit."

Captain Silver steered right for an enormous cloud—a big island in the sky with white sculpted hills and valleys. The skybergs were stitched to the cloud. A second later, a noisy wave of happy cloudies descended onto the quiet place. Tobbi was the last to get off. He complained to no one in particular, "Yeah, right! Stitch the 'bergs, stitch me. What's the difference?"

CHAPTER 29

Evil Practices

The new Manager was no longer awed by the steam cannon, he'd learned to loathe it. He made the workers practice endlessly at loading the barrel. In several seconds between the time the rock dropped and lifted, he had to get a worker with a clay container up the wall and into a barrel. Well, the workers were lethargic and containers were heavy. In his first live test comprised of three consecutive shots, the first one went fine, the second worker barely made it, and the third poor fellow was barely able to put a container into the barrel before getting smashed by a rising stone. When he reported this, a malignant fire flared in Spoiler's eyes. The Manager assured the Spoiler that he'd be ready in time. Meanwhile, his frustration and fear of the Evil Spoiler grew.

"See," he screamed over the heads of the gray workers, "see what happens if you're slow. You must do it faster! Your fate and mine depend on it. Two and two go together—you get faster and we survive, you stay slow and we all die in the soup.... Two and two...hmmm." The Manager grasped onto a fleeting idea. "Could it work...?" The Manager suddenly grinned. "Yes, of course! Come you lazy bums, we'll try something new." The Manager explained what to do. He scanned the dim gray faces, hoping to find a trace of enthusiasm or excitement. But the same dull eyes looked back at him; the same slumped shoulders and apathy was everywhere. For a second, the Manager felt a trace...a whiff of a forgotten feeling; something like...pity, but a wave of bitter, rotten contempt swept the weakness away. These good-for-nothing, dirty, unmotivated rats deserved what they got. "Go! Go back all of you. I've told you what to do and if you fail me this time—into the soup! Be done with you all, there are more where you came from.

Two gray workers stood by the pile of clay containers. The Manager swept his arm down. "Go!" One cloudie grabbed the container, while the other ran to the cannon and climbed in. There, the carrier handed him a container. The stone lifted past the opening, steam whooped, and the barrel was swiped empty. Next, the carrier became a climber and another cloudie grabbed the next container and ran it over. He was able to hand it to the worker just before the stone obscured the breech, and another gray worker was shot into the sky. The whole process was repeated again and the Manager jumped with joy. He'd done it. He ordered everyone to break and hurried off to inform the Spoiler of his success.

The Evil Spoiler was in a particularly foul mood, not that he was ever happy these days. His gray face looked crumpled and the hooked nose hung particularly low over his down turned lips. He stood on the ledge in the main chamber over-seeing the production of his cloud poison. May God help any worker who stumbled or attracted his attention in any way. Only his need to maintain a maximum speed prevented the Spoiler from boiling a few. It didn't prevent him from putting a mountain of fear into them, though. His only joy was in thinking of how he would torture the Manager if he didn't come through with his cannon shots. Just then, the Manager showed up.

"What're you doing here, underling? The Spoiler asked, "shouldn't you be saving your life by learning to shoot my cannon?"

The Manager gulped and said, "I did it, Your Evilness."

"What!"

"We can shoot non-stop. Once we start, we'll only finish if you order it."

"Are you sure?"

"Yes, Your Evilness. I'd tested it a few times and—"

"What! You dare to waste my poison?"

"Bbbbut, Master, I was only making sure that your com-

Ilya Simakovsky

mand's carried out properly. We had to test it for real," pleaded the Manager.

Evil Spoiler's anger diminished. "Okay," he said, "we're ready, then. We'll wait for my Shadow to bring me more fodder...hmm...workers, I mean, and we can start." The Spoiler jumped up, now energized.

"I've been thinking, master," said the Manager carefully, glad to be alive.

"And why do such a dangerous thing?"

"Only to serve you better, Master."

"A right response, the only response...hmm...continue."

"Well, so, okay I, well—"

"If that's a thought, then I'm the love eternal."

"No, Master, but how will the workers spread the poison in the clouds?"

"What do you mean underling?" The Spoiler was caught off guard. This was new. Could his worker see something he couldn't?

"It seems to me, Your Evilness, that they'd just fall together with the container unable to spread the stuff."

"Well, I'll be not dreaded!! You little spoiled wonder, you! That's right! I've completely missed this. You've just redeemed yourself. Dare I hope that you'd solved my little problem?"

"I think so, master."

"Thinking in my ranks! I suppose I must tolerate this repugnant idea now. So, how do we drop my beautiful poison on those appalling, unspoiled clouds out there?"

"All those, now useless, sparkling stones piled near the wall. We could collect more, there are plenty around, and give one to each worker. When—"

"Oh, YES! That'll work. As they reach the target they smash their containers and presto: storms and mayhem for the hard noses below. How simple! How magnificently Evil! Spoil what someone looks up to and their life's ruined. Simply irresistible! I ought to be congratulated for making

176

you my Manager, what foresight! What intuition! I'm beside myself. Let's go test it out."

"Eh...Your Evilness?"

"Yes, my dear Manager."

"What happens to the workers?"

"Underling! Do NOT press your luck! The thinking stops here. Besides, what's the difference? Let's go test this method of yours and tomorrow or the next day we'll start; as soon as that slow-witted Shadow gets here. There's no stopping me now!" he roared.

CHAPTER 30

All Fun and Games

The crews spread swiftly over the cloud-island, while Tobbi enjoyed a slow walk. He passed Stumble and Fumble wobbling in hyperspeed. Even though nobody poked fun at them since their heroic effort during the race, no one waited for them either. Tobbi observed them huffing and puffing for a minute and said, "You know dudes, you do fine as anchors, but walking just isn't your thing."

With the pair in tow Tobbi flew over the cloud-island that was shaped like a clown's hat with two horns. In between the two horns lay a crumpled valley. That's where everyone had gathered. Tobbi dropped his grateful friends off and drifted aside to observe. The cloudies were engaged in madness. They jumped and they kicked, and they pushed, and they bounced off walls, typical activities, say, for first graders on a class break. Tobbi was sure that in a few minutes his friends would get bored and then they could do something fun. For the ten trillionth time, the cloudies proved him wrong; they kept going and going no sign of stopping at all.

Tobbi got bored instead. "Stop!" he screamed as loud as he could. His punishment was short and swift. The cloudies added screaming to whatever else they were doing.

"Not again," groaned Tobbi and started to do some Karate forms he had learned. It worked. One by one the cloudies stopped screaming and drifted over to observe Tobbi's weird activity.

Pouch was there in a jiffy. "What's wrong? What are you doing?" he asked.

"I wanted you all to stop."

"Stop-flop. Why didn't you just say so?"

"I did."

"You did not. You screamed."

"I screamed 'STOP.' "

"You screamed."

"You should've stopped."

"No."

"Yes!"

"No!"

They stood nose to nose again like two roosters ready for a fight. Nelli's had enough of this. She grabbed cloudies and started arranging them in a circle around the battle-ready duo. This distracted the fighters who kept looking over every couple of seconds.

Finally, Pouch hopped around and asked, "What are you all doing?" Cloudies had no idea, and indicated so.

Tobbi asked, "Nelli, what's all this?"

"I'm treating my friends to a show," she answered.

"Wow, a show!?" the cloudies perked up.

"Humans have this fascination with fighting," Nelli explained. "They always gather around with music, laughter, and food to see people beating each other up. So, I decided we should do the same, since Tobbi and Pouch are so willing to fight. Let's watch, eat, and laugh. It's fun for all!" Noisy and excited, cloudies tightened the circle, waiting. Food was shared.

I'm gonna get you for this, thought Tobbi, staring at Nelli. Nelli looked back as innocent as a newborn chick.

Tobbi exploded, "We're not fighting for you. So, eat this!"

"Yeah! That's right," seconded Pouch.

The cloudies stopped stuffing their faces. Some voiced their disappointments, "And we just came...it sounded like fun...oh, come on, just a little fight...what's a couple of punches between friends...." Someone chanted, "Pouch, Pouch he's our cloud, he can do it in one round...."

Nelli said, "No, it's okay. You guys go right ahead, fight. We'll be as quiet as...clouds." She was hiding a devilish smile.

A wicked idea occurred to Tobbi. What if...this stuff looks so much like it, what if I....

"Pouch," he whispered, "do what I do."

Tobbi ripped a handful of cloud and started packing it with his hands, adding some more until he had what looked like a fuzzy snowball. Pouch also made one but was looking at it like an Aborigine at an ice skate. A puzzled hush spread over the spectators. They had another thing coming but didn't know it. Tobbi tossed his cloudball a few times. Pouch mimicked everything, still without a clue.

"You wanted a fight!? You've got one!" Tobbi shouted and threw it. His aim was true. His cloudball flew to his target far more slowly than a snowball would, but it struck Nelli on the side of her head. Her jaw dropped like a drawer in a cash register. Pouch's ball went wild, but on its flight to nowhere it encountered Button's mouth just as she jumped up. Cloudballs, like everything else in Cloudland, have peculiar properties. When you get hit with a snowball, it breaks up or bounces off; cloudballs, however, stick. Nelli's head now sported a ball above her temple. It looked like she suddenly grew a big ear. She stood there, speechless. That made her a perfect target. The second salvo was in flight and, either by luck or skill, it struck on the other side of her head. It took a couple more salvos from Tobbi and Pouch, whose aim was rapidly improving, before the cloudies caught on. The cloudball fight was on. Great fun was had by all. In the end, the results were easy to tabulate; cloudballs had transformed the cloudies into walking grapes. Despite his agility, even Tobbi took a few hits, but there was one cloudie who received the brunt of everyone's retaliation, Pouch. From head to foot he was covered with hundreds of cloudballs. He couldn't even speak, only shudder with laughter. Everyone helped cleaning him up. Then the fun truly began. Tobbi taught his friends more games, like cops and robbers, tug, spud and others. The cloudies played hard, delighted with all the new games. Hide and seek proved to be a failure, though. Once a cloudie hid and closed his eyes you could be standing next to him, heck, you could be standing right on top of him and not know it. Since the beginning Tobbi had a nagging thought that the valley between the cloud peaks reminded him of some place. Finally, it came to him: it looked like the place they went to in Vermont every winter. Here was an idea!

"Well, you guys, how about some serious fun, now?" he asked.

"It's either serious or fun. Can't be both," someone commented.

"Oh, yeah?! Watch this." Tobbi jetted up, carrying the very bewildered Dynamic duo with him. Their puppy-like yelping soon came from the very top of the left horn. There Tobbi released them. The Duo looked very nervous: see through patches winking in and out in their compact bodies.

"What?" asked Fumble. "Why?" asked Stumble.

"Do you like your feet?" asked Tobbi.

The response was immediate and negative.

"Why?"

"They're good for nothing but standing, that's why!" answered Stumble.

"Think again, Big Foot. Watch this!"

Tobbi demonstrated. Their reaction was intense enough to call a paramedic. Tobbi could hardly restrain them. He wanted to show them more, but they'd have none of it.

"Okay, have it your way," Tobbi said, "At least everything's soft. Go ahead make fools of yourselves."

Stumble and Fumble waddled to the edge of the flat spot, stepped over...and stood there, bewildered. Nothing happened. Their feet stuck to the cloud. Tobbi frowned: had he miscalculated? He gently pushed Stumble on his back. His feet began to slide, slowly at first but faster with every second. Fumble moaned, "Me...me...me...me, now!" So, Tobbi pushed him too. Soon the two were racing straight down the slope as Tobbi flew above shouting, "Use your feet, dummies!

Turn!"

It was something. As soon as they got the idea they began banking from side to side controlling their slide. Their big feet were, indeed, as good as skis. Except no skiing on earth ever looked like this. Because their feet stuck to the cloud, they didn't jump over bumps but skimmed the surface with surgical precision like a beam of light. Within seconds they became experts, using their giant feet with the finesse a few human skiers could demonstrate. All Tobbi could do was shake his head. The Dynamic Duo had found their niche. Nobody would dare calling them clumsy anymore.

Stumble and Fumble flared to a flashy stop amongst their amazed comrades and got buried in a flurry of questions. Next, Tobbi started ferrying his delirious troops to the top, fuming at himself; a ski-lift he wasn't, in spite of what they all thought. Apparently, what they all thought was more relevant because he continued to work hard.

Were they all good, though? Yet, no one could touch Stumble and Fumble; they could and did circles, around any other cloudie. The moment was theirs, and they were delirious with happiness and pride. Eventually, and to Tobbi's great relief, they all got flimsy. A mountain of delicious fluffy stuff was consumed. After the meal everyone gathered at the edge of the island and simply watched the earth rotate below. Night came and they slept. The morning found them moving in the same northeasterly direction, and since the evil finder still pointed that way, they stayed on the cloud-island and did more skiing and eating.

Next night Tobbi stayed awake after everyone turned in, fighting the overpowering darkness. Somewhere down below was North America—his home. He thought of his parents, his school, his teachers, ice cream and hundreds of other things he used to take for granted.

CHAPTER 31

Blasted Full of Holes

Tobbi didn't know when he fell asleep, except everything seemed awfully bright all of a sudden. The sun lit cloud-island was blindingly white. The cloudies, of course, were all up, playing one game or another. Tobbi sneaked away. They were moving northward, still along the edge of North America. But were they going the right way? A little further and they'd hit the Arctic. It didn't seem right that the Evil Spoiler's hideout should be in such a pristine place. Tobbi flew to the raft. The Evil finder still pointed due north. *Strange,* thought Tobbi, *in the last several days the dumb thing hadn't even twitched.* His father's ultimate law of mechanical engineering came to mind: slap-fix, he called it. Tobbi tapped the white container. The gray matter inside did-n't budge.

"Oh, well," said he "it was worth trying," and nudged it once more. The gray ball shook and shot around the perimeter of the white bawl. It came to rest, quivering and pointing east.

"Oh my!" whispered Tobbi and took off like a rocket.

On the plain, it was all fun and games. Tobbi located Captain Silver and swooped down. Captain Silver paid him no mind and kept brushing Tobbi aside. Tobbi just snatched the fair captain and flew him over to the ship. The captain thrashed around a lot and as soon as they landed started yelling. "What'd you do this for, bully? Take me back."

Tobbi pointed. Captain Silver ignored that and puffed his chest up big.

Tobbi pointed again and said, "Look."

The stored air escaped out of him all at once. Captain tumbled backwards into the mast and fell face down onto the deck.

"Sweet! One look is all it took," said Tobbi.

Captain Silver jumped up and hobbled over to the Evil finder. "What happened?"

"It was stuck. I smacked it and it points that way now. What do we do?"

Captain Silver twisted around. His elongated face drooped more than usual. Shadows appeared in shallow depressions in his cheeks and under his lower lip. His left eyebrow climbed up the forehead and his right descended onto an unsuspecting eye. He stood there listening to the sky. Finally he turned to Tobbi and said, "We've but one chance. We must move fast. Go get the others!"

"Yeah, like they'll listen to me. Did you?"

"Take me back, then," the captain said anxiously.

"Okay. Let's go."

They flew back and landed in the midst of a game. The cloudies listened to their captain well. It didn't take him a second over ten minutes to get their attention and explain the situation. By then it was almost too late. Tobbi learned later that they nearly missed the only air jet they could use. Meanwhile, he faced the difficult task of getting all the cloudies back to their ships. He didn't see any way to do it quickly. Fumble stepped out from behind the wall of cloudies. "I know a way," he said, "our ships are downhill from here. If we take the right side of the mountain instead the long way around then we can slide down...I mean, couldn't we?"

Soon both crews raced towards their awaiting ships, with Stumble and Fumble in the lead. In a frantic rush they got Skybergs on the way. The good captain really cracked the whip, not tolerating any mistakes. Now and then he would lend his ear to the sky and order minute changes. Tobbi tried to help but, after receiving a number of shoves and punches, gave up and stood next to Silver. The captain ignored him, but for one sentence. "It's going to be rough, hold on," said he. Not about to ignore another warning, Tobbi buried himself into his ship and gulped some air—his last for a while because just then the ship shuddered.

"Here we go!" someone shouted.

The wind came at an odd angle and hammered into the sails. Losing chunks, *The Raft* tipped, somebody screamed; perhaps it was he, Tobbi couldn't be sure. Next came a rodeo in the sky. They whirled, twisted, and buckled, but *The Raft* turned. The world stopped convulsing and Tobbi resumed breathing. Hearing a strange sound he untangled himself from the deck. Laughing! They were laughing. Tobbi set there in a daze but finally decided that if you can't beat them then join them. He chuckled too, but only with half a heart.

They resumed their lazy sailing, the evil finder—steady again. In time a dark land line appeared below. Tobbi figured it was the west coast of Europe or perhaps Africa. Once over the land they joined a solid sheath of cloud cover. Some time later Tobbi spotted water again. Guessing it to be the Mediterranean Sea, he confirmed it when the cloud cover broke over the unmistakable boot of Italy. Tobbi loved geography and exploration, and now was glad for the hours he had spent studying the globe and various maps. Cloudies were avid students, soaking in as much information as he could give, but, darn it, if they didn't try to teach him the language of every country he described. Tobbi's inability to speak other languages forever amused them.

Soon they passed over the eastern shore of the Mediterranean Sea, and probably either Turkey or Syria. The Evil Finder shifted from east to northeast. A skillful maneuver altered their course accordingly. The land changed from flat planes to mountains. The mountains grew higher and the going got rougher—constant up and down drafts thrashed their ships around. Despite constant repairs, the ships began to wear out, but they flew on. Once through the mountains, the Evil Finder shifted further north. The only country in this direction was Russia. Captain Silver became concerned; *The Flowerhead* had lost many sails and her decks

Ilya Simakovsky

were coming apart. Also, despite his continuous vigilance the captain couldn't find a wind that would turn them as much north as the finder indicated. Over a vast desert *The Flowerhead* became uncontrollable. The cloudies conferred and decided to move everybody to *The Raft*. Just then an outcry came from the rear of *The Raft*. Buttons was pointing at something. Captain Silver hobbled over and called an all-hands alert. Tobbi turned gray when he saw a turbulent, high wall of sand sweeping from the South across the desert. It was catching up fast, dark and menacing.

"Sandstorm," whispered Tobbi.

"Wild wind," whispered Rubex Cube coming up behind Tobbi.

Everyone went crazy. This sandstorm was both their luck and a curse. It would drive them in right the direction, but it could rip them to pieces. What of *The Flower* crew? Tobbi made a decision. "Hold hands!" he screamed over the howling of the wind.

Swiping his fist in frustration, Tobbi took off. The flying was difficult but not impossible yet. He found the Flower crew frightened but orderly. That saved them. His directions were instantly followed. Everybody held hands and Tobbi towed the chain of cloudies across the darkened sky. Against dark background they were a link of tiny white blotches, a hilarious imitation of paper-man cutouts. By the will of God or sheer luck, they made it back in time to grab onto something. The mayhem hit. This high up the sand came in separate grains, which, nevertheless, hit like bullets. *The Flowerhead* was struck first. In seconds, it was torn to shreds. *The Raft* was next. Bound not by fear of any wind Captain Silver was at the helm—his crew by his side. Their fabulous feet were buried deep into the deck. Stumble and Fumble controlled the main ropes. Using early gusts, Silver turned *The Raft*. It accelerated making the main hit less damaging. Even so, *The Raft* buckled like a frightened horse, lurched forward, and yawed right and left. Sand ripped through everything and everybody. The sail ripped and then the whole thing tore off and disappeared. Anchoring cloudies lost balance. Nelli's feet, smaller then most, came loose. Tobbi watched her sliding towards the edge in horror. Nobody noticed. Tobbi prepared to fly to her rescue, even though it seemed hopeless. Then Pouch saw it. He inflated his powerful stomach and bellowed across the deck, "Fumble, heads up!"

Fumble, the only cloudie to remain standing, looked back. Nelli's feet were hanging off the deck. She held on only with her fingers, slowly losing grip. Fumble crawled over, while the others watched helplessly. Just as Nelli let go, Fumble's long fingers encircled her arm and in one pull she was back on. Fumble's great feet saved the day again.

The strong gust ripped off a large chunk of the deck and with it three members of *The Flowerhead's* crew—Bottleneck, Charley, and Horn and there wasn't anything that could be done to save them. Soon it was over. Everyone was beat. No one moved and no one talked. Nelli still clutched Fumble with all her might. Tobbi got up and flew over *The Raft*, which it no longer was. What was left just became another unmanageable cloud. Tobbi looked around for the evil finder. It was gone.

"What do we do now?" he asked bitterly. "All the trouble's for nothing! Without the finder we can't go on; we don't know where to go!"

From a wrecked and twisted section of the deck, a muffled voice cried out, "But we do. We do. Somebody dig me out please."

"Who's this?" inquired Captain Silver, who suffered the loss of his command with quiet dignity.

"It's me, Stumble."

Fumble cried out with glee. He wanted to look for his buddy, but was unable to get away from Nelli.

"What're you doing there, Stumbi?" asked Fumble with relief.

"I'm not searching for a buried treasure, you should know. But I've got a surprise for you all. Only you can't see it if I'm six feet under, you know."

Cloudies loved surprises so in seconds Stumble was freed. Tobbi, in a foul mood, didn't expect anything good, but he was wrong. Clutched to Stumble's chest was the somewhat banged up but still functioning Evil Finder.

"You're great!" Tobbi yelped, "no, stupendous! In fact, from now on you and your partner will be known as Stumble and Fumble the Greats. Oh! I just could kiss you!" Tobbi was overwhelmed by emotions to say such an uncharacteristically corny thing. It brought Nelli back to the world of living, though. She let go of Fumble and said, "No, you won't!"

Tobbi said, "Now, Nelli, I—"

"You don't because I will," Nelli interrupted, "First you," she kissed Fumble on the cheek, "then you." She rushed over and smooched the unsuspecting Stumble. The Duo broke out with transparent blotches. There was dangerous stirring in the troops. That kissing thing teased everyone's curiosity. Tobbi prepared for trouble. Pouch saved him. Because he was totally ignored by everyone, his spirits took a terrible nose dive, followed closely by his lower lip. He coughed mightily once, twice and turned away. Nelli rushed over and hugged the big guy warmly.

"I'm sorry, Pouch," she whispered, and then yelled, "Hey, everyone, Pouch is responsible for saving me. He alerted Fumble. If it weren't for his awesome voice, I'd be a goner. So, three cheers for Pouch."

CHAPTER 32

The Taming of the Beast
or Another Way to Fly

The wrecked Raft now flew the way the Evil Finder pointed—north. Many monotonous hours passed since the sand storm and boredom threatened to murder everyone's spirit. Tobbi was nursing an idea. He picked some of the cloud material and started pounding it together. Nelli drifted over and looked on with interest. Predictably, Pouch joined her. Rubex Cube hobbled followed closely by the Great Fumble and Stumble. Buttons wouldn't miss a gathering for anything. Soon all the cloudies surrounded Tobbi. Cloudies in the back row had no clue, however.

"They're having a picnic," offered Stitch, rolling fingers nervously.

"No," said Beansprout, an oddly shaped cloudie whose long torso and neck seemed to sprout out of his bottom half like a bud of a growing plant, "they're making a secret weapon!"

"Secret from whom?" asked Twitch, a member of *The Flowerhead* crew who was never still.

"Secret from nobody, it's just a secret," interjected Smudge, stuck in the back as always, on a count of his small size.

"Unless it's a secret from someone, it's not a secret, so, I guess, it's a secret from us," said Twitch gloomily. Meanwhile, Tobbi kept pounding more cloud-matter onto the ball. When it reached the size of volleyball he stopped and looked up smiling. The smile froze as he saw the whole crew gathered around. The brave Captain Silver asked, "Well?"

"Well what?" Tobbi said.

"What is it?"

"Get real!" How could anyone not know what a ball was?

189

"It's a bomb, that's what it is."

"Duck!" Captain Silver yelled. The cloudies dropped down as one.

In the back, Beansprout said, "See, I told you it was a secret weapon."

"A secret weapon he says! Don't you understand? It's just a bomb; plain and simple—a bomb! Hhmmm, What's a bomb?" Twitch asked Fumble, twitching fearfully.

Fumble, lying several feet ahead, turned and said, "I wish I knew, but Silver thinks it's dangerous!" He tugged a cloudie in front. "Hey, what's a bomb?" That cloudie didn't know either.

Twitch asked nervously, "Did Tobbi say it's dangerous?"

Smudge shrugged and whispered, "Be quiet you two. Maybe it is something that blows things up...nah! What a silly thought."

Tobbi just couldn't take it; he explained to his shipmates what a ball was, laughing all the way. Then they all played. Volleyball was out—the ball just stuck to the cloudies's fingers. Dodge ball seemed to be everyone's favorite, it meant playing it non-stop. Tobbi, on the other hand, got bored quickly and just watched. His thoughts kept turning to days ahead. What awaited them? A wild yell brought his attention back to the game. A ball thrown by a long-armed Spindle went too far. Captain Silver hobbled backwards after it. He stumbled and fell. Tobbi watched in horror as Captain's back smashed into the evil finder's holder. It toppled and the white globe disintegrated on impact with the deck. The liberated gray globule quivered and flew right through the ranks of frozen cloudies.

"Grab it!" Tobbi yelled. The cloudies went after it. The problem was that there were too many hands with too many fingers. These fingers grabbed everything and everybody but the gray ball, which flew faster and faster. Tobbi went after it, but he was also grabbed. "Ooops. I missed," said Pouch, releasing his hold on Tobbi's leg. The gray ball accelerated off

The Raft. Tobbi couldn't catch it. He came back to a quiet ship wanting to scream, but if anybody could look more dejected than Captain Silver, they would have to work very hard at it. Tobbi took a deep tortured breath and asked, "Now what do we do?" No one said a word.

It was ten minutes into the lowest point of their journey when Buttons, the only one still wistfully watching after the escaped Finder, yelled out, "Something's coming!"

Everyone ignored her. In a minute she yelled again, "I think it's coming back." This couldn't be ignored. Tobbi flew over reluctantly, soon followed by others. Captain Silver looked on hopefully. Indeed, from afar a strange gray speck approached. Tobbi felt a whiff of excitement zip through his body. Something told him that this was it; they were about to engage the enemy.

Captain Silver lurched suddenly, knocking several of his crew backwards "It's...it's a..." he gulped hard. Everyone grayed; no one had seen the captain so scared before.

"Well, what is it?" asked Tobbi harder than he wanted to.

The captain took hold of himself. "It's a Shadow Eater— the creature that you saw in your dream."

Tobbi stepped back and looked at the approaching monster. Still far away, it was already big. Tobbi was scared, but not that scared. If it's time to fight then so be it.

"Wait a second," he said brightly, "this...thing...this Eater is our ticket in. If we can learn to control it, we can make it bring us to the Evil guy, whatchamacallit?"

"Evil Spoiler," said the captain.

"Spoiler, Broiler, whatever!"

"But how can we control it?" somebody asked, "we're tiny. It'll just swallow us."

"Well...I'll just have to ruin its appetite," Tobbi said with little conviction and no one seemed to believe him anyway. Tobbi decided not to let it bother him.

"And I'll do it too!" he stated.

Nelli came to his side, took him by the arm, and said,

"Tobbi you can't control this monster. Let it take us and we'll take our chances with the Spoiler. Or better yet, let's lay low, maybe it'll miss us."

Nelli's words infuriated Tobbi. "Yeah, it'll take us all right—for a slaughter! We must come in unexpectedly with a surprise attack. No! I must find a way! So, I'm going!"

Nelli looked into his eyes, saw a determination that couldn't be fought, and stepped aside. It was a new experience for Tobbi, usually he'd be the one giving up. His goodbyes were short. Only Nelli wouldn't take a hand wave for a goodbye. In front of everyone, she kissed Tobbi, turning him transparent with embarrassment, but somehow making the upcoming battle so much more worthwhile.

Tobbi faced the incoming nemesis. The Shadow Eater grew to an immense size, and still it wasn't near. Tobbi asked himself how he'd ever hoped to capture it. Pouch inched over, and said, "Listen, Tobbi, here's a piece of lunch I stashed for later. You need it more now."

"Wow, Pouch, you're sharing your food. That's something! I thought that food always came first; that you were a...slave...to..." Tobbi stumbled...could this be a solution?

"...food."

"Stitch!" Tobbi howled.

"What? Stitch jerked, twisting her fingers.

"Get your best spices. I'll bring some clouds over to you; make them tasty as hell. Okay? Thanks Pouch. You're the best."

"What did I do?" Pouch asked.

But Tobbi already took off, ignoring Stitch's inquiry into how exactly tasty the hell was. In several trips he brought back a dozen or so clouds. All this activity didn't go unnoticed. One of the Shadow Eater's huge eyes shifted over and zeroed on an unusual small cloud which moved much too erratically. The Eater was slow. By the time the other three eyes drifted over for a sharper look, it almost passed the area. With four eyes looking it didn't miss much and it saw the torn cloud crowded with many white Cloudtenders. What a catch! His master would be very happy. The Shadow Eater piped a low whistle and flapped its edges turning toward the cloud. It smacked its monstrous mouth in anticipation.

Something small and white zipped across its path. One eye tried to follow the strange thing, but it flew too fast. This was highly unusual: clouds just didn't fly every which way. It flew on, too simpleminded to consider it further. Again, that same cloud flew by, slowly this time. First two eyes locked onto it, then three. The Shadow Eater flapped its wings in confusion. Now all four eyes had plenty of opportunity to study it. This cloudtender was dense, had strong defined features, and could fly like the Eater—how maddening! The Eater couldn't decide: much prey further out or the one strange cloudtender right in front of it. The strange one forced the issue. It disappeared from sight and a sharp unpleasant sensation came from the Shadow's underside. The Eater flapped to a stop, puzzled: it couldn't connect the disappearance of the creature with the unpleasant sensation.

"Come on you dumb thing, go after me!" yelled Tobbi, when the thing's stupidity became apparent. Tobbi flew in and punched the Eater between the two upper eyes. This did it. Whistling like a pipe organ the Eater gave chase. Except this cloud just wouldn't stay still. Every time the Eater opened its huge mouth it disappeared and another unpleasant sensation came from somewhere in the Eater's body. What was this mad cloud?

Back on *The Raft*, the cloudies watched the aerial fight with excitement and fear. They saw Tobbi's bravery and gained hope; every time Tobbi gave the monster a slip, they cheered. Even now, the Eater made another frustrating lunge at the irritating white blotch, which suddenly turned and vanished again. The Eater flapped its wings hard and flipped over unexpectedly. Its giant tail cut through air like a whip, the thin end passing within inches of Tobbi's chest. The cloudies on *The Raft* froze, seeing Tobbi spin out of control. The Eater whistled in triumph and flapped its wings furiously, building up enormous speed. Tobbi reeled, he was nearly cut in two. From afar, he heard his name and snapped back to reality to find a gray, menacing, cave-like mouth closing in on him. Tobbi stifled a cry, dashed down, and plunged into a long thick cloud, disappearing from sight. The Eater smashed into the edge of this cloud and started ripping it apart like a rabid dog. Tobbi, meanwhile, dug down and back. He climbed out under the Eater's belly and flew to *The Raft* unnoticed. Pushing the jubilant cloudies aside, he asked Stitch if she was ready. She was. Before anything else, Tobbi stuffed himself quickly barely registering the food's extraordinary taste. He had burned a lot of fuel in his mad flying and hoped that the Shadow Eater did as well. Then he flew back ignoring all the concerns from his friends. He found the Eater still raging. The eyes were busy inspecting the torn pieces carefully. Being able to track four different objects at a time was helpful, but not enough, since the annoying enemy wasn't there.

"Looking for me?" yelled Tobbi, floating serenely at the side of the enormous, enraged gray Shadow. Was it getting a little scanty or, was it his wishful thinking? Tobbi wondered. The creature's four eyes shifted and stared dimwittedly at Tobbi, and then two of them shifted back at the cloud and back at Tobbi.

"Yes, the cloud's there and I'm here. Want to play catch again, you big ugly bat?" Finally, the Eater caught on. Again, it whistled and went after Tobbi, but was there a note of exasperation in that whistle? Was the rush a little less mad, less determined? Tobbi was chased again but dodging was definitely getting easier. There came a point after a particularly mad rush when the Eater stopped. Tobbi stopped as well. The Shadow looked at Tobbi with all four eyes. It was a strange look: intense, puzzled, frustrated but there seemed to be no hatred in it.

Tobbi backed off a little. The Shadow kept its place. Tobbi flew towards the Eater and retreated again, this time motioning for the Shadow to follow. It took two more times, but eventually the Shadow Eater got the idea. It followed Tobbi back to *The Raft*. Cloudies ceased yelling and jumping. The Shadow's eyes rolled as it saw the cloudies. It aimed for them. Tobbi flew in like a rocket and punched the Eater between eyes yelling "No! Back off." The cloudies were astounded when the giant monster backed down. Tobbi's next move was even more daring. He streaked forward and landed on the Shadows back. The Shadow Eater shuddered; its eyes rolled several times in a useless effort to see the intruder. It buckled its great back, and Tobbi tumbled off head over heels. Once more, they stared at each other. Tobbi flew over and landed on its back again. Four big, radar-like eyes keenly followed his every move. This time the giant tail flipped through the air and swept Tobbi off. The tail was surprisingly gentle and the Shadow looked goofy, his eyes shifting in four different directions.

"So, now you want to play, huh?" And again, Tobbi saddled the Eater. He leaped over the buckle, ducked under the tail smirking all the way. This time he got knocked quite a ways off by the tail whipping back. Next he had to laugh because the big bully started waggling its mile-long tail like a happy dog. Tobbi got on again and stayed on this time, while the Shadow rotated his eyes as if asking, what now?

Tobbi darted to *The Raft* and brought back one of the food-clouds prepared by Stitch. He placed it in front of the Shadow Eater. The giant eyes crossed at an impossible angle, focusing on a small cloud. Tobbi pushed it until it touched the monstrous mouth. Four stares at Tobbi—four at the cloud, and then—woof—the cloud vanished. Oh! What an effect it wrought. The big eyes rolled around like pin balls. Foamy lips smacked one another as if applauding the avalanche of flavors spreading through the monstrous gut. The menace that the Shadow Eater held for cloudtenders dissolved into a peaceful, even joyful expression that only a true gourmet could appreciate: never before had it sampled anything so tasty, rich, and good. Pouch figured it out quickly, of course. He was nodding and grinning like a maniac.

The Eater searched for more food, scanning four different directions at once. Tobbi had an agenda, however. Back on top of the Shadow, he grabbed a bunch of cloud material behind its right upper eye and stretched it into a rope, the way he saw the cloudies do with sails. The Shadow whimpered, but Tobbi directed the cloudies to throw one food-cloud to the right of the Shadow. The four eyes immediately zeroed on it. It struggled briefly and gave up trying to throw off the annoyance on its back. The taste buds or whatever it used for that purpose demanded satisfaction so, with Tobbi pulling on the right rope, the Shadow made a graceful right turn and snatched the prize, again saluting with its lips. Tobbi used the same method on the left side. Two more times, they performed these turns. The Shadow was learning. The next time Tobbi pulled on the right rope, the Shadow turned right to find no more food. It was puzzled. Tobbi pulled left—again no food. Tobbi pulled on both together. The Shadow realized it had to do something, but what? When it saw another appetizing cloud straight ahead, it knew. It flew straight ahead. It wasn't long before this command was also learned. The Shadow Eater started to change. Its grayness lessened. It now seemed playful, eager to please, and not all that nasty. Tobbi steered it to the raft and commanded the reluctant cloudies onto the Shadow's enormous back. Pouch encouraged everyone to move since he sensed a certain kindred, food-loving spirit in Shadow Eater. It didn't object to being boarded and was rewarded by the last of the tasty clouds. The Shadow nibbled at it: it was satisfied.

So far so good, Tobbi thought as he faced the colossal cloud-predator.

"Now, Shadow," he commanded, "take us back. Take us back to your master, the Evil Spoiler."

Its eyes crossed at the mention of the evil name. It grew fond of this unusual cloudtender that played with it and fed it so well. It knew what the Evil Spoiler did to the cloudtenders. Somehow, it seemed like a bad thing now. The giant's mouth angled down at the corners.

"It looks like 'no' to me," said Tobbi. "Look, Shadow, the Spoiler's bad news. He's up to no good. He holds a lot of our friends, the ones you helped capture. Help us free them now. Afterwards you can stay with my friends. And look, you'll get to eat like this all the time, how about it?"

This made an impact. They didn't call it the Shadow Eater for nothing. The two eyes on the right peered at the two on the left; it was thinking—a very slow process. Eventually the eyes uncrossed and wave-like wriggle played across the vast mouth.

"I take it as, yes!" exclaimed Tobbi. He saddled the creature, surveyed his excited but worried troops, turned, and screamed, "Onward," pulling on both ropes. The Shadow flapped its edges, and they were on the way. Tobbi didn't even notice that he'd assumed command and all cloudies now looked upon him as their leader.

CHAPTER 33

Preparing for War

The minutes stretched into hours. Cloudies stopped being weary of the Shadow, but to their adoration of Tobbi, there was no end. He got tired of their compliments and everything else. Initially he stood at the helm, so to speak, but the Shadow flew steadily forward all by itself. So, Tobbi tried to relax but every move he made was being assisted by another ridiculously helpful cloudie, as if he was a cripple or something. He'd had enough.

"Look, dudes," he said, "I did what I had to do. That's all. If you could fly you'd do the same." Objections flared. They kept trying to praise him. "Shush, you bums!" Tobbi yelled. "I'm not asking you, I'm telling you! Let it be. It's done. What's coming is far more difficult. Let's concentrate on how we're going to win, okay?" This cooled their zeal and they left him alone. So, he sat and watched the Northern horizon wandering about what to do next. Nelli and Pouch came and sat with him. "You're so brave, Tobbi," Nelli said stroking his back lightly.

"Nelli, don't you start—"

"Shhhh! I mean it, Tobbi. Whatever happens next is fine. You created a legend in Cloudland; what an incredible feat this was?"

"Oh, well, I'll admit this was...cool, but enough already. Seriously, how're we going to beat the Evil guy? I know nothing about him and his place."

"They say," Pouch said, "that the Evil Spoiler lives inside a cave on top of a mountain. He's served and protected by his workers, the former cloudtenders, whom he commands. There he makes his poison and plots our destruction."

"Well, it's all fine and dandy. How big a cave? How many

198

helpers? I need facts not sentiments."

Pouch bristled, "Who do you think I am a fortune teller! I only—"

Nelli nipped it in the bud, "Stop this immediately. This is no time to bicker. We're in this together, we're a team. That's the only way we can win. If I hear one more squabble out of you two I'll bust you heads in! I'm tired of it!"

"Wow!" Tobbi mouthed to Pouch. Pouch checked Nelli out from top to bottom. Tobbi and Pouch looked at each other and shrugged, continuing as if nothing had happened.

"So, what else can you tell me?" Tobbi asked.

"Not much," answered Pouch. Nelli fidgeted: she didn't expect to be ignored. "There's a big main cave with...fire, real fire inside—long corridors—how many we don't know— another cave with his doomsday ma...chine and...that's all I know."

"Not much to go on, dude, but better than nothing. How many workers?"

"I don't exactly—"

"Guess!"

"A hundred, maybe, but most I understand are slow and passive. there are some who are really nasty, perhaps a dozen or two. And that's really all I know."

"Well, at least it's something. Let me think now." Tobbi went back to watching the sky and thinking of a plan that began to form in his mind.

Many hours passed. The sky in the East grew dark, but on the West colors fanned across the sky like peacock feathers. The Shadow Eater, which flew steadily for hours, slowed down and piped a low whistle. A tall ridge of mountains appeared to the northwest, standing dark and massive against the dying blue sky. This had to be the place where the evil dwelled.

Tobbi flew off and positioned himself in front of the Shadow. It flapped to a stop. "We stop here for the night," he ordered. In the dwindling light of the evening he outlined his plan to the cloudies. They had a day to prepare for the battle, to rest and eat their fill. The Shadow quivered and whistled loudly, when food was mentioned, least they forget about it, but had to wait like everyone else.

CHAPTER 34

The Attack

Morning came. Nobody rushed to get up. No games were played. The upcoming battle kept things in perspective. Tobbi took his time catching the densest clouds he could find, after all, he had another mouth to feed—and what a mouth! He didn't have to fly far because the Shadow Eater followed him like a new born chick, especially after it figured out what Tobbi was up to. Stitch used most of the remaining spices to create the tastiest of feasts. Everyone had their fill except Shadow. There seemed to be no way to fill that gut. It whistled, smacked lips, and flapped wings in appreciation of the best meal of its life, begging for more. Finally, Tobbi, viewed doggedly by all four eyes, put a stop to it, stating that there'd be more tomorrow if Shadow behaved well.

They went over the strategy again. At first light the Shadow would drop them off at the entrance of the cave. Their only chance was to surprise the Evil Spoiler, sneak him away, and then find a way to help their poisoned friends. Granted, the plan was vague, but without knowing more it was the best he could do. In the evening the cloudies spread over the whole back of the Shadow Eater in quiet contemplation of tomorrow.

Tobbi sat in a forward section with Nelli, Pouch, and Captain Silver. After a short discussion, they fell silent. Tobbi brooded. Nelli sensed his mood and inched a little closer.

"What if we fail?" Tobbi whispered. "We came all this way because—" Nelli objected, but Tobbi flipped his hand and continued, "—because you believed in me. You all came thinking I'd defeat this guy. Well, I don't even know what he looks like, never mind what he's capable of! And—"

"Tobbi, there are no victims here." Nelli said firmly. "We

all came willingly, knowing that we might fail, and that's okay with us. A cloud never knows where the wind blows it. Maybe it's different for land dwellers, how would I know!? The important thing is to try; to do the best you can. Frankly, Tobbi, after seeing what you can do, we all kind of believe that we'll get the dirty cloud."

Tobbi smiled when he saw Pouch and Captain Silver nodding. He knew then, that win or lose he's with the best bunch of friends one could have. He shook his fist at the mountains ahead and yelled, "You'd better watch out, Evil Spoiler! This mean, not quite lean, cloudie fightin' machine is coming, and it'll chew you up." Cloudies cheered, of course. Then they turned in for the night.

Next thing Tobbi felt was someone grabbing his shoulder. He lurched up in alarm. Pouch was shaking him. A spurt of light over the Eastern sky hinted on dawn, but the night still ruled the world. It was against a cloudtender's nature to be up before the sun therefore every one moved slowly, as if in pain. To Tobbi it looked as if a bunch of zombies staggered all over the Shadow's back. The Shadow struggled as well, jolting and whistling in protest when Tobbi tugged on the ropes. How they reached the Gray Mountains before the sun rose was a mystery. The entrance to the cave was a dark blur on a background of gray. The Shadow Eater overshot it and bumped into the wall. Its rear section flexed and flipped the great Fumble and Stumble into the air. Their muffled squeaks disappeared somewhere high above the entrance. Everyone wanted to go after them but Tobbi whispered, "They'll be all right. We'll pick them up on the way out." Actually, Tobbi was relieved because the clumsy pair was out of his way. In double file everyone piled off the Shadow and entered the tunnel. The darkness inside was stifling, but for a faint, flickering red glow they wouldn't be able to go on. Tobbi flew ahead, but returned quickly. Around the bend the tunnel ended and a giant chamber opened up. Tobbi lead them there and crouched, observing. The red light came from a ragged crack in the floor which now and then spurted a crown of glowing red mud and fire. These licked the bottom of a giant bowl that hung from the ceiling on the end of a thick stone icicle. Inside the bowl a filthy liquid was boiling, throwing off steam in flimsy column. This was the stuff—cloud poison. There was no one around. Tobbi told everyone to move forward along the right wall, where he saw a long ledge mostly hidden by shadows. Each cloudie had to stop and gape at the fire pit which endangered their operation from the start. Tobbi had Captain Silver pass the message not to slow down: Fight first, ogle later.

Tobbi studied the cave's layout. There were two tunnels leading away from the main chamber. On the far wall he noticed openings of two small caves and another ledge that lead up somewhere. He flew to check these out telling everyone to stay put. One cave held a bunch of gray figures laying in neat rows, all sleeping. Another, smaller one was filled with small pear-shaped containers made of clay. There's no sign of the Evil Spoiler. The tunnels were next. With caution he advanced into one of them. Scared already, he nearly panicked when the walls began glowing with a deathly green light. Some kind of fluorescent mold overgrew the bare stone creating this horror movie lighting. He continued until the tunnel ended in a long and narrow cave. The pale green lighting, rows of the coffin-like niches in the walls, all created a chilling atmosphere of an ancient tomb. At the far end of the cave he observed a stage-like elevation filled with many stone pillars—stalagmites, Tobbi remembered. They were of different sizes and shapes but one looked like a large, brown throne and it was occupied by a figure the color of the dark vomit. *What a ghoul,* thought Tobbi and he shivered.

He'd found his enemy, no one but the Evil Spoiler could look so disgustingly evil. Tobbi withdrew swiftly. Time was short. In as few words as possible he explained what he wanted to do. His commands were relayed down the line and the attack began. The cloudie army advanced quietly. It was cool that quiet walking came naturally to cloudies, since humans would wake every living and not living creature in the cathedral-like cave. Giving the fire pit a wide berth they filed into the tunnel in two columns. Once inside, the cloudies took on the green sheen as well, but they looked like soldiers not hideous bugs. The lead group stopped at the tunnel's end and waited for everyone to catch up. Then they spread and advanced forward. The Evil Spoiler's back was turned. Tobbi took position near the ceiling, ready to help where needed. The cloudies rushed in. By some instinct or evil fate, the Spoiler glanced over his shoulder.

"Who...," he mumbled. A green army had invaded his domain. He swiped his hand over his eyes, but the nasty surprise was still there. Then they were upon him. The Evil Spoiler was shaken, lost because for the first time in a longest while he wasn't in control. He panicked.

"Help!" he yelped "Who are you? Where'd you come from? It's my place. Get out! Get out, you scum! Help!" He swiped at the green hornets but every time he'd shake three or four off, five or six would replace them. He was stronger, but they were many and numbers were more important. The cloudies began to take control, it took twenty or so but the Spoiler was subdued. They were about to muffle him with a cloud over the head when an evil light flared in his eyes and in a last ditched effort he twisted and threw the cloudies off, letting out a hoarse roar. Something attacked him from above. The Evil Spoiler collapsed, for the thing looked like a giant green bat. He felt it grabbing him and screamed—anything but bats! He loathed bats. He was lifted up. A voice whispered in his ear, "Not so brave with those you can't control, huh?"

Tobbi strained; the Evil Spoiler was heavy, much heavier than other cloudies, and he was tough. The Evil Spoiler lashed out and Tobbi dropped him. The Spoiler hit the floor and laid there looking at Tobbi, stunned.

"What are you?" the Spoiler spattered, malicious intent in every sound.

"Somebody who's gonna make you pay, dude. You can't enslave nowadays. It's a baaad practice. Also it's bad for you health as you're about to find out."

"A flying cloudtender!" snarled the Spoiler. "I'll have you for my slave. With you I'll be unstoppable; with you I don't need the rest."

"Think again Dirtbrain. It is I who'll have you for a door mat, you filthy beast!"

Again cloudies piled on top of the Spoiler. Suddenly a low growl echoed in the cave. The greenish-gray silhouettes were rising out of the niches on the sides. *Night of the Living Dead,* cloudie style," whispered Tobbi.

The Evil Spoiler, who managed to get free again, screamed, "It's about time, you lazy bums! Help me, foreman, or you're soup," and to Tobbi, "What do you say now, Ace?"

Tobbi looked at the advancing line of Spoiler's foremen and at the hesitating cloudies.

"We can take them, guys!" he yelled. "Give them hell! Second battalion, engage!"

Out of the tunnel came the cloudies's reserve. The battle resumed. The cloudies jumped the Spoiler and this time he was totally buried under their bodies. In a multilegged ball they rolled toward the tunnel. Those cloudie's legs that touched the ground propelled the whole group forward. The rest of the cloudies protected the rear and fought off the foremen's slow but determined attack. Tobbi stayed high, and like a jet fighter, dove down to help here and there. He held especially close watch over Nelli and Pouch. Several times he had to rescue Pouch, who often bit more than he could chew. Nelli didn't have such ambitions; she fought smart staying close to Goliath whose secret of success was his size.

Back in the tunnel they progressed faster. The cloudies fought bravely; victory was right around the corner. The melee spilled into the main cave and that's when their luck ran out. Filling the cave were ranks of gray workers. Spurred on by the Project Manager, who by shear luck or misfortune

Ilya Simakovsky

(depending on the point of view) wasn't with the Spoiler at the time of attack, the gray workers charged. They were slow, clumsy, dispirited, and ineffective, but there were so many.... Had the Manager not been there, the cloudies might've still won. But under his relentless prodding, the gray workers ripped cloudies off the Spoiler one by one and held onto them tightly. Soon only a small group remained fighting. Nelli, Pouch, Captain Silver and, surprisingly, Smudge were among them. Smudge's small size made him hard to catch and he kept sneaking up on gray workers, tripping them from behind until a few of them simply fell on him and pinned him down.

It was finished. Tobbi, flew high under the ceiling and hid in darkness there, watching with anguish and disgust as the Evil Spoiler roared, cursed, and spouted hatred and disguised fear at everything and everybody in sight. The whole room seemed to back away from him. Tobbi wasn't afraid, though. He was angry.

"Whatever it takes," he hissed, "I'm gonna get you. I'm going to get you!"

Suddenly the Evil Spoiler stopped screaming. He hopped up and down several times and shook his fists at the ceiling. "Where are you, you flying marauder? I hope you're still here, coward, and if you are, then get down here right now!" There was no answer from above. Tobbi choked when Spoiler called him a coward but stayed hidden.

"Strong silent type, huh?" the Spoiler continued, now gloating. "But what choice do you have? I know you're there. You wouldn't leave your friends—too good for that. Answer me!"

When answered with silence, the Evil Spoiler roared again, "Enough games. I'm mad and tired. Come down now or your friends are done for! All of them! Don't make a mistake of not believing me! I'll do it. I'll vaporize them all in order to get you, and I'll do it slowly, piece by piece. It'll be on your head. Now, you fly down here! Now! If you do it quickly, all will stay alive, spoiled a little, but alive and you'll live another day. Who knows what could happen? Maybe I'll die." He shook with a sickening laughter.

Now Tobbi became afraid. His options were nil. If he flew away his friends were as good as dead and if he stayed, he'd be enslaved with them. He took too long to decide. The Evil Spoiler motioned to one of the foremen, nearest to the giant pot. He held one cloudie tightly—a former member of *The Flower* crew named Blister.

"Here's a little something to help you make up your mind," said the Spoiler. The foreman took one quick step, lifted the terrified cloudie, and threw him into the boiling pot. A small puff of steam escaped to the ceiling. The cloudies wailed.

"Shut up, you unspoiled menace. Worse than bats, you are. What were you thinking!? You thought you could defeat me? ME! With your little soft fingers, your big floppy feet, and your dumb clouded brains. I'm invincible! I'm the master to you and soon—all! Bow to me, now!"

"You weren't that cocky when we had you," yelled Tobbi. "If it weren't for your helper you'd be answering to the Cloud Maker for your crimes."

"It speaks," said the Spoiler, gloating. The flying cloud-tender was here. He had feared that it was gone. "You speak the truth, Ace. The Manager did well again. He'll be properly rewarded when the time comes. And now you get down here: I've no more time to waste."

"Get away from here, Tobbi," Nelli yelled. "Don't worry about us. He needs us to work. Leave! This way you can come back and—"

"What's this?" Spoiler's growling voice easily overcame Nelli's. "Is this, perhaps, a friend? Such delicate features, even for a cloudtender. Perhaps, I'll use her as my personal attendant." He grabbed Nelli by the shoulder. "Or, perhaps, she'll be next in the soup."

"Leave her alone!" an overwhelmingly powerful voice resonated in the cave, making everyone duck. Only once before had Pouch released the full power of his throat, and again it was to save his friend.

The Evil Spoiler took a few steps back too, but quickly recovered, "How touching. Another softie, are you? All noise and no brawn." To the foreman he said, "Take them both into the soup at once!"

"Stop!" the command came from above. "Promise not to do it, and I'll come down."

"Of course, of course. Such cruelty should be unnecessary. I have use for them. The loud one would make a nice announcer, and the other one...we'll see. Well, I promise not to destroy them and, as a sign of good will, anyone else; your part of the bargain, please."

A collective sigh emerged from conquerors and conquered alike when Tobbi flew into the light. He landed a few steps away from the Evil Spoiler and instantly got grabbed by no less than five foremen.

"Yes!" rejoiced the Spoiler. "I've got you now. You'll become my ultimate, secret weapon, able to deliver my wrath anywhere, any place. Now I have true power! I'm truly awesome now!" he roared in the most scary and repulsive manner yet. Then he walked around Tobbi, observing him closely. "What makes you able to fly, huh? You're different from the rest. In all my life, I've never seen a cloudtender that was able to fly as he wished. Did that Maker of Fools come up with some secret process? I'll find out as soon as you're spoiled. Manager!"

"Yes, Your Evilness."

"Be so kind; arrange a demonstration of my power for these misguided fools. Before I spoil them, I want to see their despair. I want to savor it. I want them to crawl before me and fear me, let them see what's in store for them and their world, and I want to crash their hopes. To the ledge with them all!"

The sun was up and even though the outside ledge was

still in the shadows the sky was bright. Thick clumpy white clouds were splashed with gold from the East. The cloudies raised their faces to this beauty, soaking it, not knowing if it were for the last time. Tobbi took deep breaths, looking only at the Spoiler, setting his resolve to fight to the end.

"Check it out, fools. Look at my work and rejoice; you'll be a part of it soon."

"You're so full of yourself that if your were a toilet you'd be backing up!" growled Tobbi

"What nonsense is this?"

"Don't you know that we cloudtenders can speak nonsense, we can speak anything, and we can do anything. You'll lose in the end."

"Perhaps, dreamer, perhaps. But it can wait a millennium or two. Don't get so worked up. It'll be over soon."

A loud pop interrupted the Spoiler. Every head snapped up. A shaft of steam was expanding away from the mountain peak. A dark speck flew out and rose to the clouds disappearing there. Suddenly a gray blot discolored a golden coat of one cloud. It spread ominously through the huge cloud like gravy mixing into mashed potatoes. Meanwhile, there were six more shots and six more specks. Tobbi noticed that things were falling out of clouds: bright things, sparkling things, and dark things like pieces of coal.

The sky was changing. No longer white and yellow, the gray poison spread from cloud to cloud, causing turbulence and ugly stirrings. Soon lightning flashed and ill-favored winds raced to the lands below. In a few minutes a perfect morning turned into a nasty, stormy mess. Throughout the transformation, the Evil Spoiler laughed and talked to himself like a true madman.

He turned to Tobbi and asked, "How do you like that, Ace? These were just seven of my bombs and I got hundreds, thousands of them. The world is mine; you're mine. Mine is all!"

"Never!" Tobbi strained against the hold, nearly breaking

free.

"Talk's cheap. Let me show you, instead, what I mean."

He pulled his flask out and quickly dropped a drop on the nearest cloudie. It was Buttons. She shuddered as a gray web appeared and quickly overtook her body. Her last glance was directed at Tobbi and it was defiant. Then she was gone: a docile expression replaced the rage, and Buttons joined the ranks of gray workers.

"How about this? No sweat. I told you. Nothing to it." The Spoiler started going through the cloudies and dropping his evil poison right and left, turning Tobbi's friends into zombies. Tobbi thrashed around losing composure. When the poison hit Nelli, he screamed.

The last remaining cloudie was Pouch. He struggled and growled, but a drop touched his belly and the web began its terrifying march through his body. Its progress seemed slower than on the others. Tobbi noticed and wondered, *Was it because Pouch was big or he fought it somehow?* Incredibly, it almost stopped at his neck, but in the end he, too, was defeated. Yet, he gave Tobbi hope. His courageous struggle had shown Tobbi that the poison could be fought.

Tobbi looked the Spoiler in the eyes and said, "You're going down, Dirty Soiler," and didn't take his eyes off the Spoiler even when he ordered Nelli and Pouch to help hold Tobbi. The Spoiler expected a fight, and he expected to win.

"Ouch! That hurt, Ace." The Spoiler said coyly, getting ready. "I'm sensitive, you know. Besides, insulting your master isn't how you start to serve. The Maker's secret weapon is now mine. Dark forces win."

With that he stepped to Tobbi, who flinched, despite himself. In slow motion, Tobbi saw a drop of poison break off the round mouth of the crystal flask. It floated down stretching into a long pod, still attached to the flask. The pod broke into small droplets. The smaller droplets fell behind and the big drop rocketed toward him. Tobbi twisted away. The drop splashed on the ledge. Not at all concerned and smiling, the

Spoiler dropped another one and this time it hit Tobbi at the waist.

The world outside ceased to exist. There was only the drop and the body. The battlefield was defined, lines were drawn. Tobbi looked inward, saw the invading darkness and pushed against it. The darkness was strong, but so was he. He fought the war alone, but he fought it for everyone he loved. There will be no retreat, no surrender.

Outside the Evil Spoiler watched with amazement how the net struggled to take hold. The gray streaks sprouted out of the spot where the drop landed, but as soon as one streaked out, it would stop. This wasn't normal; this wasn't good. He dropped another drop. Tobbi became aware of another enemy. It also was trying to subdue his will. His attention split, and he fought on two fronts, then three, then four. How much could he take? He didn't know. He knew, however, that he had begun to weaken. It was getting harder and harder to maintain his will. Something new had to be done, but what? Perhaps, he should give in, perhaps it was useless to resist. Tobbi forced these poisonous thoughts out of his head and fought harder.

The Evil Spoiler was beside himself. He dropped so many drops already, enough to petrify a dozen of cloudies, but this one was fighting like crazy. "How can he? How can he?" the Spoiler kept asking and, despite himself, began to fear and admire such bravery. This strange cloudie must be his! After all, his body was already gray; only his neck and head were clear. In quick succession he dropped three more drops, hoping it wasn't too much. This thing wouldn't be any good to him petrified.

Tobbi despaired: more of the enemy invaded. Was there no end to this? His chest was so heavy. It was hard to breathe and even think. He began sliding down some slippery slope that led deep into his very core that now turned dark and was filling up with icy coldness, and...sound!? A voice? A deep powerful basso was rumbling, and it was slow-ing his descent. Was it the Cloud Maker? No, not him....

At last, Spoiler thought. The last few drops had finally produced the desired affect. The line at the neck began to move up slowly, toward the head where the victory lay.

Tobbi trembled, "Father?" he asked, "is it you?"

The voice became clear. "Are you afraid to fight for yourself, son?" his father asked.

This rattled Tobbi like the raw power of a jet engine, igniting within him a desire for home and family, and love, and empowering him beyond measure.

"No, I'm not afraid, Dad," and he wasn't anymore. He weighed his enemy and stopped fighting it. The grayness quivered and rushed onward joyfully.

The Spoiler sucked in a deep breath. He won! The relief felt sweet, indeed.

Meanwhile, Tobbi addressed the filth. "Yes, you're in me, but you're not me. I have you, but you don't have me. You cannot control me, but I can control you." Tobbi embraced his body and all that was in it. He embraced the part of him that wasn't well and commanded his body to heal it. His body tasted the poison, analyzed it and manufactured something else, that in turn, changed the poison into something trivial and harmless; he brushed it aside and became free.

The Spoiler, who looked back after turning away for a moment, jerked as if bitten: something wasn't right. All the poison he wasted on this freak; it ought to make him as evil as the worst storm cloud ever. Yet, it didn't. Tobbi's body changed, all right; it got grayer and harder, but when Tobbi's eyes snapped open they were alive, luminous with joy. The Evil Spoiler took several steps back. He was petrified and totally bewildered.

Tobbi looked himself over. He noted his own changes but also something else. The many hands that held him changed as well; the gray receded a little. *Now that was very interesting even encouraging; worthy of an experiment...,* Tobbi thought.

"Let me go!" he ordered the foreman holding his right hand. There was such power in his voice that the foreman obeyed. Quickly Tobbi pinched off a piece off his waist and forced it into the foreman's side. The Spoiler screamed for foreman to grab Tobbi. Tobbi offered his hand freely. The foreman grabbed it and looked up in confusion. The spot where Tobbi's delivered his graft was changing. The grayness retreated, and the cloudie's natural color came through. He let go of Tobbi and sagged to the ground, holding his head. Tobbi implanted another piece into the foreman on the left. Soon that guy was struggling with his change, followed by Nelli and Pouch. Jubilant Tobbi shook a finger at the Spoiler, who was shaking with rage and horror, and continued applying his antidote to everyone around. More and more cloudies behaved as if waking from a long, heavy sleep. Tobbi discovered an amazing thing: the more he gave of himself to others the more there was to give. Enormous joy filled him. He didn't walk, he hopped, and he skipped, and he danced amongst the gray workers, handing out his cure.

The Spoiler roared—an ugly and desperate sound. Yet, someone who was so feared a moment ago now was completely ignored. He whipped out a flask and started spraying the recovering cloudies with poison. They pulled away in fear at first, but the new drops absorbed harmlessly into their bodies. Soon they started comparing who absorbed the poison faster, laughing at the Spoiler's rage. This further infuriated the dethroned king. With another ugly roar the Evil Spoiler lounged for Tobbi and dragged him by the neck back to the wall—a different bottle in his left hand, a darker one. Everyone rushed to Tobbi's rescue, but the Spoiler yelled "Stop! This is my improved formula. Super concentrate! Nobody can survive this. You move and he dies right now." Everyone froze.

"Agree to surrender now, or he'll be destroyed."

"Wait," screamed Tobbi. "Don't do anything silly. He's beat. His ass is grass—we have him."

Ilya Simakovsky

"No! It is I who have you," the Spoiler hissed and tilted the flask over Tobbi's head. The foul, thick goo oozed out very slowly. Suddenly there was another kind of yell—a shrill yell—a double yell. Sliding down the mountain in an unforgettable style were the great Stumble and Fumble. They sailed over the ledge above the cave's entrance. One giant pair of feet hit the Evil Spoiler on the chest, the other swiped the flask out of his hands. The Spoiler tumbled backwards and into the arms of the retreating Manager. A mighty cheer erupted. The cloudies hugged each other mimicking what Pouch was doing to everyone he could put his paws on. They patted each other, and all were swarming on Tobbi, who for once didn't object to all the love and attention lavished on him, mainly because of exhaustion. The cheering went on and on. The Manager and the Spoiler sneaked away unnoticed while the cloudies celebrated. Old friendships were rekindled, since some of the cloudies had been lost for years. Somebody remembered the Spoiler and wanted to go after him. Tobbi said that there's no hurry, they'd get him later. This was his one mistake, for just as Nelli reached for him and hugged him warmly, the cannon popped. The Spoiler and the Manager were gone, but they were in for a rough ride, though: the sky was still very stormy. Without this place and his poison, they were doomed to wander the skies forever, and when his private stash of poison was exhausted the pure clouds would have their revenge. That transformation would be interesting to watch. The cloudies' victory was complete.

CHAPTER 35

Finishing the Job

The newly recovered cloudies ran for cover: the Shadow Eater had come into view. Tobbi flew after them and had to do some fancy talking to convince them that the Shadow had changed as well. It was now bright, playful as a kitten, and gentle as a morning breeze. It approached gingerly and everyone saw a chain of small clouds threaded on its tail. The Shadow went crazy when it saw Tobbi, flapping its wings, whistling, and smacking its lips. Tobbi flew to it causing a stir with the new cloudies. His mates enlightened the newbies: the Shadow was cool and the ride was great as well.

Tobbi scratched Shadow under its mouth and couldn't believe it when the big bully rolled its eyes up. Then he hopped onto its back, grabbed the reins and guided the Shadow to the ledge. Cloudies were floored especially when Shadow Eater whipped its tail and hurled his cloud stash onto the ledge. One hit Stitch, bowling her off her feet. Then it watched Stitch, hungrily smacking its lips. Stitch, who had lost her nervousness, got up and began flavoring the food.

The feast was filled with laughter and joy. Tobbi thanked the very proud Fumble and Stumble who no longer needed to walk anywhere: any attempt was rudely interrupted by their friends who insisted on carrying them wherever they wanted to go. Tobbi hailed their bravery, but inwardly he laughed. Who would've thought that his dismissal before the fight would come true; the fantastic pair was his reserve and they saved his hide.

Pouch and Nelli were inseparable and, after allowing everybody a little time with Tobbi, they became inseparable with him. Leaving the liberated cloudtenders to catch up on gossip, they went into the cave to look around. In the main

215

chamber, where the brew still boiled hot, a strange feeling overcame Tobbi—a sudden and undeniable urgency to leave, to go back home. He brushed it aside and turned to Pouch, who was checking out the pot of poison with his face cringed in repulsion.

"Pouch," he said, "I need to thank you."

"Thank me for what? I didn't do anything," Pouch said with a carefully hidden disappointment.

Little do you know how much you'd helped, Tobbi thought as he took his friend by the shoulder, turned him and looked into his eyes.

"Pouch, you big fool," he said warmly, "in the end when we were all alone with that monster, I was so scared. I thought I was done for. I was ready to go belly up, but someone shamed me, gave me the courage I lacked, and showed me the way."

Pouch blinked in surprise.

"Yes, it was you. You were the only one who fought the poison—the one who showed me that it could be done. Without you all would be lost. This victory is yours as well as mine. So, stop pouting and help me figure out how to destroy this place."

"Place-shmace," said Pouch, making Tobbi smile; a mocking Pouch was a happy Pouch. "How can we destroy all this? Leave it be."

"Yeah! And what if the Spoiler finds his way back, or some other nut wants to play world domination games? No, we've got to bury this place. Let's look around some more."

They found and ogled the web with its zillions of ugly, hungry spiders. Soon they would have to leave in search of food and the web would die, taking care of itself. They also found a narrow passage that led to the cylindrical cave and all its wonders. Pouch and Nelli couldn't understand Tobbi's extreme agitation when he found a mountain of the beautiful but useless sparkling stones near the top of the cave. The concept of money and purchasing power was forever beyond them but Tobbi was allowed to play with the stones for a while. But they ogled the gun and the bouncing granite slab. It continued shooting steam out of the empty barrel. Tobbi admired the genius that built this, but was thankful that they defused its evil. An idea came to Tobbi: if they could plug up the barrel, the steam pressure might blow the whole thing apart.

They went back and Tobbi explained his strategy. The enthusiasm especially from those previously imprisoned here was fantastic. Tobbi led the cloudies inside and organized a cloudie chain. They moved all of the clay containers to the main chamber and stockpiled them on the downward slope as close to the edge of the fire pit as they dared. Then cloudies build a pyramid out of loose stones behind this stockpile of poison. Amazingly, Tobbi's treatment hardened the cloudies's bodies enough to do the work. Tobbi was nudging everyone to hurry so much so that Pouch and Nelli became concerned.

At the cannon, the cloudies filled the barrel with jagged stones mixed with some clay that Tobbi found nearby. They pounded them in, jamming the barrel hard. At last everything was ready. They made sure everyone was out of the caves. The last part was up to Tobbi. The Shadow obediently allowed everyone on its back, there was plenty of room; it grew on the excellent new diet.

Tobbi steered it away and went back to finish up. He flew into the upper cave. There he opened the steam valve, fighting the insane impulse to grab a few diamonds. He did a smart thing and flew out fast. In the main chamber, he pushed on the stone pyramid which crashed forward and slammed into the stockpile of poison toppling it into the fire. He saw a hot flare impact the stone bowl. It cracked and a deluge of poison fell into the fire. For a second the fire was beaten but then it devoured the new fuel and erupted, sweeping the cave of everything, including Tobbi who hung around a second too long. He tumbled out of the tunnel head over heels. To everyone's relief he gained control and soon joined the crowd of excited cloudtenders.

All eyes were on the mountain. Nothing happened for a while. Tobbi wanted to check, but was told in no uncertain terms to cease and decease. Then there was a tremor. A few lose boulders rolled down the slope. In one large explosion, the whole top of the left peak broke off and tumbled down the mountain. Their job was done—the evil lair was no more.

The cloudies's joy and celebration was like none other, but Tobbi couldn't join them because he felt it powerfully now; he was being called home. How? Why? By whom? He didn't know but it was clear he'd have to go very soon. There seemed to be danger in delaying.

Tobbi taught Captain Silver how to control the Shadow. The cloudies were safe. He could leave now, but continued to hesitate. Night was coming, he'd leave in the morning—he could wait that long. The hardest part lay ahead; saying goodbye to his friends. Everyone turned in for the night and well deserved rest.

CHAPTER 36

Leaving for Home

Morning came unwelcome. Tobbi woke up first, troubled and not rested. Disturbing dreams kept him restless through the night, but he couldn't remember them. The urge to leave became overwhelming. It was now or never. He looked at his sleeping friends and summoned the courage. Nelli looked so peaceful, wrapped in her cloud-blanket like a cocoon. Tobbi shook Pouch gently. He growled and kicked, his giant foot nearly missing. Tobbi chuckled and shook him again staying well away from his feet. This time the big guy lashed out with both hands, knocking Tobbi back and over Nelli. Both Nelli and Pouch sat up and bumped heads. They blamed each other and argued until Nelli glanced at Tobbi's face.

"Already?" whispered Nelli. Tobbi nodded. Pouch hadn't a clue.

"All ready for what?" Pouch asked nervously. "Is there another cloud whose butt we must kick?"

"Oh! Stuff it, you dummy. Tobbi's leaving!" Nelli snapped, not taking her eyes of Tobbi.

"Leaving...." Pouch's face collapsed. The universe crashed and exploded. Its pieces plunged together with Pouch's aching soul into the endless vacuum of despair. "Leaving," whimpered Pouch, "why?"

"I knew he would," Nelli whispered, "I just didn't think it'd be now."

Tobbi felt awful. He loved these wonderful, crazy, loyal cloudies. He no longer questioned his sanity or their existence. His feelings were real enough. He wanted to stay and he wanted to go...these feelings were tearing him apart. Yet, his home was down below. His family was there, waiting, and if he didn't hurry he was sure he'd never see them again, and he wanted to, desperately.

"I must go," he said quietly but firmly.

"Oh, Tobbi" breathed Nelli, lunging forward, wrapping her arms around his neck. She kissed him. Tobbi hugged her back, but his eyes were on Pouch. Pouch sat there frozen; only his face revealed the emotions raging inside. Fear, love, and anger flashed and vanished in his face in quick succession. He nodded to Nelli and she let go, after one glance at Pouch.

Tobbi shifted over to his side. "Look, Pouch, I got family down there. My place's with them. My job here's done."

"Oh, we're just a job for you, eh?" Pouch twisted away from him. "We couldn't be your family?"

"No, Pouch. You're my friends, the very best of friends. And you'll always be my friends. As long as I live, every time I look in the sky I'll think of you. You can even fly over some day. Better than that, you have the Shadow Eater now. As long as you keep feeding it, it'll take you anywhere. I'm sure Captain Silver could find me. Butler Hill is high and always plows through clouds on rainy days. You can come and visit!" Tobbi finished excitedly.

"We could?" Pouch perked up.

"Of course we could," Nelli joined them, laughing. They hugged once more, but with hope now, no longer afraid that they'd never see each other again.

"Look, guys," Tobbi added, "I named you after my best friends at home. Every time I speak to them, it'll be as if I'm speaking to you as well. We're connected. Don't be sad. We're friends forever." It was time to go.

"Wait a second," said Nelli. "What about the others?"

Tobbi looked over the rest of cloudies sprawled all over the back of the Shadow.

"I can't," Tobbi answered, "it'll take too long. I must go now. Please tell them that I love them all and I'll miss them: Captain, Buttons, Smudge and, especially, Stumble and Fumble. And, oh, yeah! When you get back, thank the big

Head for me."

"For what?" asked Pouch.

"For getting me here, dummy. If it wasn't for him, we would've never met."

"Oh, yeah," drawled Pouch. One more hug, a kiss from Nelli, and he was off.

"Look for us in the sky!" Nelli shouted.

"I will!" Tobbi yelled back and chuckled.

The Shadow's four eyes were wide open and it was flapping hard, starting after him. "You big puppy," whispered Tobbi and flew back. He placed himself in front of the Shadow and said firmly, "Stop. No! You stay here." Shadow whistled low and his mouth sagged at the corners.

"I know you want to go, but I can't feed you all of these tasty clouds you love. But the cloudies will. Stay with them, help them get home."

The two eyes on the left stared into the pair on the right. A wavy wriggle ran right and left on the enormous lips. *Appetite rules!* Tobbi thought. Pouch peered over the edge and asked, "What's up?"

"The Shadow's going after me," Tobbi said. "This here Shadow isc a creature after your own heart. It just loves to eat. Look, Pouch, you know that problem you're having with catching the Cloud Maker's barfs?"

"They're not barfs, you idiot!" said Pouch, back to his old self again.

Tobbi smiled. "Whatever. Use the Shadow and no more cloudies will be lost."

Pouch's eyes lit up. "Oh, yeah!" he exclaimed, "wait a second," and disappeared. Before Tobbi could get impatient Pouch was back. "Here," he said, "I saved it for a morning snack, but looks like you'll need it more." He handed a chunk of a brownish cloud to Tobbi.

"Pouch, you're sharing again. This is serious stuff, my friend."

"Serious-shmerious. Get out of here, you whirlhead,

221

before I change my mind."
Tobbi saluted and took off.

CHAPTER 37

Journey Back

Flying back was all about speed, no joy or adventure, just urgency. This feeling grew with every hour as Tobbi flew westward towards the North American coast. At night he parked at a cloud, sleeping restlessly. Pouch's food lasted a day, and then he gobbled the tasteless stuff. On the morning of the third day, the ocean ended. Which way now? he wondered. Tobbi turned South on a hunch. On the way he encountered a storm. He over flew it, barely making the height to see into its swirling vertex. There was no time to marvel: the urgency became unbearable. Once past the storm he descended. An hour later he felt a surge of excitement; the land started to look familiar. He wasn't far from home! There was plenty of wind. Tobbi fought it along with the mysterious force that reappeared as he continued to descent. He felt strong and he was determined.

Tobbi saw a lake. Was it...? Yes! Crooger Lake. He and Dad loved to fish there. Tobbi screamed. He was so close. He turned southwest trembling with excitement. There it was, a sight he was so longing for. Butler Hill—a naked, rough reject of earth—bowed over the town in a timeless servitude and now it was the loveliest sight in the universe. It was circled by a road, the road that led home.

Oh, how he missed everything: the cuckoo clock in the kitchen that always screamed at ungodly hours, the stupid exercise videos Becky loved to sweat tog after school, even the annoying elevator he had to ride every day. Well, no more! He'd learned to walk again. Bummer! I'd have to give up flying, he conceded.

Most of all he missed his family. He wanted to see his mother and father; he would hug his sister and gladly go

223

through any torture she'd put him through. Immersed in memories he almost missed his house. No larger than a lunch box from this height, it sat at the top of a cul-de-sac, touched not at all by Tobbi's absence. He wiped all thoughts from his mind except one: getting down there.

He dove down, but like a helium balloon, was pushed back up. He fought the force and won a foot at the time. It seemed to take forever, but he finally reached the branches of the old gnarled oak. The house was right below. Progress was measured in inches now; the force was that strong.

But why was the house so dark? The lights should've been on at this time. Where's everybody? Intuition kicked in, urging him to fly elsewhere. He considered the dark house, broken branches cluttering the lawn, garbage cans rolling helplessly near garage doors and sighed. The force was relentless, and the wind picked up again. Reluctantly he flew on. *Where to now,* he thought, *am I too late? Why do I feel so lost?* Time was running out, that he knew, but *why...why?* Streaking along Main Street, he reached South Broadway and turned left guided by nothing more than a hunch, a sixth sense. He flew over Lark's Nest Park barely noticing benches and alleys filled with people. He was searching for something. A brightly lit window beckoned to him from the third story of a squat, square building like a bonfire to a lost ship. Tobbi hovered, unsure. The light streaming from that window flickered through the swaying branches of a tall tree; as if a hand was waving. This image was comforting, somehow. It was all or nothing now, even his endurance had limits; there wouldn't be any more detours. In a most determined way he dove for that window. The force, his enemy, attacked him in kind. The neurotic winds snapped at him from all sides like vicious, protective hounds. *Where is Captain Silver when you need him?* This odd thought came and went. But Tobbi strained and fought, fought and strained, advancing a yard at a time, a foot at a time, an inch at a time. Time lost all value, measured only in inches. Three things counted: The window, the distance, and the enemy force.

Tobbi whimpered: with every downward inch, the force got stronger and he got weaker. How could he win? A memory came out of nowhere. He and his father were on a fishing trip, when they got caught by a gale on the river. They rowed like mad but the boat didn't seem to move an inch. With their arms weak from the effort, they kept fighting and made it to the shore, exhausted but victorious.

"I want to get back," Tobbi growled and pushed, and pushed, and pushed; two inches forward, one inch back. Pain, weakness, and determination all mingled into one searing desire, the desire which required but one satisfaction— the window. Never before had Tobbi faced such a difficult task, never before had he committed one hundred percent of himself into carrying it out. He didn't believe it at first when his fingers touched the windowsill, yet there it was. He pulled himself forward and looked in. What he saw nearly broke his will and his desperate hold on the window. But shocked, frightened, and exhausted he held on, as if welded to it. Inside a drama was unfolding. Tobbi took it all in with one glance and realized what building this was: he was hanging onto the third story window of Mercy Hospital and inside... inside....

The brightly lit room was in turmoil. In the far left corner his sister stood with fists pressed to her mouth, eyes swimming in black rivers of mascara-laden tears. Near the wall, his mother was slumped in a chair with father bending over her. His initial wave of joy was crashed when he saw his mother weeping and his father's strong, typically happy face distorted with pain.

Richard Sontag tried to control his despair for the sake of his wife and daughter, but failed miserably. His eyes were glued to the bed where Tobbi laid stretched under the covers, unconscious. The desperate activity of a few days ago when an internal struggle seemed to flare inside his son was no more. The doctors and nurses did their best to awaken his boy, but now Tobbi just lay there, breathing shallowly.

Dr. Golding called the family in when his breathing became labored. Now everybody watched the monitors, hoping and praying for a miracle. His wife was near a collapse; only Richard hadn't given up all hope even in the face of despair. He believed in his son's courage. He believed that Tobbi would find strength and pull himself out of whatever afflicted him. Richard fought the malevolent doubts that kept raising their ugly heads like a mythical hydra.

Tobbi snapped to reality. His family's despair jolted him and his resolve to get inside grew even stronger. He knew that if he got in now all would be well. He pushed, but the window wouldn't give. He tried to pull on it, but couldn't. He tried to knock, but his soft cloudie hands made no sound. No options were left, yet something had to be done, but what? There was no time—no time!

Inside, Tobbi's body convulsed. The line on the heart monitor wavered. Lydia cried out. Richard's face twisted hideously. Becky covered her face, broke down in sobs, and turned her back to the room.

Richard screamed out the only thing that seemed to make an impression on his son before, "Fight Tobbi! Are you afraid to fight for yourself son?"

Outside, Tobbi read his father's lips and screamed his answer, "No, I'm not afraid," and held on despite the overwhelming attack of the force that tried to rip him away just then. He watched with mounting fear as the line on the monitor went flat; he couldn't hear the terrible, lonely whine that accompanied this.

This horrible sound wrenched all the strength out of Richard, who screamed for the nurse to turn it off. She did it, crying. Dr. Golding turned away because no amount of medical experience could diminish the horror of this moment. It hurt so incredibly deep.

Outside, Tobbi was ripped apart; the cruel force

wrenched him away, while an unbreakable power of his will kept his fingers locked onto the window frame. This couldn't go on much longer. Something had to happen or he'd be lost forever. He peered into the back of his sister's head. He put all of his heart, all of his determination, all of his desire, all of his courage into one thought; all of his love into one single thought, *C'mon, Sis! Open the window!* he commanded. *You always brag that you know what I'm thinking. Prove it now! OPEN THE WINDOW!*

Nothing happened. Tobbi screamed again, defiantly, desperately, *I won't give up! C'mon, Bubbles. Do it now!*

Becky shivered, she thought she heard Tobbi's voice. But he was lying in bed as still as.... She searched the room. Something compelled her to move to...the...window. She saw her father rip his collar, suffocating. She took one unsure step towards it.

Yes, yes, yes! Tobbi screamed, *Do it! Open it! NOW!*

Suddenly sure, Becky leaped to the window and nearly ripped the latch off, throwing the window wide open. The wind plunged in blowing loose papers from the night stand and flailing Becky's hair. She turned and stared at Tobbi's unmoving body, her eyes ablaze with hope. Why? How? She had no idea, but something was about to happen.

You did it, Bubbles, Tobbi rejoiced rushing in with the wind. In a second he was over himself, looking down upon himself, and then plunging into himself. *How strange,* he thought, *such heaviness, everywhere. This felt oppressive, stifling, not at all like the lightness of a cloud. Well, it's all right,* Tobbi thought, the agony of the Spoiler's poison invading his body was still fresh in his memory. *But why is it so quiet and stuffy in here?* A weight was squashing his chest preventing it from lifting. He would laugh if he could; how easy this was compared to what he'd faced already. Tobbi heard a loud drum beat and heaved on this command. His chest rose opening the lungs. The life-giving air filled them to capacity and oxygen flooded his blood, bringing strength and life to every remote nook of his body. Nobody saw it except Becky, who sucked in her breath in tune with Tobbi's.

Onto the next challenge, thought Tobbi, smiling inwardly. Like the Spoiler's poison, something prevented his body from obeying his wishes. And once again, Tobbi accepted the challenge, embraced his enemy, subverted it, and denied it the control of his body. The power that controlled his nervous system squirmed shamefully away, beaten forever. Tobbi opened his eyes and sat up.

Everyone around him was immersed into his or her own private hell of grief except Becky. The poor girl's lips were flapping as she struggled to speak. She stretched her arm toward Tobbi and just shook that pointed, trembling, and bony finger of hers, stuttering and mumbling. Tobbi smiled at her warmly and swept the cover off. He pointed to his legs and quietly, but deliberately stood up.

"Mom, I'm hungry," he said.

Tobbi's voice made every head snap, every eye blink incredulously, at his small figure that now stood shakily on his thin legs. Becky finally screamed.

Tobbi overestimated his strength. His knees buckled, but he took a short step to prove a point, and began sagging to the ground. A roar that would shame a lion rattled windows on the entire floor. Richard Sontag relinquished all control of his awesome voice. Tobbi never had a chance to hit the floor. A blur that Richard became was there, under Tobbi. He scooped his son up, pressed Tobbi to his chest, as the most precious thing that he was. Then he laid Tobbi onto the bed and spread himself over his son like an impenetrable force field. The rest of the family joined in a flash. There was no end or measure to their joy.

There was also no end to the pandemonium that broke a second later when the medical staff recovered and realized their responsibility. Gently but firmly, the family was peeled away and the endless battery of pocking, probing, testing, and sticking began. Tobbi took it all with a smile. It was nothing but a minor inconvenience; he was back!

CHAPTER 38

Home Finally

It took two days, but Richard eventually rebelled. After being in the hospital for weeks, the family wanted Tobbi home. Since the doctors could no longer find anything wrong, Dr. Golding released Tobbi. If it were up to the doctors, they would test him till he conked out again. He was still weak, but could walk a little; after some therapy and exercise, he'd be as good as new, that's what Dr. Golding told him when she came to say goodbye. Tobbi had to sit in the damn wheelchair again to get out of the hospital, but no price was too high.

Soon he was in the car, immersed in love and gossip. He missed a good portion of family life in the weeks he was indisposed. The family had a mystery to solve too: Tobbi kept staring at the clouds all the way back home. Lydia even began to worry again. Tobbi calmed her down. It was just nice to see the sky, he explained, after all it's been so dreadfully long since he'd seen the clouds. Yeah! Right!

Two weeks passed, and he was back to school. A hero's welcome awaited him and every student seemed to want to pat him on the back; they managed to rid his jacket of every speck of dust in just a few minutes. Nelli and Pouch, who were at his house constantly since his return, served as his body guards and ushers, managing the crowd. Tobbi was touched by all the attention, especially when he found dozens of get well and welcome back cards plastered on the walls in his class.

Everyone was shocked when a broad smile disfigured, adorned that is, Mr. Pierre's face when he saw Tobbi. A little respite from his oppression was enjoyed by all as Bulldog digressed from instructing for the whole period (which didn't hurt Tobbi's reputation any) and asked Tobbi to share his experiences with the class. Tobbi was very careful about what he said. He also began to have doubts; was it all a fantasy or a disease-induced hallucination?

It happened on the way back from school. He walked outside doggedly followed by Pouch and Nelli. The sun had been in style for the whole week now. The bright blue sky was sprinkled liberally with white clouds of various sizes. Tobbi stared wistfully into the sky, desiring to fly up and prance about a bit.

"Why do you look at the sky all the time?" asked Pouch.

"Because it's there," answered Tobbi.

"So are the toilets, but you don't go around staring at them."

"Pouch, if you find me someone who thinks toilets are beautiful, I'll marry you," Nelli said with a smirk.

Pouch perked up, "Okay. There's got to be a plumber out there who loves his work. How's next Wednesday strike you? Can you wait that long?"

"Get real!" Nelli laughed.

Tobbi said, "One day I'll tell you about our...I mean, my adventures."

"What adventures?" asked Pouch.

"Our what?" asked Nelli.

"Gees, why do I feel that we had this conversation before? Never mind that.... Say, does that cloud over there remind you of something?" Tobbi asked becoming very excited suddenly.

"Where?"

"Over there, to the right."

Indeed, a large cloud had emerged from behind Butler Hill and floated toward the school, rotating lazily. Tobbi inhaled sharply and then hiccuped. Pouch looked at the cloud and back at Tobbi, and at the cloud again. What's the big deal? So, the cloud was weird, kinda looked like a head. So what? Like he hasn't seen clouds before! It wasn't until the sun flipped a golden ray onto the cloud, that he became frightened. First one eye opened up, then another—big blue eyes with golden eyelids. They stared down at them!

"Did you ever see anything like this?" Pouch yelled, pointing up and spitting pieces of the cookie he was eating all over the place.

"Yeah, sure did!" yelled Tobbi and laughed madly, uproariously. Pouch just rolled his eyes at Nelli.

For the first time since his return Tobbi felt at peace. He waved his hand at the apparition in the sky. Next minute it was over. The eyes closed and the cloud moved on. But Tobbi was finally sure. The energy, sapped by weeks of uncertainty, returned and Tobbi jumped and hoped around like a three year old in a candy store.

"Tobbi, for a second I thought you were going to take off after that cloud. What's up with that?" asked Nelli. Pouch just looked at him as if he had just barfed.

Tobbi chuckled and said mysteriously, "This tale I might tell you guys one day if you two behave yourselves." Pouch's rumbling grunt was a fitting end to the story.

EPILOGUE

—Told by Tobbi Himself

I tell you, dudes, it's tough to keep a story like this a secret. Now, that I told it to you, I can chill out some. I don't even know if you all believe me or not. I know for a fact, though, that one person will believe me completely, once he reads this. He's been very busy inventing one thing or another—my father I'm talking about. Here's why.

Two days after coming back from the hospital, the two of us were sitting watching the news between hockey periods. Gosh, I'd missed the real sports up there! At the end of the newscast the announcer received a note. He read it and chuckled.

"This just came in; what an interesting piece of news!" He said, "In the city of Magnitogorsk, Russia, a strange thing happened several days ago. One beautiful morning the sky over the mountains darkened abruptly. A storm appeared from nowhere. Lightning flared. This by itself wasn't so strange. Anyone in the Midwest can tell you about sudden storms. But what happened next was quite peculiar. A strange, sparkling hail fell out of the sky...."

I tell you guys, I had to laugh at this point. As the announcer told everyone about what had happened I remembered the actual events. If they only knew! Imagine the ratings they'd get. The telecaster continued, "A short time later the top of the mountain exploded, so everything was attributed to an unusual volcanic activity. But now they are not so sure. A town dweller named Nikita Romanoff, found an icicle on the ground near his home. It wasn't melting so he picked it up. Imagine his surprise when he found it to be a hard, sparkling stone; would you believe a diamond the size of a small carrot? And they'd found five more—six all together,

233

lying around the town. What would you do with several mil-
lion of dollars if it fell out of the sky like this? The town's
building a hospital, I believe. How about this? Is it a Russian
version of 'Pennies from heaven'? Well, folks, that's Ripley's
believe it or not type of stuff."

That's where I really had a ball. When that guy said six
diamonds, I quickly told my dad there'd be seven, since, if
you remember, the Evil Spoiler shot seven workers into the
sky.

"Yea, right," my dad joked. Imagine HIS surprise, when at
the very end the announcer made the correction. I tell you,
friends, the expression on my father's face was worth a mil-
lion dollars all by itself. I felt great because this adventure
was all mine and I didn't do too badly up there, did I?

By the way, if any of you get a call for help in the middle
of the night, don't say no. There's much fun to be had up
there flying with clouds, making turns is kinda tough,
though. Well, see you later amigos. Got things to do; got to
fly out of here...eh...just kidding.